It's double jeopardy . . .

Two of a kind, the Virginian had called them. And that was certainly right. Not in their heritage and not in their looks and builds. But in the violence of war and during the vengeance hunts of each of them after the war was finished, they had both been reforged on different yet strangely similar anvils.

They killed without compunction and yet only in self-defense or after a fair warning had been given. They asked no favors, but if favors were granted unbidden, they ensured repayment. They didn't give a shit what anybody thought of them.

And they had survived. Physically. They had also preserved the same precious few yet important emotional responses that continued survival demanded. To enable each of them to live among other men—and with themselves. . . .

. . . when Edge and Steele ride into town!

TWO
OF A
KIND
by George G. Gilman

PINNACLE BOOKS   LOS ANGELES

TWO OF A KIND

Copyright © 1980 by George G. Gilman

A Pinnacle Books edition, published by special arrangement with New English Library, Ltd.

First printing, October 1980

ISBN 0-523-41106-5

Printed in the United States of America

PINNACLE BOOKS, INC.
2029 Century Park East
Los Angeles, California 90067

For R.G.:
A western book for him
in return for the country
one he arranged for me.

Two of a Kind

ONE

ADAM STEELE took off his black Stetson, ran the back of a wrist along his sweat-tacky brow and then replaced the wide-brimmed, low-crowned hat on his head. During the few seconds it took to accomplish this simple act a fellow human being rode into sight on the parched land sweltering under the dazzling blueness of the cloudless Mexican sky.

And immediately the Virginian became as unmoving as the grey rocks which encircled him, and as unfeeling as they were for the oven heat of the noon sun which beat down upon the Sierra Madre foothills country.

The vantage point from which he watched the rider emerge out of the distant shimmer of heat haze was midway up a gentle rise; the slope forming the south side of a shallow valley with a dry wash and a trail running along the bottom. It was the only area of broken ground on this side of the valley, whereas the opposite slope was pocked with countless depressions and featured with many patches of scattered boulders, offering, along its mile length, a thousand and one better places of concealment than that which Steele had elected to use.

But for the more than three hours he had waited and watched in this isolated pocket of cover on the valley's south slope, the Virginian had never doubted the decision he had made. And as the rider came closer and Steele cautiously prepared to kill him, the potential victim unwittingly showed the soundness of the secret watcher's reasoning. By peering only occasionally toward the south slope of the valley while maintaining a careful surveillance along the more dangerous-looking north side.

As Steele stretched out into a prone position on the arid

1

ground and eased the tip of his rifle barrel into the vee between two rocks, he parted his lips to show a smile. It was a boyish smile of pleasure that served to drop several years away from a face which in repose appeared to be much older than its almost forty years.

It was a lean face with regular features: nondescriptly handsome in the set of the coal-black eyes, undistinguished nose, gentle mouthline and firm jaw. Given character by the premature grayness of the once-red hair at the long sideburns and the deep-cut lines in his sun-and-wind-browned skin which had been inscribed by harsh living.

An Easterner come West a long time ago, Adam Steele both fitted into the barren Sierra Madre environment and was an incongruous intruder; this paradox due to the style of garb with which he clothed his five-and-a-half-feet-tall, compactly built frame. His hat, low-heeled riding boots and the skintight buckskin gloves were totally Western. Whereas his pale blue suit, purple vest and lace-trimmed white shirt would not—if they were cleaned and laundered—look out of place in the smartest section of any Eastern city.

The weapons he carried were just as much of an odd mixture as his clothing. The rifle he aimed at the lone rider below him on the valley trail was an old .44 calibre six-shot Colt Hartford revolving model with an inscribed gold plate screwed to the right side of the fire-scorched rosewood stock. In a sheath strapped to the outside of his right calf was a wooden-handled throwing knife, accessible through a slit in his pants leg. And around his neck, loosely tied in the manner of a kerchief, was a gray silken scarf with weights sewn into diagonally opposite corners—these small pieces of concealed metal turning the innocent-looking item of apparel into an Oriental weapon of strangulation. He did not wear a gunbelt and neither did he carry a handgun.

He shared the cramped area encircled by boulders with a Western style saddle fitted with all the accoutrements for rough-riding across a hostile terrain and a bedroll to which was lashed a sheepskin coat.

It had been necessary to blast a bullet into the head of his lame horse at sundown yesterday. Which was why he now took aim at the chest, left of center, of the slow-riding stranger who had approached to within three hundred yards of the Colt Hartford's menacing muzzle.

The boyish smile was gone from the weathered face now and the features were arranged in an impassive set that showed not a trace of compassion for the unsuspecting rider, as Steele thumbed back the hammer of the rifle—taking care not to move the barrel in case the slightest change of position might cause the metal to glint in the harshly bright sunlight.

Supremely confident of placing the bullet into the selected target, Steele waited until the gap was narrowed to two hundred and fifty yards.

Then squeezed the trigger.

And rasped, "Damn you!"

Steele had not shown himself. And neither had he made any sound to attract the attention of the man on the trail. Yet just as the gloved forefinger applied pressure to the rifle trigger, the intended victim began to counter the unseen threat.

He jerked on the reins to bring his slow-moving mount to an abrupt halt. Kicked free of the stirrups. Slid a Winchester rifle out of the boot. Snapped his head around and up to look toward Steele's hiding place. And threw himself in a powerful and controlled lunge out of the saddle.

The rider's moves were too sudden and violent for the horse to take without protest. The animal snickered, baring yellow teeth, in a sound and expression of rage and fear. Then, as the rider leapt clear of the saddle, the horse went up into a high, hoof-flailing rear.

And took the bullet just below the point of the right shoulder. "Shit," Steele said, his voice not a rasp with this new oath. As he saw the horse come down four-footed amid a swirl of dust, try to gallop, then stumble and roll onto its side.

A second rifle shot vibrated the searing Mexican air. But not from the Colt Hartford, even though Steele had instinctively cocked the hammer again after seeing his first shot miss the intended target. The report was in unison with the sound of a bullet impacting with and exploding chips from

3

the rock two inches to the left of where the Colt Hartford barrel rested.

He ducked his head under the spray of chippings, listened to the seemingly palpable silence for a stretched second, then peered again down into the valley. To see that the positions of the stranger and himself had been reversed.

His carefully laid and patiently tended trap had been sprung and had failed to catch anything except an injured and therefore useless horse. Leaving the rider alive on the side of the valley that gave him the upper hand, the side which provided ample cover in which to move—against a man who was forced to remain in one place, no longer secretly.

After his initial ill-tempered response to the turnabout, Steele became outwardly impassive and inwardly calm. He had tried and failed, but not through any fault of his own. Simply because the stranger hidden in the gray rocks on the lower slope of the valley's north side was not the kind he had expected to be riding along this trail.

This man was his kind.

Or, Steele acknowledged with a tightening of his mouth-line as he raked his unblinking eyes over the area in which he knew the stranger to be, his kind and better. For not by a tiny swirl of disturbed dust or the merest glint of sunlight on gun metal did the man concealed beyond the dry wash and trail reveal his precise position.

Then the Virginian was startled by a third rifle shot and his expression as his lips formed the shape of another curse he did not vent showed more than a tinge of something akin to admiration. For the stranger had secretly moved several yards away from the area where Steele was convinced he had been hidden. Higher up the slope. And east. Toward a vantage point directly across the valley from where Steele waited and watched.

The white muzzle smoke pinpointed the man's position, but the Virginian did not squeeze his trigger after swinging the Colt Hartford onto a target. For there was only solid, unfeeling rock to fire at. Instead, he glanced momentarily to the left of the aligned sights. Saw the flesh of the black stallion tremor and become still: the horse killed painlessly by a bullet placed precisely between his eyes.

4

"Hey, dry-gulcher!"

The shouted words, ringing out with perfect clarity in the silence of the foothills, drew the Virginian's attention back to the area of the grotesquely eroded rocks where the stranger was hidden.

"It was necessary, feller!" Steele answered.

His native Virginia sounded in his voice as distinctly as if he had left the state only weeks instead of years ago. The man across the valley spoke with a Western drawl.

"Like putting down a horse in pain that ain't got a hope in hell of recovering! If I don't kill you right off, I don't plan on wasting another bullet!"

First the puff of muzzle smoke and now the threat revealed the precise point where the stranger was hidden. But no part of him showed among the rocks. Which, Steele knew, meant that the stranger could not see him. Yet.

"Dumb you may be, feller! But you ain't the kind of animal I owe a favor to!"

Steele pursed his lips. Then jutted out the lower one to blow cooling air up over his sweat-tacky face. Tension as much as the oven-heat air forced moisture from his pores. As the taunt from across the valley revealed, the stranger had changed position; moved higher up the slope and closer to a direct line between himself and the Virginian. Soon, unless he showed himself in the sights of the Colt Hartford, the man would be high enough to have a clear shot down into the isolated pocket of cover on the valley's south side.

"You move like a man with some Indian in him!" Steele called.

"I've slaughtered a few in my time! But I ain't never been hungry enough to eat red meat!"

The man had not moved this time and the ice-cold fear which had triggered hot sweat to the flesh of Steele drained away. Maybe the man was now pinned down to the same extent as he was; had moved into an area of cover he could not leave without showing himself. In which situation the advantage swung back to the Virginian, who had ample supplies of food and—more importantly—water. While the stranger's saddlebags and canteens were still on the dead horse.

Then the gentle mouthline tightened again. The man had already proved himself an expert in one aspect of the art of survival. And he was not likely to take any uncalculated risks for a drink of water during the long afternoon. Then would come evening and full night, when the shadowy darkness would again give him the upper hand.

"Hey?" Steele called.

"I'm still here!" the stranger responded, obviously aware that his words revealed his position on the rocky slope.

"I can pay you for the horse!"

"What I aim to make you do, feller!"

"I mean in money!"

"It's a long walk to any place I can use that!"

Steele experienced a stab of hot anger and struggled to subdue it. But did not succeed until after he snarled. "This is crazy!"

"I wasn't mad until you shot my horse from under me!"

It was just such calm, evenly spoken responses from the stranger which had triggered sparks from the Virginian's latent but usually tightly controlled hot temper. But now, as Steele relaxed his vise-like grip on the rifle and made the conscious effort to reform his features out of the ugly snarl, he acknowledged the man's attitude as an encouraging sign for exploring talks as a way out of the dangerous stalemate. He was intelligent and a man of his intellect ought to be able to see reason.

"You know what I mean!" Steele called, and his voice held no trace of anger. "I've got no reason to kill you anymore! And you've got very little to gain from killing me!"

He waited for several stretched seconds. Then blinked sweat beads off his eyelids as he strained to catch a glimpse of the stranger moving.

"You hear me?"

"I hear you, feller!" He was still in the same place. "You just ain't said anything worth answering!"

"What have you got to gain? Revenge for a dead horse and a little more than he was worth! I'm a long way from being rich!"

"We're both a long way from anywhere, feller! You want to toss your rifle out of the rocks?"

"What, then?"

"Stand up and head down to the bottom of the slope!"

"That's a big order!"

"But you can fill it, feller! If you don't, I figure I can wait until dark to collect!"

Steele nodded once, acknowledging to the inanimate rocks his respect for the stranger's appraisal of the situation—which matched his own. But would such a man gun him down in cold blood? Further words could not provide a trustworthy answer to this. Only actions.

He rolled over onto his back, cracking his eyes almost closed against the brightness of the blue sky. Then he thrust the Colt Hartford above his head to the full extent of his arm's reach, folded up into a sitting posture and came full erect. For long moments his back was toward the stranger and the muscles from waist to shoulders were knotted in expectation of the vicious impact of a bullet. The silence lengthened and the only pain he felt was from the strain of the taut sinews in his back.

He turned slowly and although he now looked toward the opposite slope from a higher level than before, he still could not see the stranger.

"The rifle means a lot to me!" he called. "I don't like to throw it around!"

"You don't keep it where it is, I'll see it's close by you when I leave you for the buzzards, feller!"

Steele picked his way carefully out from among the rocks and kept his pace just as slow when he was on the uncluttered down-grade. After a few moments, he abandoned the futile exercise of keeping his gaze fixed upon the area of rocks where he knew the stranger to be. And tried not to wrinkle his nose as the nostrils were assaulted by the rancid odor of his own sweat-drenched body.

He came to an abrupt halt at the side of the shallow dry wash, as the stranger unfolded to his full height some twenty feet above and fifteen feet to the left of where Steele stood—his cocked Winchester canted casually to his left shoulder while his right hand hung close to a holstered Frontier Colt.

"Lucky it wasn't a tall order I asked you to fill," the stranger said, the even tenor of his tone more pronounced now that it was unnecessary to shout. As his piercingly blue, heavily hooded eyes raked over the frame of a man who stood more than a head shorter than he.

Steele tested the boyish grin on his face and it felt comfortable enough. "Some people say the best things come in small packages. My name's Steele."

The stranger did not alter his impassive expression in response to the grin. "Edge, feller."

The Virginian licked beads of sweat off his upper lip. "Sounds like we were made for each other."

Edge directed a small globule of saliva at a rock. "Maybe. But after you cut down my horse, I ain't so keen on you."

TWO

AS the man called Edge came slowly down the slope, having to watch where he set his feet among the rocks, he could guess something of what was running through the mind of the disheveled-looking dude below him. With neither man aiming a gun at the other, it was a matter of conjecture which could get the drop. And several times, as Edge concentrated on his footing, Steele seemed to have the better chance.

When he reached level ground and just the dry wash and the trail were between the two men, Edge said, "I got no way of knowing if you made the right choice, feller."

"About showing myself or not trying to kill you from here?" the Virginian asked.

"The first saved us a lot of time. The second saved a life. What I got no way of knowing is whose life. Warn you now, though. You ever aim a gun at me again, make the shot count. Or I'll kill you."

Steele nodded, and lowered his arms, continuing to grip the rifle in both gloved hands but across the front of his thighs now. "Reason you didn't warn me before was because you hoped I'd try?"

Edge fixed the Winchester into his armpit and the crook of an elbow then took the makings from a short pocket and began to roll a cigarette. "Hope ain't something I ever have, feller."

He was a tall man, standing six feet three inches and although he weighed close to two hundred pounds, the solid flesh was evenly distributed over his frame so that there was a lean look to his build. He was in the same late-thirties age group as the Virginian and the flesh of his face had been weathered to a similar extent, although the tone of the heavily lined skin was several shades darker.

This was due to the Mexican blood inherited from his father. From the same parent he had drawn the jet-black coloration of his hair, which grew thick and long enough to cover the nape of his neck and brush his shoulders. His mother had been an immigrant from Scandinavia and it was from her bloodline that he had derived the light, ice-blueness of his permanently narrowed eyes.

These eyes, which surveyed the world with a total lack of expression and yet seemed not to miss the most insignificant detail in the whole of what they saw, were the most prominent features of a face that could be considered either handsome or ugly. Beneath them were high cheekbones flanking a hawk-like nose with slightly flared nostrils above the merest suggestion of a Mexican style moustache. The mouth was narrow and set in a line that revealed the possibility of a cruel streak within the man. Below was a firm jaw which stretched the skin taut from the cheekbones.

Like Adam Steele, Edge had not shaved for several days and there was a dark expanse of stubble on his cheeks and jaw and throat. Also like the more slightly built man, the half-breed wore clothing which had seen many better days. But his garb was entirely Western in style. A gray Stetson, kerchief and cotton shirt. Black denim pants and spurless riding boots. A scuffed leather gunbelt with a bullet slotted through every loop, the holster with the Colt in it tied down to his right thigh.

Unseen by the Virginian was another weapon—a straight razor which Edge carried in a leather pouch at the nape of his neck, the blade and its sheath held in place by a beaded thong which encircled his throat.

"Reckon you won't take my hand and accept an apology, Edge?"

The half-breed struck a match on the stock of his Winchester, lit the cigarette and blew out a stream of smoke. "I can't ride your hand to Southfields and you being sorry won't ease the way my feet are going to ache while I'm walking there."

When the tacit truce had been called, both men had clicked forward the hammers of their rifles. Now Edge

10

showed the extent of his trust that Steele would honor the truce by turning his back on the Virginian, to move along the trail and drop to his haunches beside the dead stallion. But he was not so casual as he appeared to be: Below the surface of his calm exterior he was poised to draw the Colt and whirl to face any threat the smaller man posed. Trusting his highly developed sixth sense for danger more than he trusted Steele.

Flies buzzed angrily and launched themselves into the air, off the areas of rapidly drying blood around the two bullet wounds, as the half-breed began to uncinch the saddle.

"You're not the kind of man I expected to see riding this trail," Steele said.

Edge looked back at him and caught the final flicker of a quizzical expression before it left the coal-black eyes of the Virginian. "Figure you ain't the kind I'd expect to bushwhack me."

He returned his attention to removing the gear from the carcase. And did not look up for several seconds after he heard Steele's footfalls. By which time the Virginian was well on his way back to the cluster of rocks on the valley's southern slope.

Edge dragged everything except for the bridle and reins off the dead horse, grimaced as he tested the weight of the gear over four or five paces, and dropped the saddle. By which time Steele had emerged from the rocks and was coming back down the slope. The Virginian, too, carried just his rifle, saddlebags, canteens and bedroll.

"Reckon twenty miles or so to Southfields," he said as he crossed the dry wash. "With nothing but rocks and dust between here and there."

"Plus a band of renegade Mescaleros," Edge added as he started slowly along the trail.

"So that's it."

"That's what, feller?"

"Why one of us isn't dead. Two guns are better than one if we run into the Apaches."

Edge arced the cigarette into the pebble bed of the wash. "There's that, too."

"What else?"

11

"You did like I told you and didn't try to pull anything. To kill you then would've been almost as bad as shooting a man from ambush. Just to get his horse."

He directed a brief sidelong glance at Steele and saw the Virginian react to the soft taunt with a grimace. Which ended with a soft sigh.

"If I stole a man's horse, I couldn't leave him with a gun, feller. Usual run of men riding this kind of trail are either bounty hunters or bounty hunters' prey. Man without a gun and horse in this area is better off killed cleanly. Even more so if what you say about renegade Indians is true."

"The Federale patrol I heard it from were short-handed, feller. On account of the Apaches killing four of their men."

"How many in the party?"

"Ten or a dozen. Kill crazy with nothing to lose. On the run from the US army, the Federales and from Geronimo."

"Geronimo?"

"Right. They raised some hell around his camp before they hit a supply train out of Fort Huachuca. Then crossed the border and raided a Mexican pueblo up near Fronteras."

Now that there was no reason to watch each other, the ill-matched—in stature—men maintained an apparently casual but actually careful surveillance over the barren terrain ahead and to either side of them. Each of them aware of the other's distrust of the rocks and clumps of dusty cactus plants, the rises and depressions that offered cover to anyone in need of it. Each of them aware, too, that it was only such innate caution, allied with some indefinable sense for menace, which had saved the half-breed's life further back along the valley.

"You must have good reason to get to Southfields," Steele said after a long, easy silence.

"I came down to Mexico to meet a man that didn't exist," Edge answered.

"Didn't exist?"

"He sure enough doesn't now. He's dead. But I didn't have to kill him."

"You've lost me."

"Doesn't matter, feller. It's none of your business. Heading for Southfields because there's nothing in Mexico for me. And I've already been to the nearest border town."

"And to hell with the Apaches?"

"Them or me'll go there sure enough if we meet up and they ain't had their fill of killing."

"I'm looking for a Swede named Sven Karlsen. Caused some trouble for me up near Ogallala. Way it turned out, the trouble's over already. But I was told Karlsen has a son living in Southfields. After hunting the Swede this far, I reckoned to see it through to the end."

"And to hell with the Apaches?" Edge echoed the other man's earlier comment.

Steele grinned. "Two's company. Especially if the Indians try to crowd us."

Edge nodded and another silence lengthened between the two men as they ambled easily along the little-used trail, small puffs of gray dust rising from under their booted feet, occasionally running a hand or a shirt cuff over sweat-tacky faces.

The tall, lean, narrow-eyed half-breed was totally at ease but sensed a degree of discomfiture within the other man. Sensed it and understood the reason for it. For he knew that Steele, although he did not look it, was of a similar breed to himself. An independent, self-assured man who lived his life by rules which he lay down. One such rule was that he should avoid being in the debt of another. And when a favor was taken, it must be returned as soon as possible. No man could be granted a greater favor than to have his doomed life spared.

"Mind telling me something?"

Such men as they were spoke little and cared even less for the circumstances of others—under normal conditions. But this situation was not normal for Adam Steele and the Virginian was obviously using talk as an exercise to keep his mind from dwelling on the debt he owed.

"I don't have a thing to hide—anymore."

"You didn't know I was up on the south slope because you saw me. Yet you knew somebody was there before I fired the shot. Where did you learn to do that? In the war?"

"Right, feller."

"Union?"

A nod. "And it sounds in your voice that you were on the other side. You picked up the same trick the same way, uh?"

"That's right. As a cavalry lieutenant."

"I made captain."

Another, shorter silence. Then Steele said, "I'm from Virginia. But accents didn't mean so much back then. My Pa worked as a secret agent for Lincoln. This was his rifle."

Edge glanced at the Colt Hartford which the Virginian had sloped to his right shoulder while carrying his gear over his left forearm.

"Maybe one day you'll be able to afford a new one, feller."

Steele's mouthline tightened and tiny flames of rising anger flared briefly in his dark eyes. But he brought the emotion into check. "This one suits me fine," he answered evenly.

"No sweat," the half-breed said, aware that he had touched a sore point.

"Only thing on the whole plantation that was left to me after the place was burned to the ground. And a group of hot heads lynched my father. Rebels all of them."

Edge might have started to contribute his fair share to the conversation. By telling Steele how he had returned to the farmstead in Iowa to find his kid brother murdered and the buildings razed by fire by men he had commanded throughout most of the war. It was unlikely, but he might have done so—had he not come to an abrupt halt and peered fixedly toward a point on the north-eastern horizon.

Steele was only a part of a second later in matching the half-breed's attitude.

"You see something?"

"Yeah, Reb. Smoke."

Because of their side by side positions, it had been tacitly agreed that the Virginian should watch the ground to the south of the trail while Edge surveyed the north. It therefore took Steele a few moments to rake his eyes over the barren terrain and focus on the mushroom-shaped cloud of smoke which had captured the half-breed's attention.

It showed against the sky where the blueness of infinity became blurred by heat shimmer above a line of low ridges. These ridges marked the horizon at the far side of a desert plain which stretched away east, north and south from the mouth of the valley. The dry wash petered away into nothing here, but the trail was still clearly defined, running straight as a prairie railroad toward a point below where the smoke columned up from among the ridges and then spread out to the sides under a current of warm air.

"Ten miles, maybe fifteen," Steele suggested.

"About that."

"Be full night before we get close enough for anyone over there to see us."

"Unless they start to head this way after they finish eating." Edge uncapped a canteen and took a frugal swallow of tepid water.

"You always look on the black side, Edge?"

"Yeah, Reb. That way I'm never disappointed. Sometimes get nice surprises."

The half-breed recapped the canteen and started forward.

Steele fell in beside him and said, "Be grateful if you didn't call me Reb. War's been over a long time."

"When we were fighting it, I outranked you. And when it was over, I was on the winning side. Way things stand, I figure I still outrank you. Not just because you lost. You know what I mean, Reb?"

The Virginian had to make the effort to control his temper again. This time it was easier, though. And not just because the taller man had shown self-control without seeming to try. Edge had, Steele acknowledged, good reason to be aggrieved. He always had, since the stallion was shot from under him. But now, with the flat-topped column of white smoke signaling a potential new danger, the loss of his horse was of greater importance. For if they did meet up with trouble riding far out on the desert floor,

15

without a horse between them they would have little chance of survival.

"I reckon I know what you mean," the Virginian replied after a pause. And added, "Yank."

"No sweat with that," Edge allowed evenly, not letting the column of smoke keep him from watching the rest of the country. "I even ride with the occasional bastard or sonofabitch these days. Just don't call me or any other Mexican greaser or Mex."

"Any other rules I should know about, Yank?" Steele asked with a grimace.

Edge produced a chunk of jerked beef from a saddlebag and bit into it. "Figure you live by the same rulebook as me. I like to stay alive and I don't like to have my old man's nationality insulted."

Steele nodded. "I have just the one beyond the usual." He raised the Colt Hartford an inch off his shoulder and the inscribed gold plate on the stock glinted in the afternoon sun. "Value this rifle second only to my life."

"It's a horse you owe me." the half-breed answered. "Nothing else I want from you."

This exchange prefaced the longest yet silence between the men as they set out across the desert which was featured only by cactus, mesquite and countless washes which showed no sign that water had ever run along their beds. The hottest part of the day was over now but the temperature seemed to rise after they had moved from the token shade—which they had never used—of the rocky valley. It was a dry heat that evaporated the beads of sweat as they squeezed from constantly open pores. The sun blazed down upon their heads and backs with an intensity which made them feel naked, without any barriers of hats and shirts between the burning rays of their flesh. Their eyes were strained by the brightness of the desert light and the need to distinguish the realities of the landscape from countless mirages. Their burdens seemed to grow heavier with every step. The temptation to take more than a mere lip, mouth and throat-moistening sip of water at long intervals was increasingly hard to resist.

Once, Steele said, "If those ridges are ten miles away, it means they're halfway to Southfields."

Edge made no response. But much later, he drawled, "You figure to kill the Swede if you find him in South-fields?"

"Depends," the Virginian answered.

Then, later still, the leading arc of the sun touched the distant peaks of the Sierra Madres to their left and behind them. And gradually, with the changing colors of the sky and the fading light, the horizons receded and the desert landscape showed up more clearly, the tough vegetation and rugged rocks standing out starkly against their backgrounds of arid earth and long shadows.

And the two men saw smoke again. Maybe from the same fire or maybe not. It was impossible to tell, because of their altered viewpoint from the last time they had seen it.

"Mealbreak?" Edge suggested after the sun had plunged to a crimson death and full night encroached across the desert.

He did not wait for agreement before dropping his bedroll and lowering his rump onto it. Steele chose to unfurl his and stretch out on it full length for a full minute, flexing his weary muscles. While the half-breed opened a can of beans and started to eat them without relish—watching the dark hills and from time to time raking his hooded eyes in other directions.

"Figure twenty miles was nearer the mark, Reb," he said as Steele sighed and folded up into a sitting posture. "Covered something over half that."

The Virginian rubbed gloved fists against his eyes, trying to ease the painful effects of the long day of dazzling light from them. "Reckon so," he agreed after glancing along the trail.

If the fire was still burning, its smoke was lost against the night sky.

A bright quarter moon hung low in the east and more stars than it would take a lifetime to count gleamed against the entire enormous dome of infinite blackness. The cool air was a luxury the men enjoyed without expression—just as they had endured the hardships of the blisteringly hot day.

They ate in silence, washing down the food with meager

17

draughts of water. Then Edge rolled and lit a cigarette and lay out full length on the ground with his bedroll as a pillow. Steele accepted the chore of keeping watch without complaint.

"You out of makings, or is it you don't smoke, Reb?" the half-breed asked, a hand going to his shirt pocket.

"Grateful to you, but I don't use tobacco."

"That what you grew back in Virginia?"

"Tobacco and cotton both."

"Came west after the war?"

"Got as far as Tennessee before I caught up with the men who lynched my father."

"They paid, Reb?"

"They paid, Yank!" Steele came back forcefully, obviously recalling bitter memories.

"Something you don't want to talk about?"

The Virginian sighed out of an emotion that was a wasteful drain on his diminished energy reserves. Then shot a quizzical glance toward the totally relaxed half-breed. "I reckon you hardly ever talk about anything unless there's reason?"

Edge came up into a sitting posture and flicked the remains of the cigarette far out across the desert.

"We've seen smoke twice," he said evenly. "Maybe from two fires in two different places. But not far away from each other. Big fires. Not from house smokestacks."

"I'll go along with that."

"Close to the border. Not so far away from Southfields."

Steele nodded. "Chances are, cooking fires at a camp. A camp made by people with good reason not to go into town."

Edge spat a piece of tobacco off his lower lip. "Chances are, the Apache renegades."

"Who saved my life, in a manner of speaking?"

The half-breed said nothing. But there was a question in the slitted blue eyes which glinted in the moonlight—like short lengths of gun metal—through the shadow below his hat brim.

"You were an exception, Yank," Steele said tightly, resenting the doubts of the taciturn man. "Because the circumstances were exceptional. I only once before did something I'll be ashamed of for the rest of my life. That circumstance was out of the ordinary, too. Whatever kind of trouble we meet up with between here and Southfields, I'll do my share of handling it. You can either accept my word on that, or I can pay you a fair price for your horse and we can part company here and now."

Edge looked hard into the grim set profile of Adam Steele as the Virginian stared toward the ragged ridges of the northern horizon. And experienced a mild pang of regret that he had voiced uncertainty about the man's courage. It was not the half-breed's way to prejudge a man, with words or actions. But there was something about this man—a certain quality that was totally at odds with the sneak attack he launched a few hours ago. That had been the act of a desperate man and yet Steele did not seem to be in desperate straits. But because of the kind of man he was, it was difficult to decide what fears or joys he experienced behind his impassive exterior.

Anger sometimes. That was plain enough to see when a word was spoken to trigger his quick temper. And this an emotion that was more often than not directed inwardly, as if the Virginian felt a greater resentment toward himself for allowing his emotions to show than at the object of his rage.

Edge could understand this. From personal experience. Was this why he sought, uncharacteristically, to discover more about Adam Steele? To find more common ground they shared?

"I wouldn't know how much to charge for a dead horse, Reb," the half-breed said as he rose to his feet and gathered up his gear.

The final eight or nine miles of desert walking was easier in the coolness of the moonlit, star-bright night. And they covered the ground at a faster rate—the more slightly built Virginian able to keep up with the longer striding half-breed without showing any more signs than he of weariness.

No words were spoken—even when a column of smoke was seen, white against the darkness of the moon-shadowed hills. For each man was aware the other had spotted it, knew it was from a freshly lit fire, less than two miles away and in the same area where two other fires had been lit during the day.

"Late supper," Edge murmured when they were in the hills and close enough to the fire to detect the scent of woodsmoke.

"Or early breakfast," Steele countered.

"No, don't!" a man screamed, terror pitching his tone to a high shrillness.

"Or maybe someone playing with fire," the half-breed growled as the piercing words of the terrified man caused both of them to come to a halt.

They were still on the trail, but could see only thirty yards or so along it now. For in off the flat desert it took the line of least resistance among the rocky rises and ahead of them it curved to the right between the folds of the hills, swinging away from the smoke column which they had been walking toward for the past hour.

Another sound of depthless fear split the night silence. This time not a word. Just a scream. High pitched and long lasting then abruptly curtailed.

Edge turned his head to look at Steele, lips parting to voice a question. But he held back on the query, puzzled by the frown on the other man's face.

"Something, Reb?"

"Two words. Sounded like they were spoken with a foreign accent, wouldn't you say?"

"I wasn't listening that hard. You figure your Swede?"

"I listened hard enough to want to take a look?"

Steele's tone of voice added the question mark.

Edge nodded. "We just guessed how far to Southfields from the smoke, feller. You check the man. I'll look over any horseflesh that's around."

There was no word or sign of acknowledgement. The Virginian merely started forward and Edge went with him. Off the trail and up the hillside which was the first obstacle between them and the fire.

As they neared the crest they crouched and then went down on all fours, abandoning all their burdens except for the rifles. They covered the final few feet on their bellies, using elbows and the toecaps of their boots to propel themselves forward. They pushed their hats down their backs to the full extent of the neck thongs before they slowly raised their heads.

The looked briefly down into a shadowed, empty draw, then across it to where an Indian brave sat on his haunches at the top of twenty-feet-high rock face. The long haired, naked-to-the-waist brave cradled a rifle in the crooks of his elbows resting on his thighs as his gaze shifted lazily from a section of the trail visible at the eastern end of the draw to the area down on his left where the fire burned.

With just the far side of the draw—perhaps forty feet away—between the two white men and the fire, they could see a dull, dome-shaped glow from the flames now. And hear low whimpers and moans vented by a suffering man.

Edge was closer to the Apache sentry than Steele, but it was the Virginian who moved to deal with him, after glancing briefly across the fifteen feet of hilltop that separated them. Their eyes locked for a part of a second, allowing no time for a tacit message to be transmitted and received. Then Steel bellied away, careful to remain off the rim of the draw.

The half-breed spent a few moments looking between the Apache and the white man, then eased down the slope a few inches, put his hat back on his head and rolled over onto his back. He took the makings from his shirt pocket and when the cigarette was finished he hung it, unlit, in the corner of his mouth. Then, with his hat pulled forward, he peered up at the darkness of the brim and listened to the anguished sounds from the throat of the man enduring Apache torture. While in his mind, he watched images of Adam Steele as the Virginian made his lethal approach on the unsuspecting brave. Going away from the sentry at first—back along the draw to where he could safely climb down into it and up the other side. Then back toward the Apache, maybe able to look down onto the area where the fire burned. But he would not spend more than a moment indulging his curiosity, would move as fast as the need for complete silence allowed, closing with the bored sentry.

If he made the slightest sound, he would be dead. Maybe he would take the sentry with him, but that wouldn't make him any less dead.

Edge moved the unlit cigarette from one corner of his

mouth to the other. And pondered briefly on the prospect of what the Virginian carried in his saddlebags. Perhaps something of value to pay for the dead horse. For the Apaches would certainly strip his corpse and steal his rifle.

For ten minutes the half-breed lay on his back, at ease, content that the Indians would not come looking for another white man if they killed Steele. Then, with the sounds of agony from the torture victim diminishing, he pushed the hat off his head, turned over and inched back to the point from where he could look across the draw.

His timing was good. For the Virginian had bellied to within six feet of the bored sentry. And here he left his rifle on the ground and eased forward empty-handed.

Instinctively, the half-breed nestled the stock of the Winchester against his shoulder and drew a bead on the squatting brave. He rested a thumb on the hammer but did not click it back.

Steele interrupted his intent concentration on the back of the Indian to spare the briefest of glances for Edge. Then he rose onto all fours and reached down to his right leg. On the occasions they had rested out on the desert, the half-breed had seen the slit in the Virginian's pants seam and spotted the bulge of a sheathed weapon at the lower calf. Now he saw that Steele was careful to shield the polished metal from the moonlight as he drew the weapon.

Maybe the Virginian made a sound—breathed too loudly or caused a tiny pebble to roll from under a hand, knee or boot. That, or the brave sensed a menacing presence behind him.

But the Apache had time only to tense and move his head just a fraction of an inch. Before Steele powered forward—both arms stretched to their limit. The left gloved hand curled around the neck of the brave, clamped over his mouth and nostrils, and forced him to topple backwards. As the right, fisted around the knife handle, went up and came down in a blur of speed. For a part of a second the blade glinted in the moonlight. Then was buried to the hilt in the throat of the Apache.

The brave's body spasmed once and became inert as Steele pressed himself as close to the ground as his victim. The moans which rose with the fire glow from the ground beyond the draw diminished further. As if the effort to give vocal response to agony was a greater drain on the man's reserves than the infliction of the torture.

All else was silence.

Steele moved his head, to look down at the fire. Then withdrew the knife from the dead flesh and signaled with it for Edge to approach the Apache camp by way of the trail. The half-breed followed the suggestion, collecting his own and Steele's gear on the way. Not hurrying, because there was no need—the Virginian's gesture not transmitting urgency. He took time to light the cigarette and had smoked it down to the smallest stub before he reached a point where he was able to see a man dying slowly, Apache style.

He had to amble some fifty yards beyond the mouth of the draw before he located a gully along which he was able to approach the encampment secretly. He did so with just the Winchester in his hands, having placed his own and Steele's gear beside a rock at the side of the trail.

The fire was set at the lowest point in a shallow basin, with four US Army pup tents erected in an arc around one side of it. Because the draw to the south rose higher than any other ground for at least a half mile in all directions, the single sentry posted up there had been sufficient. Until the Virginian's knife had proved otherwise. For the brave had been able to keep watch on the trail where it ran by the mouth of the draw, and a long stretch of it north toward the border. And had the two white men been riding instead of walking from the south, he would undoubtedly have been able to hear them long before he saw them.

Edge looked for long seconds up toward the area where the sentry had been posted. And failed to see the corpse or the very much alive Steele against the moon-shadowed rock. Until the Virginian raised his rifle against the sky to acknowledge that he had spotted the half-breed.

From the stolen pup tents came the sounds of men, sleeping. Deep, regular breathing. Snoring. The smacking of lips. These noises competing with and often louder than those vented by the dying man.

A big man—at least six feet six inches tall who must weigh more than two hundred and fifty pounds. With wide shoulders, a broad chest and a bulging belly. Held prisoner in a spread-eagled position, wrists and ankles lashed to the tops of stout poles which protruded two feet out of the ground. His rump and lower back sagged to the earth. And he was fast losing the struggle to keep his head from lolling downward, onto the glowing ashes of the fire. He was naked and the effort of keeping his head off the fire rather than the heat of the fire itself caused every pore to ooze sweat beads. Runnels of salty moisture coursed down over his face, made white marks through the soot on the top of his head where his hair had been seared off, and hissed into extinction in the embers.

During the stretched seconds Edge studied the agonized man, he saw that the slow death by fire was the culmination of other tortures the hapless white man had suffered at the hands of the renegade Apaches. His crotch was a pulpy mass where his genitals had been cut off, his eyes had been gouged out and he no longer had any ears. His chest, belly and thighs were covered with shallow knife wounds which looked as if, before the blood ran and congealed, the cutting blades had inscribed the marks of Indian sign language.

A weaker man would undoubtedly have died from shock and loss of blood long before the final anguish was inflicted. Which explained why all save the sentry had bedded down—bored by the length of time it was taking their vicitm to die. Lulled to sleep by the sounds of his agony— the reason they had not pulled out his tongue. Their dreams given images, too, by pulque, the sickly sweet odor of which was almost as strong as that of scorching flesh.

The half-breed, familiar at second and first hand with the suffering resulting from man's inhumanity to man, looked at the torture victim, the tents, and the remuda of ten ponies and a horse with the same cold, compassionless glint in his narrowed eyes. Then concentrated his attention between the tents and the man moving down the slope on the other side of the basin.

The Apache's prisoner jerked from head to toe, and vented a strangled cry as his head sagged low enough for the crown to make contact with the glowing wood fire. The

24

veins and tendons at the side of his neck stood out like pulsing lengths of thick cord.

The louder sound drew grunts from some of the sleeping braves—involuntary reactions to having their rest disturbed.

Steele froze on the fringe of the light from the fire. Then raked his rifle back and forth, covering the tents.

Edge waited, his Winchester still held in two hands, diagonally across his chest. And watched as, when the sounds settled down to the same level as before, Steele continued his advance. Moved up beside the tortured man and craned his neck to look down at the punished, contorted face. Just for a moment or two. Then he looked across at the half-breed and gave a curt nod.

Edge moved forward, came to a halt on the opposite side of the fire, dropped to his haunches and rested the Winchester across his thighs. So that, with free hands, he was able to grasp the unburnt ends of two lengths of timber and draw them out of the fire. He mimed tossing them toward the tents and the Virginian showed the flicker of a smile before he followed the squatting man's example.

For a moment, the animalistic instincts within man triggered a clear spot within the tormented mind of Sven Karlsen and the Swede swung his head from side to side—turning his eyeless sockets toward Edge and then Steele.

"Finish me off," he rasped, the words mere scratches on the silence.

"First things first, feller," Edge murmured. And hurled his two pieces of glowing timber at the tents.

"And there are no seconds to waste," Steele added grimly, powering to his feet after tossing his missiles toward the other two tents.

As the glowing sticks spun through the air, the slipstream caused the embered ends to burst into flames. And it was as blazing torches that two struck the canvas and dropped to the ground as the other two crashed through the flaps.

The braves, their minds dulled by alcohol and blurred by sleep, came awake with yells of fear and whoops of rage. As two tents began to burn from the inside and the other two from the outside.

"Blast them, Reb!" Edge snapped.

"Shove your orders, Yank!" Steele snarled back.

And the half-breed had fired two shots into flaming canvas before the Virginian triggered his first—electing to wait until an Apache jerked aside a flap and showed himself.

Both men stood in half-crouches, rifles leveled from their hips—identical killer grins pasted to their faces, the expressions fixed to their lips not reaching up to their eyes. Eyes which glinted—Edge's brighter than Steele's—in the firelight that spread higher and wider with each second.

"They sure appeared to be fired up about something, don't they?" the Virginian yelled as he pumped off two more shots, the cracks of exploding bullets cutting across the crackle of burning canvas and the yells of the pained and terrified Indians.

"On account of the heat's in tents," the half-breed growled. And triggered and pumped the Winchester's action three times—one bullet burrowing into the side of a brave who broke clear with his hair in flames and the other two cracking into the black smoke and yellow and red tongues rising from the remains of a tent.

Ponies snorted and whinnied, tried to break from the remuda in their panic but stumbled or fell because of their hobbles. Panicked by the leaping flames, billowing smoke, the screams, the gunfire and the stench of slaughter.

Two, or maybe three, wild shots were exploded from out of the fires. Or perhaps the cracks were simply the detonations of overheated ammunition. Certainly no bullets came close enough to the crouching Edge and Steele to give them pause for thought.

The Virginian emptied the six rounds from the Colt Hartford and reloaded without haste, watching while the half-breed expended the shells from the larger-capacity magazine of the Winchester.

The tinder-dry canvas of the tents, the bedrolls and the clothing of the Apaches had almost burnt to nothing by then. And the blackened corpses of the braves could be seen slumped among the pyres. But because there was a chance one or two of the Indians might still be clinging to life, a Colt Hartford and a Frontier Colt were swung across the gruesome scene for a few moments.

26

Then the final flickering flames went out and Steele growled, "Grateful to you for the help, Yank."

"Didn't do it for you," Edge replied, holstering the revolver and looking across to where the ponies and the horses were calming.

Steele grimaced. "Killing a whole bunch of men for a mount is all right? If they're Indians."

"Don't matter what they are, Reb," the half-breed answered, feeding shells through the loading gate of the rifle, and turning toward the dying man as the Swede groaned. "Important thing is not to kill the horse."

Sven Karlsen died. He screamed one more time, as his head fell back into the fiery embers. Then, as the two men cradling rifles watched, his overheated skull split open and the soft contents spilled out, the gory liquid spitting and hissing and steaming as it doused the area of the fire where it ran.

"Worth it for you?" Edge asked evenly.

"People back in Ogallala were wrong," Steele said, stooping, drawing his knife and cutting through one of the ropes which trapped the corpse to the stakes. "They reckoned he didn't have much brain."

Edge spat and turned to go toward the remuda. "He sure didn't have enough to put the fire out before it was too late."

THREE

THEY rode into Southfields in the light of the false dawn. Edge was astride the dead Swede's saddle cinched to the gray gelding of the man who had died so badly at the hands of the Apaches. While Adam Steele rode an Indian pony, just a blanket between his rump and the pinto's back. The limp, mutilated corpse of Karlsen was wrapped in another blanket, lashed over the back of a bay pony which the Virginian led by a line.

They could see the town from more than a mile away, as they crested a rise and started down a long, gentle slope. A town which, even over such a distance, they were able to see was comprised of two distinct sections—with the adobe buildings of the Mexican area on the south side of the board east-to-west main street and the frame and brick and stone construction of the American style architecture on the north side.

The crude shacks scattered to either side of the south trail, each of them set amid a few acres of meagerly cropping dusty soil, suggested only poverty—a style that had no nationality. Something else they had in common was that they were all sited north of the American-Mexican border—this marked by a wooden sign with faded lettering nailed to a post at the side of the trail halfway down the long slope.

No windows showed light and there was no smoke rising from the chimneys when the two living men and one dead one came slowly over the ridge. But by the time they reached the limits marker—*Southfields, El. 901 ft. Pop. 1307*—the town was stirring. Wisps of smoke tainted the clear air, kerosene lamps were flickering into life, pots were rattling, cocks were crowing and dogs were barking.

28

But out on the streets, only the newcomers were moving, the clop of shod and unshod hooves drawing attention to the strangers. Perhaps idle curiosity at first, the early risers in the Mexican section of town relieved to have some diversion from the routine morning chores. Then any face that showed at a window was abruptly drawn back out of sight, expressions of indifferent inquisitiveness instantly changing to shock and fear—at the sight of hands and feet swinging limply from under the humped blanket over the back of the pony on a lead line.

The two heavily bristled, weary-eyed men showed no sign that they knew they were a center of frightened interest. And appeared totally indifferent to every aspect of their surroundings as they rode along the curving side street that cut through the Mexican section of town, reined their mounts to a halt where it ended at Southfield's main street.

"That's my first stop," Steele said, nodding in the direction of a single-storey, stone-constructed building with a sign reading *Sheriff's Office* above the doorway.

"Ain't nothing to me where you stop or go, feller," the half-breed answered, looking directly across the street to the impressive façade of a wide-fronted, two-storey frame-built hotel called the Town House.

"You'll have a long wait for the sheriff, son," a man muttered, and then was shaken by a wracking cough.

Both newcomers had been aware of the slightly built, bald-headed and thickly bearded old man who was curled up asleep in the doorway of the cantina to their left as they halted at the intersection. Now as he rose unsteadily to his feet, having to press a hand against the wall to stay upright, they eyed him with the same lack of interest as the first time.

"A deputy will do if the top man is out of town," Steele said.

The old man, who walked as if he was still drunk and looked to be in his eighties, squinted his bloodshot eyes against the first rays of the rising sun. He opened his mouth to respond to the Virginian's comment, then saw the blanket-shrouded corpse for the first time. He did a shocked double-take, swallowed hard, spat out a stream of brown-stained saliva and rasped, "Jesus Christ!" As his feet

29

dragged to a halt on the dusty street and he had to reach out for the wall again to keep from toppling over.

"This feller was burned, old man, not crucified," Steele said.

The bearded man in the ragged shirt, patched pants and split-open boots shook his head, fisted the grit of sleep from his eyes and shot a frightened glance across at the Town House. "Mr. Clinton Merritt ain't gonna like this one little bit."

"Ain't here for anybody's benefit but our own, feller," Edge said.

"Then the best thing you two can do is head on out. And take the stiff with you. Bounty hunters ain't welcome in Southfields."

"It's a long time since I was a bounty hunter, old man," the Virginian answered, and drew a sidelong glance from Edge as the half-breed recalled what Steele had implied the previous day about men who tracked down others for blood money. "Merritt the sheriff?"

Another shake of the head, as the old man forced himself to look away from the blanket-draped corpse. "Mr. Clinton Merritt's the owner of Southfields. Lock, stock and barrel."

"What about the sheriff?"

"He left. Him and his three sidekicks. What's today?"

"Friday."

"Then it was Wednesday they left."

"When are they due back?"

"They ain't."

The coolness of the night was now completely gone. And in the first heat of the new day's sun the air was fast becoming tainted with the smells of smoke, brewing coffee and cooking food. These aromas were generated from both sections of the town, but beyond the group of three men and three horses on the corner, there were no other signs of life along the main street. This because it was lined with commercial premises which would not be open for business for some time.

West of the Town House was a bank, a newspaper office, a line of five stores and a stage line and telegraph office. East was a livery stable, a blacksmith, a barber's

30

shop, the law office and jail, a seed merchants and a boarding house. Aligned along the south side of Southfield's main street were three cantinas, two stores, a church, a restaurant and a gunsmith. The restaurant and one of the stores looked to be abandoned.

"Like standing at the gates of hell, ain't it. Reb" Edge muttered as he heeled the gelding across the street.

"Uh?" Steele grunted.

"Just one damned thing after another."

"I'm used to it, Yank!" the Virginian called after the half-breed, as Edge swung out of his saddle in front of the stooped entrance of the Town House.

"Hey," the old-timer said. "Them look like Indian ponies."

"That's what they are," Steele told him absently, watching Edge as the tall, lean man from Iowa hitched the gelding to the hotel rail and stepped up to try the double doors.

"You and that feller have a run in with 'Paches, mister?"

"We did better than him," Steele answered, jerking a thumb toward the slumped corpse.

The hotel doors were locked and Edge moved along the stoop and sat down with a sigh on one of the four rocking chairs, lay back and tipped his hat forward over his eyes.

"Oh, well that's different, mister. If you ain't bounty hunters. Why, Mr. Clinton Merritt might even be pleased to see a couple of fellers like you."

"We don't come as a couple," the Virginian drawled, shifting his gaze to the stage line depot which incorporated a telegraph office. He nodded in that direction. "What time they open up down the street?"

"John Clements sleeps out back, young feller. If you got an urgent message you want sent, you can wake him any time you like."

"Grateful to you. Guess you have a mortician in town?"

The old man chuckled, obviously relieved that Clinton Merritt would have no cause to be disturbed by the appearance of the strangers in town.

"Mortician and doctor both. Same man, I mean. Lots of folks don't trust a man that does them two jobs at once. Harry Pollock is the man you want. Office in back of the

31

Town House for doctorin'. Place out behind the livery where he does what's necessary to bury his mistakes."

Another chuckle.

"Reckon you heard that from your grandfather when you were very young, feller," the Virginian said, and heeled the pony into movement, tugging on the reins to head him toward the livery.

"Hey, I figure all that information I give you oughta be worth the price of a drink, young feller," the old-timer called after him." Wouldn't you say?"

"Cheaper to disagree with you."

The dishevelled oldster spat again, directing the foul-colored saliva into the tracks left by the two unshod ponies.

An upper-story window of the Town House was banged open and a gray-haired man leaned out. There was gray hair on his naked chest, too. And he had grayish-tinged skin. Colored with the red of anger as he fumbled to place a pair of wire-framed spectacles on the bridge of his nose and hook them over his ears.

"How'd you get to be drunk this time of day, Shep?" he called in a snarling tone.

"I ain't drunk, Mr. Merritt sir!" the old man responded, resentment changing to nervousness.

"Then why're you hollering loud enough to wake the dead?" He shifted his gaze from the apprehensive old man to focus it through the thick lenses of his glasses on Steele. And exploded, "Damn it, a stinking bounty hunter!"

Steel dismounted from the pony and peered up at the window where Clinton Merritt was fuming and saw that the man was twisted awkwardly in the frame—as if he was held fast to the chair that allowed him little freedom of movement.

"It'll be the corpse that will start to stink in this heat," the Virginian corrected. "Unless I can get it buried soon."

The shouted exchange caused more windows and some doors to open, as citizens of Southfields below the stature of Merritt but higher on the success scale than Shep sought to see and hear better what was happening at the center of town.

"Nobody gets planted in my town unless I say so!" Mer-

32

ritt snarled. Then turned away from the window and yelled, "Wanda, bring me my frigging clothes!"

"Been easier to have left him for the buzzards, Reb," Edge said from the rocker on the stoop.

"We left them breakfast, Yank," Steele reminded. "Even cooked it for them."

"Sounds like you could be in for a roasting, too."

This as the doors of the hotel rattled and were thrown open, by a sleepy-eyed, tousle-haired short man with a paunchy belly and bandy legs who was still pushing his shirt tails into his pants as he stopped on the stoop.

"Somebody need burying, did I hear?" he asked, his voice strangely squeaky.

He was looking at Edge, for Steele had led his own and the corpse burdened pony into the alley between the hotel and the livery. The half-breed raised his hat on to the top of his head and rocked lazily forward to come to his feet.

"I'm nobody," he said to the rudely awakened Harry Pollock. "It ain't my funeral." He jerked a thumb. "In back of the livery, feller."

Southfield's doctor and undertaker managed to regain some composure. And chided pompously, "You shouldn't make jokes about the newly dead, sir."

"Understand that's part of my charm," Edge replied as he turned in through the hotel entrance while Pollock stepped down off the stoop.

The lobby of the town house was large and plushly furnished, still fresh-smelling with the cool air of night. So that as he crossed the thick pile carpet toward the unattended reception desk, Edge could smell the staleness of old sweat on his flesh and clothing.

There were a half dozen thickly padded armchairs, three polished tables, a number of floor-standing ashtrays and a few plants in pots on the wall-to-wall carpet. Two crystal chandeliers hung from the carved ceiling and the walls were wood panelled. A door on the left was labelled *Restaurant* and on the right were double doors marked *Bar*. The lettering was gold-blocked. To the right of the reception desk which had a bead-curtained archway behind it was an impressive curved stairway with highly polished

33

banisters and to the left was a doorway size opening in the wall with ropes hanging inside.

When Edge banged the bell on the desk the ropes began to move and there was a rumbling sound from above. And a small, doorless elevator car dropped into sight, just big enough to carry a man in a wheelchair.

A tall, thickset man of about fifty-five with a gray complexion and hair. Wearing thick-lensed, wire-framed spectacles in front of green eyes. He had a fleshy face, deeply wrinkled on the forehead and at the sides of his small, slightly pouted mouth. His torso and arms were heavily padded with flesh that bulged against the fabric of his expensive white shirt, but his legs looked to be emaciated within the white pants. The hands with which he propelled the chair out of the elevator were gnarled.

He swung the chair into a turn and stopped it, glaring angrily at the half-breed. "You ain't him!" he accused.

"I'm me, feller."

"I want to see that bounty hunting sonofabitch!"

"I want a bath, breakfast and a room."

"See Wanda about that," Clinton Merritt snapped and spun the wheels of his chair to head for the street doorway.

Beyond this, the cripple made a sharp left turn to trundle himself along the stoop.

"Him and Doc Pollock gone down to the morgue, Mr. Clinton Merritt sir!" the town drunk called across the street.

"Two fifty a night and you can take as many baths as you like, mister. Town House restaurant ain't open, but you can get good food across at the Mexican place."

She came down the stairway, her feet bare, as dishevelled by recent sleep as every other citizen of Southfields as he had seen this early morning. A slender redhead in her mid-twenties. Close to six feet tall with the kind of face which could be made to be pretty if the right cosmetics were wisely applied. Her eyes were a paler green than those of Merritt and her lips had a slightly more accentuated pout. Her skin was pale and blemish-free, except for the dark half-moons under her eyes. The shapeless blue dress she wore was high-necked and reached to her ankles. It fitted her where it touched and the contours of her body

34

it did follow suggested a slim but well-proportioned figure.

Her gait was as weary as her appearance and voice as she moved behind the desk and produced a register from below.

"Obliged," Edge said, taking the pen she handed him and signing the book she opened.

"Payment in advance . . ." She turned the book to read his name, ". . . Edge."

The half-breed took some bills from his hip pocket and asked, "Who do I see about taking care of my horse, lady?"

"Dave Pollock runs the livery. The animal outside?"

"Yeah."

"I'll have him see to it. You pay Dave when you leave." She reached under the desk again and brought up a key, looked at the numbered tag with her dull eyes and added, "You're in room five if that's all right. It's at the front. One of them over the restaurant. Bathroom's at the end of the hall. I'll have the Negro fill a tub for you." She took the money from him, made change and asked, "Anything else you want?"

"What else is there?"

She shrugged her thin shoulders and for a moment the fabric of her dress hugged the small, conical breasts revealing their firmness. "Bar'll be open around ten. You want a woman, there are a couple over at the Cantina Plata."

She puckered her lips, as if giving information about the whereabouts of the town whores left a bitter taste in her mouth.

"Reckon that's about all Southfields has to offer people passing through."

"Wanda!" Merritt yelled.

"Shit," she rasped, then glared at the half-breed as if challenging him to take exception to her use of the word.

"Guess the place for that is out back of the hotel?" Edge asked.

"Wanda, come get me back on the stoop!" Merritt bellowed.

The woman scowled, brushed aside a few of the stranded beads in the archway and directed her ill-temper toward an unseen and undeserving target beyond. "Leroy! Get your stinking body out of your stinking bed and fix a hot bath for a guest in room five!"

"Yes, ma'am, I'm comin', ma'am," the Negro answered.

Wanda squeezed her eyes tight-closed and bit down on her lower lip, as if she regretted taking out her feelings on the black man. But then, as Merritt yelled again for her, she re-adopted the scowl, whirled out from behind the desk and muttered bitter words under her breath as she went toward the door.

Leroy, with skin as black and shiny as washed coal, tightly curled hair, a broad mouth, widely flared nstrils and inflated cheeks, was in his early twenties. He thrust just his head through the bead curtain and his big, round eyes drew no comfort when, after searching the lobby, they failed to find anyone except the tall, lean, impassive half-breed.

"I'm sorry, sir. I'll just get my pants on and I'll be right with you."

"Obliged to you, feller," Edge told him and made for the foot of the stairway.

The soft-spoken response which contained no direct or implied insult caused the Negro to pause in the act of with-drawing behind the curtain. Then to smile in relief and make haste in undertaking the chore he had been given.

The stairs and wide hallway which ran off to left and right at the top of them were as plushly carpeted as the lobby below. There was also carpet on the floor in the fifteen-by-fifteen room which the half-breed had been allot-ted. The walls were white-painted, like the ceiling. There was a single bed made with crisp-looking linen. An easy chair by the lace-curtained window. A three-drawer bureau with a basin and pitcher on a sampler which covered the top. A closet for hanging clothes. To the right of the bed-head, a low table with a kerosene lamp on it. The necessi-ties with a few added luxuries—plain, simple and clean.

The neatly made bed looked inviting but, conscious of his dirt-ingrained skin and trail-dusty clothes, Edge moved to the window and looked down on to the street and out over the Mexican section of town spread along and back from the other side.

The sun was well clear of the eastern horizon now and

36

the air it heated was thick with the smoke from cooking fires. The fearful interest which Edge and Steele had caused by their entry into town with the corpse of Sven Karlsen had now been lost. Three scrawny dogs scavenged and cocked their legs, watched with embittered eyes by the old-timer who leaned against the front wall of the Cantina Plata, hands in his pockets. The half-breed had to look further—out to the scattered dirt farms—to see other signs of life. Where men and some women were making an early start to the daily chores of tending their crops.

Then, just as knuckles rapped on the door of the room, he heard the clop of slow-moving horses, approaching town on the trail from the east. Three horses.

"Tub's all filled, sir," Leroy announced.

"Obliged."

He remained at the window for long enough to glimpse the three riders as they steered their mounts across the intersection. Heading for Shep, who came upright from the cantina wall and licked his lips in anticipation of doing better business than he managed with Steele. Which probably meant that the heavily stubbled, trail-dusty trio were also strangers to Southfields.

Then he went out of the room, and almost collided with the Virginian, who was in the act of stacking Edge's bedroll, saddlebags, canteens and rifle against the door.

"Feller who runs the livery said to tell you he only looks after horses. he's about as friendly as everyone else in this town."

Edge shifted his gear from the hallway into the room. "Friendship what you're looking for?" he asked.

"A bath and some sleep is about all that appeals to me right now. After that, maybe we can talk horse prices?"

The half-breed nodded and as he moved along the hallway he heard Steele open the door of the room next to his. Then the rumbling sound of Clinton Merritt's personal elevator as the car was hauled to the top of the shaft.

"I don't like the look of it, girl!" the gray-faced cripple growled. "These gunslingers are gathering. Like vultures gather when they know there's easy pickings."

As Edge began to close the door of the bathroom, he

37

saw Merritt roll his wheelchair out of the car and Wanda appear at the top of the stairway.

"Quit worrying until you know for sure, Pa," the woman said with a sigh, turning to go along the hallway, where she swung open a door.

"A dead man don't have any worries!" her father countered sourly, as he swung his chair into the doorway.

And Edge closed the bathroom door after locking his eyes on to the abruptly anxious gaze of Wanda Merritt for part of a second.

In the steam-filled room he stripped off everything except for the razor pouch and beaded thong that held it in place. Then sat in the tub and lathered his body with a fresh cake of soap. He washed his hair and shaved by feel, giving no expression to the feeling of relish which he experienced from clean flesh and a bristle-free. Dressed in the red, sweat-stained longjohns, he shook his top clothes free of dust before donning them and stepping out of the bathroom.

Adam Steele was leaning against the frame, the Colt Hardford rifle canted to his left shoulder. "You given any thought to how much I owe you?" he asked.

"Live horse for a dead one seems a fair trade to me, feller."

"The gelding belonged to Karlsen. I pay my own debts."

Leroy, tall and gangling, turned from the top of the stairs and carried without any show of effort two four-gallon pails of steaming water. "Message for you two gents," he announced. "Miss Wanda would be happy for you to join her in the bar at ten o'clock."

"You sure it wasn't her Pa asked for us to join him?" Edge asked.

Leroy shook his head vigorously. "No, sir. I wouldn't make no mistake like that."

The Virginian eyed the half-breed quizzically as Edge stepped across the threshold to go toward his room, turned at the doorway and said with a wry grin, "Just seemed to me it was him who was coming apart."

FOUR

IT was close to noon when Steele opened his eyes to the bright sunlight flooding in through the curtained window. He came awake easily, with his right hand curled loosely over the frame of the Colt Hartford rifle which lay beside him under the single sheet. Not roused by any sound or sense of impending danger and thus for a few moments he felt relaxed and contented. Enjoying the simple comforts of the hotel room, the clean feel of his body and the well-being derived from recent untroubled sleep.

But then he recalled the events of yesterday—the way he had tried to kill a man, shot a horse instead and the repercussions of this which had driven him deeper into the debt of the tall, lean, impassive faced Edge. A man whose motive for not accepting money in repayment of the debt he was reluctant to even guess at.

And soon his mood of sensuous pleasure was dissipated and he felt the beginning of cold anger at the pit of his stomach. At the first directed toward the half-breed, but quickly turned inward. Because of his stubborn insistence upon tracking down Sven Karlsen even after it had been made clear to him that there would be no murder charge awaiting him should he ever elect to return to the jurisdiction of the Ogallala law office. Had he not been so intent upon finding the Swede and returning him to the railroad town up north, he would not have been desperate enough to try to kill a man for his horse.

For what, as it turned out? The mutilated corpse of his quarry who had suffered a death a thousand times worse than from the noose of a hanging rope.

And there was the moral issue, too. Concerning the attempted murder of an innocent third party in the pursuit of a guilty man.

Grimacing, the Virginian tore the sheet off himself and swung his feet to the floor. As he pulled his pants on, coins rattled in a pocket. Just two of them. Pennies which were all the Swede had left after killing his wife and stealing her money before heading away from the Wyoming rain toward the Mexican sun.

By the time he was fully dressed, sweating from the exertion of the simple chore in the stifling heat of the room, he had calmed his anger. What was done was done and there was little to be achieved by dwelling on the past. Except the learning of lessons for the future, maybe—if a man chose to believe he had a future.

He carried the Colt Hartford out of the room, along the empty hallway and down the stairs to the lobby. A youngster of eighteen or nineteen was behind the desk, reading a newpaper and needing to mark each line with a moving forefinger. He had sandy hair, pale-blue eyes and a face scattered with freckles across both cheeks. When he looked up and saw Steele he showed dislike for a moment, then got his expression into neutral to announce, "Miss Wanda said to tell you your partner's over at the Cantina Plata, mister."

The boy, who was tall and skinny, resumed his difficult reading chore.

"Message of the lady, son," Steele said as he crossed the lobby. "Edge and me aren't partners."

Wanda Merritt appeared on the threshold of the bar, a large room made to look almost cavernous by the emptiness of it spread out behind her. "Me and Pa ain't the best of\ friends," she said dully. "But we're stuck with each other."

Since the Virginian had last seen her, the woman had changed into a blue dress with a low neckline and narrow waist that made the most of her sparse figure. She had also combed her hair, painted and powdered her face and put on shoes. With a bright smile instead of a bitter frown on her face she would have looked almost beautiful.

"Everyone has problems, ma'am," the Virginian said.

"And neither of you give a damn about ours," she

growled. "The Negro said he give both of you the message."

Steele stopped in the sunlit doorway, waving a hand in front of his face as the wheels of a passing buckboard raised a billow of gritty dust. "Why should we give a damn about your problems, ma'am?" he asked.

"Money!" She spat out the word as if it had a foul taste.

"That causes more than enough of its own," the Virginian countered, and stepped out onto the stoop.

"Specially when you ain't got it!" the freckle-faced kid behind the desk called sourly.

Steele gave a short nod of acknowledgement, unseen by the boy, as he surveyed the main street of Southfields. It was busy with people, on foot, astride horses and riding on wagon seats. Mexicans and Americans intermingling, buying and selling supplies and services as dictated by needs, irrespective of which side of the street the stores or offices happened to be.

Townspeople, most of them. Plus some who looked like they had come in from the dirt farms. And some more— most of those with wagons—who looked like ranchers and farmers, or their hands, who had ridden in from bigger and more prosperous spreads further out in the country.

As he strolled along the sidewalk, nobody on the street showed more than a passing interest in the Virginian. Many nodded in friendly greeting or wished him a good day. But he did sense a less than amiable surveillance of his progress from elsewhere—the shadowed interior in back of the open doors of the Cantina Plata.

Edge? Or the owners of the three travel-stained horses hitched to the rail in front of the place? Maybe even the old-timer named Shep who had failed to bum the price of a drink off him.

He entered the stage-line depot, which seemed to be doing the least business of all the enterprises on the street. It was crowded only with heat.

"Noon stage left on time, stranger," a short, blond-haired, round-faced, heavily sweating man of about fifty announced, explaining why he had the place to himself.

The depot was divided into public and private areas by a wall-to-wall counter which crossed the room at a midway point. A wooden partition rose from the counter top to the ceiling, concealing most of the private area, except where it was interrupted by a grille of iron bars. The man who had provided Steele with the unwanted information sat on a stool at the counter behind the bars, looking like a prisoner in solitary confinement not particularly concerned with his lot.

"Want to send a wire to Ogallala, Territory of Wyoming," the Virginian said as he crossed the public area, which had walls lined by uncomfortable looking bench seats.

"Can do that." He reached to the side and slid a pad of message blanks in front of him, took a pencil from behind his ear and licked the point. "Mind if I fill it out? Some folks don't write so good."

"Fine, Mr. Clements. It is John Clements, isn't it?"

"Sure is. What'll I sign the wire?"

"Steele. Adam Steele." He lay the Colt Hartford along the counter top, the inscribed plate uppermost. And pursed his lips as he considered the wording of the intended message.

"You prefer Adam to Ben, uh?" Clements asked, his head twisted so that he could read what was etched into the gold plate. It read: *To Benjamin P. Steele, with gratitude, Abraham Lincoln.* "But that says your middle name starts with a P?"

"Adam has to be better than Ben, feller. Seeing as how he's still alive."

"My mistake," Clements said quickly, licking the pencil point again.

"Everyone makes them, feller. You ready?"

"Sure."

"Address it to the sheriff's office in Ogallala." He paused to allow the man to write the words. Then, more slowly, dictated, "Sven Karlsen died as a result of Indian torture in northern Mexico yesterday. He is buried in the potter's Field of Southfields, Arizona Territory. Adam Steele."

Clements hurried to complete the signature then blurted, "Hey, you're one of the two guys I heard about."

"What did you hear, feller?"

42

"Rode in early like a couple of bounty hunters and nearly give Clint Merritt apoplexy."

"He made a mistake, too. How much for the wire?"

Clements did a word-count, told Steele the cost and accepted payment.

"Them Apaches really give that poor guy hell, didn't they?"

"There are easier ways to die," the Virginian allowed, canting the rifle to his shoulder.

"Was them Indians really camped south of town waiting for Kelly? Or was this . . ." He glanced down at the printed message ". . . this Karlsen guy one of Kelly's men who run into trouble?"

"Tell you something," Steele said as he turned from the grille.

"What?"

"I reckon you know more than I do."

"Only rumors, Mr. Steele. Ain't nobody in this town knows anythin' for sure."

"They say ignorance is bliss, feller."

Clements scowled. "Then this oughta be the happiest little town in the whole damn country."

Steele moved out into the direct glare and heat of the sun and as he retraced his steps back toward the intersection in front of the Town House he looked more closely into the faces of the people around him. And saw, here and there, signs of the same kind of anxiety which was troubling John Clements.

Then he turned his mind to other things, for the troubles of Southfields were not his. Hunger pangs disturbed his stomach and the problem of clearing his debt to the man called Edge was yet to be solved.

The Mexican restaurant which earlier had looked abandoned was now open for business, the aromas of cooking food emanating from it far more inviting than the appearance of the place. Subtler, but harder to ignore, was the intangible emanation of malevolence directed toward Steele from within the Cantina Plata. And it was toward the bar that the Virginian headed as he stepped down off the sidewalk. Then halted as a glass-sided hearse drawn by two black horses with black plumes fixed to the bridles came out of the alley between the Town House and the livery.

The paunchy Harry Pollock was up on the seat. Looking much fresher and neater than he had after his rude awakening, attired in a black frock coat and high top hat.

He reined his team to a halt when Steele raised his free hand, gloved palm open. And the Virginian became aware of a much broader streak of anxiety running through the town as the hearse with the plain pine casket in the back rolled to a stop.

"You want to come see the minister put him down, mister?" Pollock asked.

Steele approached the hearse and took the two pennies from his pocket, thrust them up toward the undertaker.

"Two lousy cents? For what?"

"They were his."

"He can't take them with him."

"So put them in the church poor box or something, feller."

Pollock accepted the money and said with a sneer, "The minister will be real grateful, mister."

"Gratitude can't be bought, feller. At any price."

Pollock set the hearse rolling again and spat into the dust raised by the hooves of the team. Some men removed their hats and a few women bowed their heads as the funeral wagon without mourners moved slowly by. And almost without exception, the Mexicans on the street crossed themselves. Then the early afternoon business of Southfields continued, but with less natural vivacity than before. The change of mood due to something more than the mere sight of a funeral and the thought that this inevitably implanted in the mind that at some time in future, there would be a coffin for everyone.

The black horses with their plumes, hauling the dead man in the glass-sided wagon, triggered a more urgent concern within people who had previously been able to subdue it with the day-to-day chores of peaceful living. And Adam Steele was aware of antipathy directed at him from many sources as he crossed the street, his exchange with Harry Pollock having marked him out as the man who quite literally had brought death to town.

But the Cantina Plata was still the point from which the

most powerful bad feelings came. And as he entered the shaded, liquor-and-tobacco smelling place, he shifted his apparently unconcerned gaze between the scowling faces of the two men who hated him. Then made an unhurried survey of their surroundings as he crossed to where Edge sat.

It was a large, white-walled, low-ceilinged room with a crude bar counter along one side, glass and bottle lined shelves behind. There was ample space for the ten-chair-ringed tables on the floor which was scattered with old sawdust. There was a doorway behind the bar and another in the rear wall.

A fat, bald-headed Mexican in a sweat-stained undershirt leaned on the bar, massive arms folded and eyelids blinking rhythmically. Shep stood at the far end of the bar, elbows on its top, shoulders hunched, staring down into a glass a quarter full of flat beer. Edge had about the same amount of beer in a glass on the table where he sat, back to the side wall where he could watch every door in the cantina and a section of street through the two windows.

Two of the three men who had entered Southfields soon after the half-breed and the Virginian this morning sat at a centrally placed table. Both were in their early thirties, tall and with muscular builds. Attired for rough riding across southwestern trails, carrying guns in low slung holsters, the ties released now that they were seated. They had square faces, still unwashed and unshaven, and dark-colored eyes which, after meeting the incurious gaze of the Virginian, resumed a watch on the street through the held-open batwing doors. Their beer glasses were empty.

"A man, he does not get rich with customers such as this," the fat bartender said to no one in particular as Steele pulled out a chair at Edge's table and sat down opposite the half-breed, his back to the room.

"You sell coffee?" Steele asked, as he leaned the Colt Hartford against his chair.

The Mexican spat out across the counter top, the saliva adding a new stain to the sawdust on the floor. "I sell liquor and beer and my two daughters, *hombre*."

"Live it up while you can, punk," the unshaven man with a livid knife scar on the right side of his jaw said evenly.

"On account of time's runnin' out for you," his blond-haired partner added.

Steele looked away from the half-breed's impassive face to glance over his shoulder and saw that the men sitting in the center of the cantina were still gazing out at the street. When he returned his attention to Edge, he raised one eyebrow to convey a tacit question.

"They don't like you, Reb."

"Something I did, Yank?"

"Edge jerked a thumb toward the disconsolate Shep. "You didn't give the bummer the price of a drink. Seems he had to go elsewhere."

"All I done was tell the truth, mister!" the old-timer growled without turning from the bar. "Told these guys and their buddy it was you brung in the dead man. And run an errand to Doc Pollock to find out the name of the deceased."

"Common knowledge," Steele said. "Was no need for you fellers to pay money for the information."

"Jerry and us got more important things to do than poke around askin' questions."

"When our friend here was willin' to do it for a lousy dollar."

Steele pursed his lips, then gave a curt nod. Said to Edge, "Seems there's a chance I could die sometime soon, Yank. I'm sure hungry enough to eat the hearty meal a condemned man is supposed to have. Like to get my debt settled first, though?"

The half-breed took a sip of his beer, vented a low whistle through clenched teeth, and replied, "You have any kin?"

"No."

"So where there's a will, there's a way. Guess there's no need to write it out. The four witnesses we have here should be enough to give me title to what you leave."

"What's on me and in my room over at the hotel."

Edge glanced at the other men in the cantina. "You fellers hear that?"

"Sí, hombre."

"Sure did, mister." From Shep.

"You could catch what's gonna ail him," the scar-faced man growled.

The glint in the blue silvers of the half-breed's eyes seemed suddenly more intense and his mouthline tightened for a moment.

Steele showed a fleeting smile, took hold of his rifle and stood up.

"Sit down, punk!" the blond-haired gunman ordered. And drew the Remington from its holster, rested the base of the butt on the table and aimed the revolver at the Virginian's back. Clicked back the hammer.

"A man does not get rich. He gets only trouble." The Mexican moved only his head, to look toward the open doorway in the rear wall.

As Steel resumed his seat, not needing to turn around to know there was a gun aimed at him, instead looked blankly at Edge who continued to reveal his latent viciousness in the glinting eyes and cruel mouthline.

"Now you're here, Jerry wouldn't like it for us to let you go." the scar-faced man said. "Best you take your hand off the rifle."

"That's right, Brad," a man agreed from the doorway at the back of the room as he stepped across the threshold. "I've about used up all the energy I got for a while."

He was five or so years older than his partners. Shorter and less heavily built. Dressed the same way they were, but with his shirt unbuttoned to the waist. Still in process of buckling his gunbelt into place. He had eyes as blue as those of Edge, but his face was fleshier and his hair was the color of rusted iron.

"Chico, he did not pay us!" a woman complained.

"He ask everything and give us nothing!" another one added.

They stopped short in the doorway; two black-haired Mexican whores in their early twenties. Short and slim, with slatternly attractive features. Dressed in white shirts and black skirts. Sweat-sheened and dishevelled from providing their services to the man named Jerry. Their anger giving way to fear when they saw the aimed Remington.

"I am in no position to ask for what is owed," the Mexican bartender growled.

Jerry laughed, showing tobacco-stained teeth, and began to button his shirt as he reached the bar. "Give me a tequila, Mex," he demanded. "And put it on the tab I ain't gonna pay. Greaser liquor is like greaser women. It ain't worth havin', but it has to do when there ain't nothin' else available."

Steele showed another fleeting smile, as he saw the ice-cold anger take a firmer grip on the lean features of the half-breed.

"Anyone mind if I leave?" Shep asked, a croak in his voice. And half-turned toward the doorway from which the whores were backing away.

Chico turned to the shelves, lifted a bottle and shot glass, and placed them on the bar top. He slid the glass toward Jerry.

"Kill 'em, Jerry?" the man with the aimed revolver asked.

"Figure Clark would appreciate that, Dave. Come on with the bottle, Mex."

"Your right," Edge rasped. To Steele.

And fisted a hand around the butt of his Colt. Thumbed back the hammer as he swivelled the holster. Squeezed the trigger a split-second after the Virginian had hurled himself sideways off his chair. To his right.

The bullet cracked out from under the table top after blasting a hole in the toe of the holster. Then drilled another hole—in the base of Dave's belly.

The man yelled at the impact of lead against his flesh. And half-rose to gaze down at the bloodstain that blossomed around the wound.

Jerry was turning by then, the hand that had reached to stop the sliding bottle falling to fist around the butt of the holstered gun. The barrel was just clear of the leather when Edge fired a second shot—his own gun out in the open now as he unfolded to his full height.

Shep, his reflexes in the pursuit of liquor as fast as any of the younger men, encircled a scrawny hand around the neck of the bottle. He showed a toothless grin as he thrust the bottle into his shirt.

Jerry's expression was pained, and it became his death

mask as the bullet tore in his heart and lodged there. It swung him around so that his back was to the bar. Then his legs bent under him and he dropped down into a sitting posture, head lolling forward.

Certain of a kill, Edge snapped his glinting eyes back to the center table. And was in time to see Dave fall backwards over his chair, the handle of Steele's knife protruding from his chest, left of center.

"I ain't—" Brad started to say, powering to his feet and thrusting his arms high into the air.

Edge stayed his finger to the trigger of the Fontier Colt. As the Virginian, up on his haunches after a roll, cocked the hammer of the Colt Hartford and held back from squeezing off a shot.

But Chico had committed himself to using the short barrel shotgun he snatched from under the bar counter. It bucked up off the top as he fired it, but the scatter pattern of the shot was wide enough to flay flesh and splinter bone from the side of Brad's head and his shoulder and upper arm. And to send the man as a limp, blood-spraying corpse across the table and into a heap on the floor.

"Bravo, Chico!" one of the whores shouted.

While the other clapped her hands in glee. As both of them came into the cantina, allowing space for Shep to escape into the back with his booty.

For stretched seconds, the fast clapping of hands was the only sound in town, the gunfire having brought the business of Southfields to a shocked halt.

"Did I do right, *hombres?*" Chico asked and swallowed hard, blinking at a more frenetic rate and with fresh sweat stains spreading across his undershirt at the armpits and belly. Breaking his eyes away from the trap of Edge's icy stare only to have them caught by the hard darkness of Steele's. "With men such as these, I think it is better to shoot first and ask questions later, no?"

"You don't get to hear a lot of answers that way, feller," Edge answered, and ejected the two spent shells from the Colt's cylinder.

"They are with Chris Kelly, *hombres*," the Mexican said. "To know this is enough."

Edge pushed fresh bullets into the empty chambers and holstered the revolver, as Steele straightened up and went to retrieve his knife from the chest of Dave.

"It sure enough is," the gravel-voiced Clinton Merritt agreed from the doorway.

His green eyes were bright with happiness. While behind him, her hands on the grips of the wheelchair, Wanda surveyed the scene of slaughter and the survivors with grimacing repugnance. And had to turn away from the sight of the Virginian wiping blood off the blade of his knife on the shirt of its victim before replacing it in the boot sheath.

Chico grinned his pleasure that Clinton Merritt approved his action. "Free drinks for everyone!" he announced and brought a bottle of the best bourbon up from beneath the bar top.

"Grateful to you, but I'm not a drinking man," Steele said.

"Then take your pick of my daughters," the fat Mexican offered, waving a hand toward the eagerly smiling whores. "Either or both."

"Did it for peace of mind, feller. Not for a piece of ass."

Chico and the women all scowled at the even-voiced ingratitude.

"You *hombre*?" Addressed to Edge. "What is your pleasure?"

"Just indulged it. Twice."

"Killers of the worst kind!" Wanda Merritt rasped.

"Better than three I knew for a while, lady," the half-breed countered.

"Go tell Pollock to dig three more graves while he's out at the cemetery, girl!" her father ordered. "And to keep his spade handy now we know for sure Chris Kelly and Ludlum are planning to come back."

He waited until she had whirled away and stalked out of sight, her petticoats rustling. Then he clenched his gnarled hands over his emaciated thighs and smiled more brightly than before as he gazed with hungry eyes at the blood run corpses and said, "I got a proposition that might interest you men. Be glad to talk to you about it over lunch."

"Food sounds good," Steele allowed.

Merritt looked questioningly at Edge and drew the response, "My belly sounds empty, feller."

"Then you'll both do me the honor?"

"Eat your food and listen to you, Mr. Merritt," the Virginian drawled.

"Sometimes I'm an agreeable kind of feller," the half-breed added and moved in the wake of Steele toward the door.

His smile now a combination of pleasure and satisfaction, the cripple backed his wheelchair out of the doorway and turned it to face across the street. Which was a lot less busy now, most business concluded or abruptly curtailed by the burst of gunfire.

"Jerry used the wrong words about Mexicans," the Virginian said as Edge fell in beside him.

"And if you moved fast enough, Reb, the other feller's gun would have been pointed at me."

Steele grimaced. "Whatever, I'm deeper into you now, Yank."

Edge grinned. "No sweat, feller. I'm in line to collect a legacy."

The Virginian showed a matching expression—the lips curled back from the teeth, but the eyes remaining cold. "Over my dead body, as they say."

"Guess that gives you a will to live?"

FIVE

ALTHOUGH the Town House restaurant was not open to the public, a table by one of the three large, lace curtain-hung windows was set for four. And Leroy was standing nearby, attired in a crisp white waiter's tunic, black pants and highly polished shoes. The Negro's teeth, displayed in a broad smile, gleamed as brightly as the silver cutlery and condiment set on the table.

"Miss Wanda won't be joining you, sir?" he asked, drawing a napkin from a wine glass and placing it in Merritt's lap as the cripple eased his wheelchair up to the table.

"Maybe, but we won't wait for her. Start serving, boy."

Both Edge and Steele showed they were equally at ease at a rich man's table as they had been in the squalid cantina on the other side of the street, taking off their hats, draping the napkin from the correct side of their plates over their laps and obviously not overawed by the wide variety of cutlery before them. Only the Virginian seemed intrigued by the half-breed's easy acceptance of the surroundings. But then the curiosity in his dark eyes was replaced by hardness.

"Leroy has to be at least twenty-two," he said as the Negro moved across the plushly carpeted floor between the unset tables.

"What's that you say, Steele?" Merritt came back.

"Figure the Reb objects to what you called—" Edge started.

And was interrupted by the Virginian with, "I can do my own explaining, Yank. And the Negro question was just a side issue of the war."

The half-breed acknowledged both points with a slight

nod. Then showed a quiet smile as he said, "And I figure I'll know which eating irons to use when Leroy brings the food."

"Shit!" Merritt growled. "I didn't ask you men over here to discuss table manners and how to address blacks."

"Be polite and I'll listen to what you have to say, feller," Edge offered.

"Reckon so," Steele agreed.

The man in the wheelchair removed his glasses, cleaned their lenses on a handkerchief and reset them on his nose. As Leroy, sharing a secret smile of thanks between the Virginian and the half-breed, served bowls of good smelling soup.

"I'm a rich man," the cripple opened. "I seen you talking with that old sot Shep Mallison, so I guess you've been told a few things about this town."

"He talks only for money," Steele pointed out.

"And talk's cheaper than that if a man needs help," Edge added.

"Help is sure what I need. And since I collect rent on every square inch of real estate inside Southfields limits, I'm in a position to pay high for it."

Sunlight from the window he faced bounced off the newly polished lenses of his glasses as he gazed bitterly across the street to where Doc Pollock and Chico were bringing the bullet-shattered corpses from the cantina and tossing them unceremoniously into the rear of the hearse. Edge on Merritt's right and Steele on his left glanced briefly out at what had captured the cripple's attention.

"That was personal," the Virginian said and returned to his soup.

"Don't kill for money, feller," Edge said. "Sometimes kill people who try to stop me earning it."

Merritt shook his head. "What I want to buy is protection that's all. For me, my daughter, the people of this town and the town itself."

"From Chris Kelly, a feller named Clark Ludlum and whatever kind of help they can afford?" Edge asked.

"So you have heard?"

"Cantina talk," Steele put in. "Just the names." He looked quizzically at Edge.

"Nobody said a word to me until you showed up, Reb."

Out on the street, Pollock set his hearse rolling. As the fat Mexican bartender dusted off his hands, displayed a smirk of satisfaction and turned to re-enter his premises.

"Frankie's Pa is sick again," Wanda called from the lobby. "I'll take over the desk."

The tall, skinny, freckle-faced youngster moved hurriedly across the window outside and after he had gone from sight the street looked empty in the bright, hot, early afternoon sunlight. Making it pointedly obvious that there was no need for anyone to stay at the Town House reception desk—unless the unwelcome alternative was to share a meal with two guns for hire and a man who could pay highly for such services.

"Chris Kelly was sheriff of this town until a few days ago," Clinton Merritt said, pushing his hardly touched soup away from him. "And Clark Ludlum was his deputy. A boy in the true meaning of the word." He looked at Steele. "No more than nineteen years old. But he was good at his job. Had a fine teacher in Kelly. It was almost a father-adopted-son relationship. Kelly's about forty-five, I'd say."

"Elected to office of sheriff?" Steele asked.

A nod. "Came to town a year or so ago. Was a Texas Ranger from San Antonio on the track of two men who robbed a bank. Found them here in Southfields. Along with a lot of other outlaws and villains. He had to kill the two he was after. But would have been backshot himself by one of their buddies if young Ludlum hadn't intervened."

Leroy came to the table to remove the soup bowls. Replaced them with warmed plates onto which he served fish on top of which he ladled white sauce. During this interlude, Merritt frowned out of recollections of bad times. Then continued:

"We had a sheriff in those days, but the only men he ever had in his jail were those that paid him for a roof over their heads when everywhere else was full up. It was that kind of border town, gentlemen. No villain on the run from justice was ever arrested or shot in Southfields until Chris Kelly rode in."

"Those he didn't shoot, feller?" Edge asked.

"Formed themselves into a bunch and went gunning for him and young Ludlum. Would've got them, too. If I hadn't rallied some help for them. Doc Pollock, John Clements from the stage and telegraph office. Chico Lopez and a few others. Including Ed Heller, Frankie's father who ain't enjoyed good health since that day when he took a bullet in the belly. Town lost three men dead. But seven outlaws are buried out in Potter's Field. And the rest of them scattered south into Mexico."

He frowned again, a greater bitterness magnified by his spectacle lenses this time. "I tell you, it was a day to remember. Marred for me by this damn infirmity that kept me on the frigging sidelines!"

"You own the town in those days?" Steele asked as Merritt's appetite for the fish went the same way as for the soup.

The cripple sighed. "That I did. And if there had been a man like Chris Kelly with me when I started to build it after the war ended, it would never have become a bolt-hole for the scum of Texas and the territories. But all I had was money—and you can't buy the Chris Kellys of this world." He was speaking in the present of the distant past, and abruptly realized the implication of what he had said, "No disrespect intended to you two gentlemen."

"So what made him resign the Rangers to run the law office of Southfields, feller?" the half-breed wanted to know.

A small smile of remembered pleasure paid a brief visit to Merritt's mouthline. "He liked what he saw here. The town, the people in it—especially my daughter—and the chance it gave him of a good, settled life. And when he made it known he was interested in the office of sheriff, Jake O'Rourke turned in his badge and left on the first available stage. And Kelly was elected on a show of hands with every man in the county on the street!"

As Leroy served the main course of roast beef and fresh vegetables, the man in the wheelchair continued to talk, his temporary happiness with events of the past plain to see and hear. "It took a little time for the news to spread and for a while Kelly and Ludlum had to deal with the occasional fugitive or trigger-happy bounty hunter who rode in

55

still thinking Southfields was the way it used to be. But it wasn't long before this place became just like I'd always planned it should be."

"What happened last Wednesday?" Steele asked.

"Nobody knows for sure," Wanda Merritt said from the restaurant entrance, her embittered tone completely at odds with the mood of her father—but immediately infecting him as he shifted his gaze to her. "Chris and Clark just up and left before dawn. Only person to see them go was old Shep Mallison."

"And Kelly gave the sot a message," the man in the wheelchair continued. "Said to tell everyone in Southfields to leave within ten days. If they wanted to stay alive."

"Just that?" Steele asked.

"The way Mallison tells it, Steele. And when he's not drunk, he's not stupid. In the early hours of morning, he's never drunk."

Edge looked across the restaurant at the woman. "Nobody knows for sure, lady, is what you said. Way your father spoke a while back, you were one of the reasons Kelly pinned on a badge in this town."

"We were walking out together," she allowed dully, and in the sunlit room it was possible to see a sheen of moisture in her eyes. "And I guess I was closer to him than anyone except Clark Ludlum."

"So what don't you know for sure, ma'am?" Steele asked as he and Edge finished eating and lay down their forks on their empty plates.

"That Chris didn't want to be paid any more than Jake O'Rouke because the job of Southfield's sheriff wasn't worth any more. So he bided his time for a year, finding out just what kind of money can be made by a man running a town like this. And when he knew enough, he started to make his move. But he needed help. Most people hereabouts have respect and liking for Pa. He charges a fair rent and allows people to get into arrears if there's good reason for it."

"And they like Southfields to be the way I planned it should," her father added.

"We got fresh fruit and ice cream or we got some cheeses," Leroy offered.

"Enough, feller," Edge said, taking out the makings.

"Like some coffee, Leroy," Steele responded, as Clinton Merritt shook his head and waved away the almost untouched main course.

"But they're not prepared to defend the way it is," the Virginian drawled.

"I haven't asked them and I don't have to," the cripple said, bristling with barely controlled anger. "But you've seen enough of them to know what kind of people they are. Storekeepers, dirt farmers and clerks. Most of them with wives and families. Last time the chips were down they stood up to be counted and lost three dead. Toll would've been a good deal higher if Kelly hadn't been leading them. This time Kelly'll be heading up the men against them. With you two prepared to take on Kelly and whoever he brings with him, there won't be any need to call for volunteers. You seen proof of that already. The way Lopez over at the Cantina Plata lent a hand against those three gunslingers."

"How much are you prepared to—" Steele began.

But was interrupted by the shattering of the window pane. The crack of a rifle shot. And the clang of a bullet as it ricocheted off a silver dish-cover on the dessert cart which Leroy was pushing away from the table.

"Oh my, I'm bein' shot at!" the Negro shrieked, and sent the cart trundling across the carpet to crash into a chair as he flung himself to the floor.

As the glinting shards of razor sharp glass showered over the vacant chair left for Wanda and ripped at the tablecloth.

Clinton Merritt vented an obscenity and gripped the wheels of his chair to power it backwards. His reactions as fast as those of Edge and Steele as they came erect, the half-breed drawing the Colt and the Virginian snatching up the rifle.

"It's started!" Wanda moaned, lunging across the room to go to her father.

While Edge and Steele spared part of a second to get a bearing on the bullet's direction from the point where it hit the piece of silver before spinning off to imbed itself in the far wall.

"Across the street to the left," Edge growled as he flattened himself to the wall on the left side of the broken window.

"A roof, I reckon," Steele added, as he folded away from the wall, rifle angled from the hip, to look out through the lace curtain.

The fabric swayed, almost imperceptibly, with the final movement caused by the bullet and glass fragments ripping through it. Questions were shouted, in Spanish and English, by people who had heard the shot and its shattering aftermath. But nobody showed within the Virginian's range of vision until Chico Lopez and the two whores advanced anxiously to the threshold of the cantina.

"Nothing," Steele murmured. And shifted his gaze to watch Edge take long strides across the room and go from sight in the lobby.

Then the Virginian pulled aside the tattered curtain and glanced along the stoop when he heard the half-breed's footfalls at the hotel entrance.

"Any of my services needed inside?" the squeaky-voiced Harry Pollock called from the livery stable.

"Maybe you'll be wanted some place else in a while," Edge replied as he crossed the stoop and stepped down into the street.

The Virginian showed himself fully at the window, tracking the barrel of the Colt Hartford along the uneven line of the building roofs on the south side of the street. Covering the half-breed as he walked directly across the intersection toward the top of the narrower street which curved through the Mexican section of Southfields.

Both men were aware that they were being watched tensely by more than just the dark eyes of Chico and the two whores.

"Which one of you was he firing at, *hombre*?" the big-built bartender asked.

"It's my aim to find that out, feller," Edge answered.

And heard loose shards of glass fall to the hotel stoop and then be crushed underfoot as Steele stepped over the frame. After which the half-breed made to continue his advance following a pause to respond to Lopez. But halted after one pace when he heard the slow clop of a shod horse, being ridden through the town from the south, toward the curve in the narrow street where mount and rider would come into sight.

Edge holstered his revolver and Steele canted the rifle to his shoulder. But remained poised to respond to a threat under their nonchalant exteriors.

The horse was a black gelding, dusty from a long ride but with no sweat or lather on his coat. The rider was tall and thin, pushing fifty and with a demeanor which suggested that during his near half-century of living he had learned to pace himself slower than the average. He had a sun-burnished and time-lined face that would probably look distinguished if he was washed up, shaved and had a haircut and moustache trim. He did not rein in his horse when he saw Edge and Steele, made no move at all except as a result of the motion of his mount until he was within thirty feet of the half-breed. When he raised a long right arm and flicked a finger away from his thumb to hit the underside of his Stetson brim. Dust coiled up from it as he said:

"Afternoon. Way I heard it, this was supposed to be a quiet town."

"It was, until they lost their peace officer," Edge answered.

"Careless of them," the tall stranger said as he steered his horse around the half-breed.

"You see anyone who looked like he might be careless enough to try to kill a man and miss?" Steele called as the rider kept horse on a course toward the hitching rail out front of the Town House.

"Saw some dirt farmers. Heard the shot. Then didn't see anybody until you two fellers." He swung lazily out of the saddle. "I can get a drink inside?"

"We're closed to anyone who hears shooting and still keeps coming!" Clinton Merritt snapped from within the hotel lobby.

"Over here, *hombre*!" Lopez called. "I am open for business to anybody!"

The stranger did a slow double-take at the cantina entrance, then said to Steele, "Selling liquor ain't his only business, or have I got those two women wrong?"

59

The Virginian had resumed his concentration on the rooftops across the street. "You got the urge, all you need is the money and you've got the women, mister."

The man grinned, showing big, ugly teeth. "Wish you fellers good huntin'," he said as he unhitched his horse. "Figure I've found what I'm lookin' for."

Edge had already started along the curving street, right hand hooked over the blckle of his gunbelt as his narrowed eyes surveyed the alleyways between the sunbleached adobe buildings on his left. The rifle shot might have come from the roof of any one of them, or any of those which contributed to the patternless sprawl of crude dwellings behind them. For the Mexican area of Southfields was built on the lower slope of the hillside that reached across the border—making it more elevated than the American section which was sited in the flat bottom of a broad valley, its streets and alleys laid out to a symmetrical plan.

"Anyone get killed?" Shep Mallison asked, and giggled.

Edge half-turned toward a garbage-littered alley, but had not moved his hand toward his gun before he recognized the voice of the town drunk and saw the old-timer move among the trash. To wave the now-empty tequila bottle.

Footfalls sounded behind the half-breed, but he had been in the company of Adam Steele for long enough now to recognize the light tread of the small-of-stature Virginian.

"I guess he didn't see anything, Yank?"

"Well guess again, smart ass!" the old man crowed. And attracted the close attention of Edge and Steele.

The toothless grin was displayed. "I saw the elephant. Lots of elephants. All of them pink!"

A bout of cackling laugher became a coughing fit and Mallison slumped back into the garbage.

"Like looking for a needle in a haystack," Steele drawled as he surveyed the sun-bright walls and shadowed windows of the adobe buildings.

"Anyone who fires a shot that comes that close sure gives me the needle," Edge answered.

"I reckon you're stuck with it," the smaller man said wryly.

Then matched the actions of the half-breed as Edge swung toward the mouth of a side street twenty yards south. And both were in time to see the freckle-faced Frankie Heller slouch around the corner.

"How's your pa, kid?" Edge asked.

The boy had his hands in his pockets, shoulders hunched, and his head hung down. He came to a sudden halt, snapped up his head and was momentarily provoked to fear by the sight of the two men. Then he showed a frown of irritation as he started forward again.

"What do you care?" he snapped.

"You weren't headed in this direction when you left the hotel, boy," Steele pointed out evenly.

"Up yours," the youngster muttered, and made to go through the gap between the two men.

The half-breed's right hand moved into a blur of speed from his belt buckle to the chest of Heller. Where it formed into a fist, clutching a bunched up section of the boy's shirt front. With easy strength, as Heller yelled in mixed anger and fear, he lifted him up onto the toes of his boots and swung him in an arc, which came to a sudden halt as the boy's back thudded against the front wall of a grocery store.

"You open your mouth again, kid, you'll be polite or you'll choke on the bad mouthing when I shove it back down your throat."

Edge kept the youngster up on his toes, hard against the wall, and spoke into his pained face from a distance of just a few inches.

"Hell, mister, you could've broke my back," Frankie rasped.

The half-breed nodded "Possible, kid. But one thing I never do is break my word. And I just made you a promise."

He released his grip on the boy and stepped back. As the high heels of a woman's shoes rapped against the hard as cement street surface.

"Leave him alone, you damn great bully!" Wanda Merritt called breathlessly. "Why are you beating up on Frankie?"

"He was where he should've been at the wrong time, ma'am," Steele replied.

The woman came to a halt, her upper body rising and falling from the exertion of running, her complexion high-colored and with a sheen of sweat on her skin. "That's right, he is, in his father's eyes," she agreed with vehemence. "Frankie's walking out with a Mexican girl and if his pa knew that, the shock would like as not kill him." Her green eyes flashed a venomous stare from Steele to Edge and back again. "Satisfied?"

"Reckon so, ma'am," the Virginian allowed.

As the half-breed struck a match on the grocery store wall and lit his cigarette. His glinting slits of eyes raking the length of the curved street he could see, noting that Southfields was slowly getting back into its afternoon routine following the violent interruption of a gunshot.

"No, lady," he growled. "I won't be satisfied until I find out who that sharpshooter is."

"Get back to work, Frankie," Wanda told the boy. "And don't worry. There's no reason your father should find out you were in the Mexican quarter."

She distributed another equal quota of tacit dislike between the two men then turned and went with the Heller youngster back toward the Town House.

"Reckon I'll go to work as well," Steele said.

"For Merritt?"

"Sure. I feel like you about a man who takes a shot at me and runs. Since the feller has offered to pay me to stay in town, be foolish to turn him down."

Edge nodded as the two of them retraced their footsteps back to the main street of Southfields. Then said, "Mostly I work alone, Reb. When I do have to work with others, I do things my way. So do the others. My way."

"You like to be the top man?"

They reached the intersection and were aware of Clinton Merritt in his wheelchair on the hotel stoop, the sun glinting on his spectacle lenses as he stared intently at them. The two men made a half-turn to the right, heading across the street in the direction of the abandoned law office.

"In this case we have us a precedent, feller," the half-breed said.

"Only thing we ever did together was walk to this town and get mixed up in——"

"Not talking about you shooting my horse and me helping you out of that scrape in the cantina. Mean we were in the same war."

The Virginian pursed his lips and nodded. "And your side won, that it?"

"Not only that, Reb. I made captain and you stayed a lieutenant." They reached the law office and Edge tried the door, found it unlocked. He smiled tightly at the expression of distaste on the smaller man's face. "Rank is bad, uh? You think my idea stinks?"

"So does crap, Yank," Steele growled, as Clinton Merritt ran his wheelchair down the ramp at the end of the hotel stoop and steered it into a turn to head for where they stood. Then showed a grin of his own as he added, "But I try not to wrinkle my nose when you talk."

SIX

"WANDA tells me there was no sign of that yellow-livered bastard who took a shot at me," Merritt rasped as he stopped his wheelchair against the sidewalk opposite the law office.

And the two men who stood there made no offer to lift him up onto the boarding.

"Just the Heller kid stealing time from you to see his girl," Edge answered.

"And not making time with her from the look of his face," Steele added.

Merritt waved a gnarled hand in a gesture of impatient dismissal. As the glass-sided hearse hauled by black-plumed horses rolled out of the alley between the livery and the Town House. "Young Frankie and Juanita deserve all the encouragement they can get. Way Ed hates the girl just because she's a Mexican sticks in my craw."

"Warn the boy's father to keep his feelings to himself if he ever meets up with the Yank here," Steele said, looking bleakly toward the rear of the hearse with its load of three plain pine coffins.

"Uh?" Merritt grunted, his impatience showing again as he glanced in the same direction. Then he put the matter out of his mind to ask, "You boys being here mean you're gonna take the jobs I offered?"

"How much you paying, Mr. Merritt?" the Virginian asked.

"You'll get two-and-a-half thousand each next Saturday night if this town is safe forever from Chris Kelly. And you'll get a thousand each in advance today. For you to keep, whatever the outcome. And I'll make another five thousand available for you to hire help. You'll pay the help whatever you think fit. How does that sit with you?"

"Clements, Pollock and the others who threw in with Kelly a year ago, Mr. Merritt?" Steele said.

The man in the wheelchair shook his head. "I don't want any townspeople involved in the fighting. That's the reason I've allocated funds to hire outside help. Three innocent men died the last time. I refuse to have a repetition of that. Kelly will come with professional guns. I intend for him to be faced with like."

"If some local men apply for the jobs?" the Virginian asked.

"Then you will accept or reject them as you think fit. Anything else?"

"When will the first thousand come?"

Before he replied to Steele's query, Merritt turned from the waist to look along the street, which was beginning to stir with people, horses and wagons, throwing long shadows in the afternoon sun. As the cripple looked toward the hotel, his daughter rose from the rocking chair on the stoop. Then, in response to his outstretched hand, thumb extended skywards, she stepped down into the street, obviously complying with the prearranged signal with bad grace.

"Wanda is on her way to the bank to collect the money now, sir," Merritt said with a glint of self-satisfaction in his lens magnified eyes. "Is that all gentlemen?"

Edge flicked his cigarette out into the street and watched as its fire was crushed out under the wheel of a sack-laden flatbed wagon. "The old-timer said Kelly left with three side-kicks, feller. One was his boy deputy. Who were the other two?"

Merritt's mouth became set in a line of grim loathing. "Hoyt Shaw and Lester Noon. Couple of drifting ranch hands who were working out on the Bar-M spread for the past few months. Hard-drinking pair who used to wind up in the cells out back of this place most Saturday nights. But for some reason Kelly took a liking to them. Entirely different types." The man with the well-built frame and wasted legs shook his head as he reversed his wheelchair away from the sidewalk. "Just ain't any accounting for it sometimes. They way men who ought to have a dislike for each other takes to each other."

"Reckon there isn't," Steel drawled as he went into the law office.

"Mutual interest is the usual reason, Reb," the half-breed supplied as he followed the Virginian inside and closed the door, breathing the hot, stale air which had been trapped since the last occupants had left.

The office was about twenty by twenty feet with a barred door in the center of the rear wall. There was a desk to either side of this doorway with a padded leather chair behind each of them. A gun rack on the wall to the left held six Winchester rifles, secured in place by a padlocked bar running through their levers. Nearby was a table with a straight-back chair at either side. Against the opposite wall was a neatly made single bed and two filing cabinets. Pinned to the wall above the cabinets was a well-drawn street plan of Southfields and beside this a commerically printed colored map of Cochise County.

While Steele looked at the street plan, Edge crossed the spartanly furnished office to check on the cells.

The Virginian saw that the main street of town was called Main Street and that the thoroughfare which curved through the Mexican section was less appropriately named Via de Bello. While the half-breed saw a row of three narrow cells containing just a cot and a bucket. Bars ran along the front of them and divided them. The rear and side walls of the cell section were of brick, with a single small window high up in the center cell. Like the frame-built law office, the cell area was layered with the dust of several days but beneath this was basically clean and tidy.

"Looks like Kelly's Texas Rangers training stayed with him," Steele said as he laid claim to the desk on the right of the barred door by dropping into the chair behind it.

"He sure didn't go in for too many trimmings," Edge replied as the unglazed door between the two street-facing windows swung inwards.

"Chris was content with the simple things of life!" Wanda Merritt snapped, her almost pretty face set in a frown of angry sullenness.

66

"So why did he take a shine to you, lady?" Edge asked evenly.

"Uh?" she grunted as she advanced far enough into the office to toss a fat envelope onto the desk in front of each man.

"I think he means you're not simple, ma'am," Steele explained. "Intelligent enough, anyway, to know that your beau must have good reason to want to change things around here."

"I don't know what that reason is!" she snarled at the Virginian. "And I'm not so sure that old Shep Mallison told the truth about what Chris said to him! Or if Chris said anything at all!"

She seemed like she wanted to say more. But could not find the words she needed to convince the two impassive-faced men seated at the desks.

Edge nudged the bulky envelope in front of him with a long, brown-skinned finger. "This is just part payment from your father," he said evenly. "How much were you going to put up? And for what?"

"Uh?" She was still trying to find vocal expression for her feelings.

"You wanted to see the Reb and me earlier. We didn't keep the appointment."

"It doesn't matter now," she snapped, and spun around. But at the open doorway she halted and looked back over her slim shoulder. "I couldn't afford a part of what Pa plans on paying you men. But I was ready to give you everything I have if you left Southfields. It was the only way I could think of keeping my father and Chris from maybe killing each other."

She strode out of the office and slammed the door behind her.

"A telling phrase," Steele said as he drew the knife from his boot sheath and used the point to slit open his envelope.

"Killing a man is simple enough," Edge drawled. "For a man trained by the Texas Rangers." And watched for a few moments as the Virginian drew the fifty- and hundred-dollar bills from the envelope and started to count them.

Then said, "Money you don't really need, Reb. Unless that isn't a bankroll padding out your hip pocket?"

Steele leaned back in the chair, feeling the bulge in his hip pocket pressing against his flesh. "I made some money out of a poker game in Chicago a while back, Yank."

"I ain't ever been to Chicago."

"It's not my kind of town."

"New York didn't strike me as so wonderful. Figure they're much alike."

"Never have been in New York," the Virginian answered, adding the new money to the old. "Don't you aim to get rich?"

"What you've never had, you never miss."

"Reckon it was just a small place you had in Iowa?"

"Big enough to bury my kid brother on."

"Big enough to miss?"

The half-breed showed a wry grin. "Small enough, if you don't know what you're looking for."

"What are you looking for?"

"If I knew that, maybe I'd have stopped looking by now."

Steele sighed, leaned forward and began to open the drawers in the desk. "You and me both, mister."

In one of the drawers was a big green fly, weak from being trapped without food for so long. But it summoned the energy to take flight into the sunlit office—only to become helplessly caught up in a spider's web spun across the gun rack. The spider did not emerge from shadowed hiding until the fly had ceased to struggle and its irate buzzing had been silenced. By which time the Virginian had located a box of a dozen tarnished tin deputy badges in another drawer. And the half-breed had begun to work with pen, ink and some paper located in a drawer of his desk.

"This make sense?" Edge asked, holding up the sheet for the other man to read as Steele up-ended the box to spill the contents across the desk top.

Help wanted, the Virginian read. *High risk work for high pay. Apply law office. Any man not applying or not selected is required to turn in his gun. This ordinance cov-*

ers town of Southfields and radius of ten miles in United States territory.

"They had schools in Iowa," Steele said lightly. "Not a word spelled wrong and all of them in the right order."

"Obliged, teacher. But you know you ain't answered my question."

"I wouldn't turn in my gun, Yank. Especially not if I reckoned there was going to be lead flying."

"And especially not if you were backing Kelly to win. And had decided to keep your preferences to yourself instead of riding out with him and the others last Wednesday."

Steele nodded and pinned a badge to his shirt front. "I reckon it makes sense," he allowed and tossed a badge across to the other desk. "Likely also to make trouble."

"Trouble is what peace officers are appointed to deal with. Says deputy on this star, Reb."

"Same as on this one, Yank. They say right is might and I guess we have to believe that right's on our side?"

Something harder than a fist banged on the door, after footfalls had rapped heavily on the sidewalk. Then the door swung open and the loose-limbed, lazy-moving stranger stepped across the threshold, in process of sliding his Remington six shooter back in the holster.

"Hear tell you people are hirin' on help," he said evenly. "On account of there's trouble brewin'."

"News travels fast in this town," Steele answered.

"Not near so fast as I can draw and shoot this gun, Mr. Steele."

"What at, usually?" the Virginian asked as the man used a boot heel to close the door. Then he took a chair from beside the table, turned it and straddled it to rest his elbows on the back and lean his chin on his hands. He grinned at both newly installed lawmen. "The other side. And they ain't around to make me an offer. You guys gonna make me one?"

"You know what's involved, Mr. . . . ?"

"Deed, Mr. Steele. Charlie Deed." He shrugged. "Girl down at the cantina said as how the one-time lawman here aims to make a comeback. But he don't wanna be just the sheriff no more."

"He's about as well informed as we are, Reb," Edge said, and began to print out another copy of the notice.

Steele frowned at the half-breed. "You sound like you're leaving the hiring up to me, Yank?"

Edge showed a cold grin. "If you take my meaning, firing's more in my line."

"What's your line, Mr. Deed?" the Virginian asked the man with the big and ugly teeth who had witnessed the exchange with a quizzical expression in his soft brown eyes as they shifted from one speaker to the next.

"Was a deputy sheriff up in Dodge City for a few years. Then took to holdin' up stages and robbin' banks. But I'll be fifty next birthday and that's too old to be hittin' and runnin'. Come here with the intention of buyin' a store and settlin' down. Like the way the town is now, though. Got no objection to earnin' a little cash keepin' it that way."

"What do you reckon, Yank?" Steele asked as Edge began to print out a third notice. "A good Deed turned bad who wants to reform?"

"Toss him a tin star, Reb. Sounds like a feller who's earned a Merritt badge."

SEVEN

WITH Adam Steele and Charlie Deed doing a share of the chore, ten identically worded notices were produced and tacked to telegraph poles, sidewalk awning supports and the bulletin board out front of the office of the Southfields Reporter newspaper. This meant they were all displayed in Main Street positions. But they went up during the late afternoon of Saturday and as the daylight faded the evening was succeeded by lamplit night, enough local citizens saw the notices to ensure their contents would be communicated to everyone concerned by Sunday morning.

The newly installed lawmen, working to an agreed duty roster that kept one in the sheriff's office, another out in the town and the third free to rest up, awaited the response with no preconceived notion of what to expect. And did not convey to each other their feelings when, by the time the moon was high and bright, close to a hundred assorted handguns, rifles, carbines and scatterguns had been handed in to be stored in one of the cells. Without a single application for work being received.

At eleven o'clock, while Deed was playing solitaire in the law office and Edge was eating a meal of tacos and chili beans in the spartanly furnished but reasonably clean Mexican restaurant—with the intention of crossing to the hotel and bedding down after he was through—Adam Steele patroled the streets of Southfields.

It was a warm night, the broiling temperature of the day reduced not solely by the coming of darkness. For there was a pleasant breeze blowing down from the hills to the northeast, strong enough to stir the air but not to raise any dust.

The Virginian, freshly washed up and shaved, wearing a

71

vest and the jacket which matched his pants, made a complete tour of the town, seeing in reality the impression of Southfields as a whole he had gained from the plan in the law office. He moved at an easy pace, the Colt Hartford canted to his left shoulder.

At this time of night, only the premises on Main Street and Via de Bello were open for business, and a lot of these, he guessed, would have been closed had it not been Saturday. But because it was the weekend, much the same mixture of people who had thronged the mid-town area this morning were back again. Families, couples, groups and loners. Cleaned up and wearing their best outfits, intent upon pleasure as a reward for a week of working.

The three cantinas on the south side of Main Street were doing good business from men without women, who went to Chico Lopez's establishment if they were interested in whores as well as liquor, the Estrella next to the church if they liked to gamble while they were drinking, or the Golden Guitar at the extreme western end of the street if they preferred tequila with music.

The employers of the men who used the cantinas chose to drink in the bar of the Town House. While families ate in the restaurant on Main Street or one of the three on Via de Bello before discovering and sometimes buying trinkets in any of the several stores in town.

Lovers strolled in the warm night air.

Devout Catholics made their way to the mission church for midnight Mass.

One man made plans to kill another.

For a while as he patroled the quiet side streets and noisier main one, the Virginian wondered why he was doing it—why he had accepted the job offered by Clinton Merritt. He had no need of the money, no particular regard for the man who was paying him and no vested interest in the town he was being paid to protect.

So, inevitably, the reason had to be the man called Edge. And the debt he owed this man. A debt that could not be discharged with money. For on two occasions Steele could have died had it not been for the actions of the glinting eyed, taciturn half-breed. So in order that he could rest easy at nights and be at peace with himself during the days, the Virginian had to return what he had been given, in kind. And to do that, he had to be where Edge was.

As he started along Main Street from the western end, Steele cleared his mind of the side issue and concentrated his attention on the business in hand, immediately became aware of the atmosphere—which had nothing to do with the climate—which surrounded him. As he strolled the sidewalk on the north side of the street, he sensed animosity and respect, ambivalence and indifference. Some of the passers-by and the people behind lamp bright windows were pointed in their attitude toward him and others surreptitious.

He recognized the faces of several men who had turned in their firearms, some with relief, others with almost obsequious meekness and others still with reluctance. A number of men—ranch hands from the outlying spreads—walked the streets and sidewalks with revolvers plain to see in their holsters.

For the time being, Steele elected to respond to those who offered friendly or respectful greetings and to meet levelly and impassively any hostile glances directed at him. Often, he was conscious of resentful whisperings, but no one with real or imagined cause to feel malevolent toward him ever said anything to his face.

Until he turned in through the open doorway of the Cantina Plata at a time close to midnight when business had slackened. There were about a dozen customers in the place including Doc Pollock, Shep Mallison and Frankie Heller. The others were a mixture of town merchants, dirt farmers and ranch hands. All of them, seated in groups, pairs or alone had almost empty glasses in front of them, but from the bleary eyes and slouched postures it was obvious the glasses had been filled and refilled many times over.

Leaning with his arms akimbo on the bar top, Chico Lopez had the satisfied look of a man who had been enjoying good business. The two whores—who had features similar enough to be sisters but bore no resemblance at all to the fat man who called them his daughters—sat idly at a table apart from the customers. They looked drained and sweaty, as if they had served their purpose several times.

73

"Evening, *hombre*," Lopez greeted. "All is quiet to-night."

He looked pointedly at the area where three men had earlier died. If the blood of the dead men stained the floor, the marks were concealed by fresh sawdust.

The Mexican's words drew attention to the Virginian as he moved between the tables to the bar. Several men had difficulty in focusing on the newcomer. Most abandoned the attempt, others resumed their drunken slouches with indifference to Steele. A few watched him with varying degrees of interest. Two of these carried Frontier Colts in their holsters.

"Hey, *Señor* Steele," the shorter and more flashy whore called, sitting up straight in her chair, pulling her shoulders back and taking the sag out of her breasts. "If it's too quiet, I can liven things up for you, uh? If you changed your mind since today?"

"Be a charge, though," the other woman added. "You lost your chance, *gringo*."

"But not my mind, ma'am. Which I never change."

The slimmer whore scowled.

The other one shrugged and growled, "You should be a priest, not a lawman, *señor*. It does not matter, though I like my men to drink and smoke and—"

"So does the undertaker, ma'am," Steele cut in as he rested the Colt Hartford on the bar top.

"As a doctor I can bear that out," the squeaky-voiced Pollock contributed. "Liquor except in moderation attacks the liver. And it is my belief that every pack of tobacco should carry a printed warning—"

"Having a gun without a deputy's badge to go with it can be a really bad health hazard in this town," the Virginian interrupted, looking at Lopez.

"You mean my shotgun, *hombre*?" the Mexican muttered, satisfaction replaced by the threat of anger on his fleshy features. "If you mean my shotgun, I tell you I need it, running the kind of business I do."

"Get into another business for a while."

"He means me and Beale, too, Chico," one of the Colt-carrying ranch hands said. "You mean me and my buddy, don't you, dude?"

74

Steele turned sideways-on to the bar so that he could see everyone in the smoky, sweat-and-liquor-smelling cantina. And nodded at the two beefily built, rugged-featured men seated at either side of a centrally placed table. "Turn them in at the law office or convince the man down there that you'll make good deputies."

"It's a stupid, unworkable law, if you don't mind my saying so, sir!" This from a city-suited, short, balding man of about fifty who shared a table with Pollock and the Heller youngster.

"No law against free speech, feller," the Virginian answered.

"*The Southfields Reporter* is here to ensure there never is!" the man retorted. "And to campaign against all infringements of civil liberty."

"This is Gilbert Reade who owns and runs the town newspaper," Pollock introduced.

"In the next issue of which there will be a damning editorial concerning your attempt to rob Southfields citizens of their right to bear arms."

"Aw, come on, Gil," the paunchy doctor-mortician protested. "All these lawmen are asking is for men to stand up and be counted. Or stand down out of the firing line so they can do their job properly."

"Lawmen?" Reade countered. "Who said they are? In the past, this town has always elected its peace officers by democratic vote."

"Damn right!" Frankie Heller said, and his voice was slurred. He tried to grip the edge of the table, and had to make two attempts at it. "This *deputy*—" he made the word sound like an obscenity "—and them other two are no better than the kinda scum used to walk the town streets before Chris Kelly cleaned up Southfields."

"Them other two ain't here right now," Beale said with meanace in his tone and his dark eyes, a smile on his thick lips. He glanced at his drinking partner. "And with Chico not about to lend a hand this time, I figure we got us a good chance of rubbin' this guy's nose in his own bullshit. How say you, Rob?"

Rob, who had hair the color of dirty ripe wheat, looked toward Lopez. Who scowled in the direction of Shep Mallison and growled, "This time I have interest in protecting only what is mine."

"Aw, I told you I'll pay," the toothless old-timer groaned.

As Beale and Rob rose to their feet, causing the legs of their chairs to scrape on the floor. Both showed menacing smiles now, enjoying the attention they drew, and anticipating success.

Even the most drunken patrons of the cantina were able to see every detail of the tableau clearly, sobered sufficiently by the near-palpable tension which had slowly built up in their fetid surroundings.

Steele did not move as the two taller and broader men advanced on him and halted less than three feet in front of him. His left hand remained loosely hooked over the front of the bar top while his right hung at his side.

"You see my gun, dude?" Beale said, and pushed his right hip toward the Virginian. "Take it."

"Mine, too." Rob invited and matched his partner's attitude. "Because I sure as hell ain't gonna walk down to no law office and hand it over like I was givin' Maria two dollars for a screw."

Steele was certain Chico Lopez would not intervene, whatever happened. Harry Pollock expressed sympathy for the Virginian's position but would obviously offer nothing more tangible than words and looks. And everyone else in the cantina showed the same kind of moral support—for Beale and Rob. Frankie Heller more than anybody.

"Well, dude?" the blond-haired ranch hand growled impatiently.

Beale vented a short, harsh laugh. "Or can't you cut the mustard without your buddy along to—"

Steele, his lips pursed and his coal-black eyes expressionless, had slowly raised his left hand to scratch the side of his jaw. "Well, I'll truly tell you," he said softly and evenly. "Edge and I, we aren't all that close."

He moved his gloved left hand down to his neck, scratched once under the silken fabric of his kerchief. Then seemed to throw a punch toward Rob's jaw.

Both Rob and Beale took a startled step backwards, right hands clawing for the jutting butts of their holstered

Colts. But their surprise at the Virginian's sudden move—his violence erupted from an attitude of totally unaggressive calmness—forced their haste to be hampered by awkwardness.

Steele's action was not a punch; his fist was merely clenched to take a firm grip around one weighted corner of the scarf he wore as a kerchief. And as the weight in the free-flying corner caused the scarf to curl around the nape of Rob's neck, the Virginian jerked up his right hand, caught the scarf and crossed his arms. Then interlocked one elbow with the other.

Professional gunmen would have had their revolvers clear of the holsters by that time. But these two men were not gunslingers.

Rob was the faster on the draw, but he did not have time to cock the hammer of his Colt before a more urgent need consumed him. The need to get free of whatever was cutting into the flesh of his neck and constricting his windpipe. And he let the revolver clatter to the floor so that he was able to raise both hands to the source of his pain, this as he was jerked forward and half-turned. To come to a halt tight up against Steele, whose back was hard to the front of the bar counter.

"We never have been as close as this," the Virginian said, over the shoulder of the suddenly purple-faced Rob to address his comment to the perplexed and frightened Beale, who had backed away until he was halted by a table at his back. "How close are you two? You want to try to blast me and maybe put the bullet in his back? Or do you want to wait until I've strangled him so you'll have a clear shot."

Rob was already weakened. His fingers merely fumbled at the fabric enclosed between the ridges of flesh around his neck. And he was sagging as his knees started to bend.

"Throw your gun away, man!" Gilbert Reade urged.

"Or he'll be dead in less than ten seconds!" Harry Pollock augmented.

Beale licked his lips, swallowed hard and then tossed his gun to the side. "Sneaky bastard!" he snarled.

Steele let go of one corner of the assassin scarf, unlocked his elbows and jerked the fabric clear of Rob's throat to drape it loosely around the back of his own neck. Then stepped to the side as the big man dropped hard to his knees, the air which had been trapped and turned bad in his lungs whooshing out of his gaping mouth.

"Elected or not, I figure we got us a fine lawman here, Gil," Harry Pollock said. With triumph and even pride that he had made known his support for the Virginian.

As Rob toppled over on to his side, moaning and gasping for breath, big work-scarred hands rubbing his pained flesh. And Steele casually lifted his rifle off the bar top and canted it to his left shoulder, raked his unblinking eyes across the faces turned toward him in the silent, lamplit cantina.

Out on the streets of Southfields hooves clopped, wheels turned and footfalls rapped on sidewalks as some of the last of the many Saturday-night revelers made their way home.

The bell of the Mexican church began to toll as the time for Mass drew close.

"Violent and vicious!" the city-suited newspaperman snapped, getting to his feet. "I have no time for such men!"

Beale's anger was giving way to concern for his partner, who was still in pain and having trouble drawing breath on the floor. Of the rest of the people in the cantina, only Frankie Heller responded with blatant malevolence to the mildly questioning look in Steele's eyes.

"If you have me, *hombre,* I take a job with you," Chico Lopez said without enthusiasm.

"Consider yourself employed, feller," the Virginian said and moved further down the bar as Pollock crossed from his table to drop to his haunches beside the suffering ranch hand. Then nodded to Beale that he could do likewise. "First duty is to collect up the two revolvers."

"*Sí, hombre.*"

"For a man that doesn't drink, you sure do cause a lot of trouble in barrooms, Reb," Edge said as he stepped on to the threshold of the cantina, and struck a match on the doorframe to light a cigarette.

"Wasn't any trouble for me, Yank," Steele answered in the same level tone.

Lopez was out from behind his bar and had retrieved the Colt dropped by Rob. As he began to straighten up,

78

searching for the gun Beale had tossed away, he froze and yelled, "No, boy!"

Edge had begun to turn away from the cantina entrance, right hand raised to pick a loose tobacco leaf off his lip.

Steel was still at the bar, watching Lopez, seeing the stiffening of the Mexican's body in response to fear. And he reacted in a blur of speed when he saw the reason for the man's sudden tension.

Except for that part of a second a few moments earlier when the Virginian had looked at the scowl of hatred on Frankie Heller's freckled face, no one had paid any attention to the youngster. But all eyes swung toward him now. After he had had time to reach down and pick up Beale's still cocked Colt from the floor beneath his chair. His movements had been slow, were suddenly fast—as he whip-lashed up into a sitting posture. The placement of his chair making Edge, rather than Steele, his first available target.

The half-breed had time to snap his head around. And drop his right hand three-quarters of the way to his holstered revolver. As people seated between Heller and the doorway hurled themselves off their chairs to the floor.

The Virginian's rifle pivoted down from his shoulder, a gloved thumb cocking the hammer. A gloved finger squeezed the trigger an instant after the other gloved hand had fisted around the barrel.

The report silenced the shouts and curses which had vibrated the strong-smelling air of the cantina.

The crack of the Colt was like a weak echo of the rifle shot. The bullet from the handgun took the heel off a dirt farmer's boot before it buried itself in the floor, less than six feet from where it had blasted from the Colt barrel.

Frankie Heller was probably already dead by then. Even though he was on his feet: his shocked nervous system having jerked him upright as the rifle bullet drilled into the left side of his head, tunnelled through flesh and brains and smashed clear at the right side amid a spray of blood, tissue and stark white fragments.

The silence which followed the two shots was much deeper and harder than that which preceded the explosions. Until the dead boy fell heavily back into his chair and then went sideways off it to the floor.

And Edge raised his right hand to his face again and took the cigarette from between his lips to say, "Obliged, Reb. Figure that pays for this morning."

The Virginian acknowledged his agreement with a nod.

As others in the cantina vented pent-up breath and eased terror-tensed muscles.

And from beyond the walls of the building came the sound of raised voices demanding to know the result of this new violent episode.

"Attend to your patient, Harry," Gil Reade said tautly, shifting his gaze from the inert form of Heller to Pollock—who had made to turn away from Rob. "Ed's boy is a client for your other business."

Steele ejected the spent cartridge case from the smoking chamber of the rifle's cylinder and reloaded. "Finish your job, deputy," he said to Lopez.

As the newspaperman shared a look of revulsion between the Virginian and Edge. "Places like Southfields," he muttered dully, "all over the west—they used to be nice peaceful towns until violent men like you came along!"

The half-breed nodded. "So I been told, feller. And pretty dull by all accounts."

Reade made a wet sound of disgust in the back of his throat, but held on to the saliva as he attempted to elicit some sign or word of regret from the Virginian. "A professional gun like you, you could have just slightly wounded him and achieved the same result. You didn't have to do what you did to Ed's son."

"Just did what's expected of me, Gil man," Steel answered evenly.

"Wake me at four, Reb," Edge said as he turned and started across the street toward the Town House, the group of people in front of the cantina parting to allow him a wide passage between.

"So you get tired just like normal folks, uh?" Gil Reade sneered. "But you never tire of killing, do you?"

"Quit it, Gil!" Harry Pollock snapped after a glance at the Virginian. "Or you could wind up talking yourself to death."

The newspaperman twisted his mouthline into a more firmly set sneer as his eyes locked on those of Steele. "I'll say a lot more about him, Harry. In print. The pen's a great deal mightier than the sword."

He strode across the cantina and out into the night. As the Virginian calmed his rising temper, a sign of which Pollock had detected.

"Don't pay any attention to Gil Reade, Mr. Steele," the squeaky-voiced man urged. "He talks a lot, that's all. And when he's not taking, he's writing it all down to run in his newspaper."

"Sure," Steele said, taking the two handguns which Lopez held out to him. "He'd have to throw more than words at me for me to take him out of circulation."

EIGHT

THE CITIZENS of the border town bedded down peacefully. Although, while Steele took his turn of duty behind a desk in the spartan law office and Charlie Deed walked the deserted streets, the lazily strolling man with the big and ugly teeth sensed a degree of restlessness behind the locked doors and shuttered windows of many of the buildings which flanked his route.

He mentioned this to Edge after the half-breed had been roused and Steele was sleeping in the Town House.

"Put your feet up at the office, feller," Edge said as he emerged from the hotel, Winchester at his left shoulder, and Deed came across the intersection from the top of the Via de Bello. "I'll do some walking."

"Streets are quiet, but early on there was a lot of talk," the older man reported. "Heard just the sounds. Not the words. Figure a lot of people ain't happy with what's happening in this town."

"If they were, we wouldn't have jobs," the half-breed pointed out.

"And the Heller kid would still be alive," Deed answered gravely. "I wasn't there. But a pro gun blastin' a local . . . I guess that don't sound good to anyone who wasn't there to see."

"Ask the question, feller," Edge invited.

Deed looked as if he regretted having started this line of talk. "Guess it was a matter of . . ."

"Murder or suicide, feller," Edge filled in the pause as the other man clamped his lips over his big teeth. "Heller tried to murder me. While Steele was around. Meant Heller committed suicide."

"Pretty close, you two?" Deed suggested as Edge started along the street in the direction of the law office.

"You could say that once we walked out together, feller. Now we're just business associates."

"I ain't meanin' to pry, mister," the older man said quickly, suspicious of the half-breed's tone.

"It's part of your job, long as you're looking in the right direction."

"Sure. Like I said, all's quiet. Only light showin' except for the one in the law office is in the window above Ed Heller's shoemaker store. Maybe the old man's holdin' a vigil for the dead."

"Where is it?"

"Twenty yards up the street between the seed store and the boardin' house."

"Obliged," Edge acknowledged and did not break his easy stride as Deed hesitated in front of the law office, then stepped up onto the sidewalk and crossed it to push open the door.

The half-breed's attitude did not alter when he was alone. He continued to seem nonchalantly impervious to his surroundings while in fact he kept close watch on the town in front of and either side of him, and his ears strained to pick up any sound from behind that might signal danger.

Thoughts of Charlie Deed were immediately banished from his mind when the man had gone, but his reference to Steele triggered a line of thinking which had kept the half-breed from drifting off to sleep the moment his head had hit the pillow in the hotel room.

Two of a kind, the Virginian had called them. And that was certainly right. Not in their heritage and not in their looks and builds. But in the violence of war and during the venegeance hunts of each of them after the war was finished, they had both been reforged on different and yet strangely similar anvils. And had survived. Physically. Had also preserved the same precious few yet virtually important emotional responses which continued survival demanded. To enable each of them to live among other men—and with themselves.

They killed without compunction and yet only in self-defense or after a fair warning had been given. They asked no favors but if favors were granted unbidden, they ensured repayment. They didn't give a shit what anybody thought of them. Unless the thinker be one of their own kind.

Edge allowed his lips to draw back from his teeth in a quiet smile as he turned off Main onto the narrow side-street that ran north to a dead end at the eastern side of Southfields.

This was what riled Adam Steel. The Virginian had broken the code, for it was stretching the self-imposed rules of survival to try to kill a man simply to steal his horse. The situation had just not been desperate enough to merit such an act. And now Steele was trying his damnedest to right the wrong he had committed in the eyes of one of his own kind.

The smile vanished from the half-breed's lean face, his mouthline suddenly set in an expression which came close to being melancholic. As, once more, he considered his own attitude toward Steele and wondered if the Virginian dude shared another common factor with him, that of never making a friend of anyone—man or woman—who you truly felt a rapport with and an affinity for.

Because, in the experience of Edge, such relationships were doomed to reach a violent and often lethal end. For the fate which moved him along trails marked by the blood of past and future victims was cruel enough to extract from him punishment for such deeds preordained by his destiny. And he had learned from countless brutal lessons to abandon desires for the good things of life. To come to terms with being a loner.

And if they really were two of a kind, then Adam Steele was also a loner.

The narrow street was short, lined on the right by a row of small houses and on the left by a grocery store, the premises of Ed Heller and a large barn with a sign which labelled it as a wagon repairer's establishment. The sole light along the street gleamed from an upstairs window of the two storey, narrow building which at ground level had a door with a faded sign beside it proclaiming: *Heller's Best Ladies and Gents Boots and Shoes.*

84

There was an alley between the Heller place and the barn, from which an outside stairway rose to the upper level.

As he went up the stairs, making no attempt to tread lightly, he heard a woman sobbing. The sound was abruptly curtailed when he was halfway to the top. And the woman asked in Spanish:

"Who is that?" There was fear in her tone.

"What's that you say, girl?" a man demanded gruffly. "If you wanna talk to me, you speak my language."

"Shush, somebody is coming up the stairs outside, *señor*."

"So open the friggin' door for them! There ain't nothin' to be afeared of now we got such powerful lawmen protectin' us!"

A wedge of light from the opening door fell across the half-breed as he reached the head of the stairs. And he touched his hat to the pretty, slim, eighteen-or-so-year-old Mexican girl who peered anxiously out at him. She stood no more than five feet tall so he was able to see directly over her head and he nodded to the man who sat in the room behind her.

"Like to talk with you, Mr. Heller," he said.

"Talk's cheap, mister," the father of a newly dead son answered as the Mexican girl's anxiety expanded to fear, her dark eyes moving from Edge's face to the star on his shirt and back again "Most as cheap as human life in this town."

"*Asesino*," the girl murmured and clutched at her throat.

"My language, girl!" Ed Heller growled. "You talk my language or you leave my house, Juanita."

Edge stepped across the threshold and Juanita backed away from him. Then, with a choked cry she turned, ran into the room and crouched down beside the high backed, thickly padded armchair in which Heller was sitting.

"She thinks I shot your son, feller," the half-breed put in before the girl could force words around the lump in her throat. He closed the door behind him. "Happens she's wrong. Another feller wearing a star pulled the trigger. To keep your son from killing me."

Heller's leather-textured, dough-gray face did not alter

its expression of deep-set misery: the lines which cut away from the sides of his mouth, his nostrils and his eyes suggesting that he had been indulging such a mood for many of the fifty-some years he had lived. It was a thin face under an almost hairless skull atop a body of near skeletal sparseness—his clothes hanging on him much as Merritt's pants draped the bigger man's wasted legs.

The room in which this shadow of a man sat with the frightened girl at his side was small, clean and tidy. A frugally furnished parlor which smelled faintly of death, perhaps because the shriveled, old-before-his-time man was clost to the end of his allotted span, or maybe emanating from the half-open door in back of the chair where Heller sat.

"Don't matter who killed Franklin," the man said in the same growling voice he had said everything else. "He's dead, and neither the law nor me is in any fit state to see that his killer pays."

Juanita, drawing moral strength from the nearness of the physically weak man nodded in emphatic agreement, her eyes directing hatred at Edge.

"Didn't come here to make any excuses, feller," the half-breed said. " But since I am here, you should know—"

"Doc Pollock told me how it happened, mister," Heller interrupted. "When he brung Franklin up to spend his last night in his own bed. Way him and me had his ma here with us when she passed on. And I ain't disputin' what the doc said."

"You and the other man with badge!" the girl hissed, pointing a finger at her small left breast. "You have to kill a *mozo*? A boy?"

Heller lashed out with one of his thin but work-scarred hands, caught the girl on the temple and sent her sprawling to the floor, away from his chair. "Keep your mouth shut, or leave my house, slut!" he snarled, anger erupting two blotches of crimson at the center of his pallid cheeks. "Hadn't been for you, Franklin would be alive still. Tryin' to be a man before his time. Just to show off for the likes of you."

Juanita had merely gasped in response to the blow. Now, eyes that looked cried out, spilled fresh tears. As she pulled the fabric of her mourning black dress over her exposed legs, got to her feet and ran through the half-open door to the back room. She slammed it closed behind her, blocking off the sounds of her sobs.

"Something I should tell you, feller," Edge said evenly.

"What?" Heller snapped, and sucked in deep breath as if he thought this would help calm his anger.

"When I'm around, don't insult her just because she's a Mexican. My pa was a Mexican."

"So are some of my best friends in this town, mister. But I wouldn't want my son to marry one."

He directed a challenging stare at Edge, and did not flinch when the half-breed advanced across the room toward him. The big, comfortable chair in which he sat was to one side of a bureau; on top of which was arrayed several framed photographs. Of Franklin at various ages, of a handsome middle-aged woman and of a younger, stronger Ed Heller in the uniform of a Confederate artillery sergeant.

"No!" the man in the chair croaked as Edge stopped in front of him. And began to swing his free hand.

But hand and arm swept across the bureau top and sent the family mementoes crashing to the floor. Some of the thin-glass protection for the photographs shattered.

"My ma married one," the half-breed said, his slitted blue eyes glinting as sharply as some of the shards in the lamplight. Then he took a backward step and lowered his boot heel here and there to complete the act of destruction. Breaking more glass, snapping frames and tearing the photographs. "You got the smell of death about you, feller. And I figure you've taken enough lumps to last you what life you've got left. Best you be polite about Mexicans in what little future you have, uh?"

The lines of misery deepened in the tough, white skin of his face as his eyes got a sheen of moisture, gazing down at the mess around the half-breed's feet. "Why did you come here?" he croaked, clawed fingers digging into the upholstered arms of his chair.

"Ask if your son owned a gun."

"You said he tried to kill you with one."

There was a less comfortable chair on the other side of

the bureau. Edge sat in it and rested his rifle across his knees as he dug the makings from a shirt pocket. "You said Pollock told you what happened at the cantina, feller. Figure he told you all of it. Was another man's gun your son grabbed."

"I do't know!" Heller growled, dragging his gaze back up from the floor to stare venomously at Edge.

The half-breed nodded after he had licked the paper and as he ran thumbs along the cigarette. "Means I'll have to search this place, feller. And I may get a little clumsy with any other souvenirs I come across."

He struck a match on the rifle stock and lit the cigarette, blew out the flame and replaced the dead stick in the box.

"Somethin' I ain't ever come across, mister," Heller muttered. "And I been around some before I settled in this town. That's a bigger, meaner bastard than you are."

"More I get shot at, meaner I get," Edge allowed levely.

"We got an old Henry repeater rifle," Heller said with a sigh, closing his eyes tightly and opening them. "No more than another souvenir, mister. I took it off a dead Yankee after Chancellorsville. Why?"

"Like to see it."

The man was suddenly angry again. And suspicious. "Hey, mister! You ain't sayin' it was Franklin took that shot at the Town House restaurant yesterday?"

"I ain't saying anything," the half-breed countered, getting to his feet. "Except that a shot was fired. And that your son sure tried to kill me later."

Heller set his mouth in a firm line. But winced and had to put a hand to his belly as he came erect. "In the room where we sleep, mister. In a trunk and likely covered with dust. Maybe don't even fire no more."

He walked with difficulty, still pained by the year-old damage a bullet had wrought to his intestines, dragging one foot after the other as he went to the door the Mexican girl had slammed.

The room beyond the door, furnished with a double bed, two closets, a bureau and chair was now dimly lit by a ceiling-hung kerosene lamp with the wick turned low. The girl sat on the chair, head bent and hands clasped in an attitude of prayer, beside the bed. The body of Franklin

88

Heller lay on the bed, contoured by a single sheet which draped it completely. The smell of burning oil masked the odor of death which had previously been rising from the slowly decomposing flesh of the corpse.

The one window of the room, which offered a moonlit view across the rooftops of the mostly single-storey buildings along and behind the north side of Main Street, was closed and had the drapes drawn back.

"What new evil do you intend?" Juanita asked dully as she rose from the chair after crossing herself.

Both men ignored her, as Heller pointed a shaking hand toward one of the closets. And Edge went to it and opened the double doors.

There was a large tin trunk inside and he leaned his rifle against the wall, needing both hands to drag it out into the dim light.

"It'll be under all the other stuff," Heller said as the half-breed unfastened the clasps.

"What is he looking for?" the girl asked anxiously.

And was again ignored.

Edge raised the hinged lid. And saw the neatly folded uniform of a Confederate artilleryman.

"Appreciate it if you wouldn't do no more damage," Heller asked dully as he went to the window and stared out. "A man's memories are better when he's got somethin' he can look at well as think about."

Edge complied with the request, taking care not to disturb the folds as he removed the tunic and pants from the trunk. Beneath were two caps, a belt and cartridge cases, a ribbon-tied bundle of letters still in their envelopes, a cord-tied package of other papers and a white dress ornate enough to be a bridal gown. He took all these out with as much care as he had handled the uniform. To reveal a number of books with gold-blocked lettering naming them as diaries for the years 1848 to 1869. These layered the base of the trunk.

"Well, mister?" Heller asked, his back still to the room, as Edge came erect.

"You have to remember Chancellorsville with just what's in your mind, feller."

Heller turned slowly from the night beyond the window

and nodded, looking smaller and older and sicker. "Thought it might be so, mister. But I couldn't bring myself to come look in the trunk after Doc Pollock brought my son home and told me how it happened. Kinda makes Franklin out to be a coward, don't it?"

The girl caught her breath.

Edge said, "There are times when a man can convince himself that he has to do something wrong to make something else right." And had a brief image of Adam Steele rising out of the rocks, rifle above his head—realized he had just made an excuse for the Virginian as well as Franklin Heller.

"My son came home early afternoon," Ed Heller said, eyes misty and voice quavering. "Didn't come in through the workshop below like usual. Up the outside stairway. Called out he'd spilled somethin' on his shirt and needed a change. Didn't think nothin' of it. Except I tried not to think he wanted to pretty himself up to go see his Mexican girl. Franklin didn't know I knew about her."

"He came to see me," Juanita confirmed, her mind as far away from the present and her present surroundings as that of Heller.

"Ain't nothin' makes it right for one man to bushwhack another," the frail, suffering Heller went on in the same absent tone. "Reason I always wanted to be infantry or cavalry in the war. Never seemed right to me, firing those big twelve-pounder howitzers at an enemy you couldn't see. And who couldn't see you."

"Know why he took that shot at me in the afternoon, feller?" Edge asked. "And made another try later?"

His glinting eyes shifted from the man to the girl and back again.

Juanita licked her lips as a sign of nerves, as Heller shook his head, but this gesture was not in reply to the questions. "Not so much at you, mister. Did what he did on account of the Masonville Massacre and—"

The sounds were a repeat of those which had curtailed the lunch at the Town House restaurant.

The shattering of window glass.

The crack of a rifle bullet.

The thud of a human form hitting the floor.

But unlike Leroy, Ed Heller went down not of his own volition. And the blossoming bloodstain on his glass-sprinkled shirt-back showed that he would not get up un-aided.

Juanita stood rooted to the spot and vented a single short scream. As Edge reached the window in three long strides, dousing the light as he went below it. And Ed Heller used his dying breath to rasp:

"Least my son died in the open. Out-numbered by . . ."

The words were swamped by the death rattle in his throat. As Edge peered out of the darkened room and saw the black shapes of many buildings suddenly squared by the vivid yellow of windows illuminated by freshly lit lamps. And voices were raised, in anger and fear. Too many lighted windows with silhouetted forms at them for the half-breed to learn anything from his vantage point.

He turned away to look at the Mexican girl. Who seemed on the verge of hysteria, but controlled it by stoking her hatred for Edge.

"It's the shoemaker's window got broke!" somebody yelled.

"More trouble for Ed!"

"That guy just don't seem to have any damn luck!"

Edge relit his cigarette and asked, "The kid fired his rifle from your place *señorita?*"

"*Si*," she spat the answer. While my mother and father were out. Afterwards I hid the rifle out in the back yard. Are you going to arrest me?"

"It's there now?"

"*Si*."

"You won't be arrested if you turn it in to the law office."

There were voices out on the street in front of the building. A banging on the door. Then footfalls coming up the outside stairway.

"You know why he did it?"

"He said it was better I did not know. He said it would all be made plain to everyone when Chris Kelly returned to this town."

"He say who it was he aimed to kill?"

"No. He said a man who did not deserve to go on living."

"Ed, what's happening here?" the squeaky-voiced Harry Pollock called after springing open the door at the top of the outside stairway.

"Obliged," the half-breed said to the girl as he went to the door giving onto the parlor from the bedroom. "Don't forget to turn in the rifle."

The town doctor and mortician, Charlie Deed and a man Edge did not recognize were grouped on the threshold of the outside doorway. Pollock, dishevelled from sleep and hurriedly dressed, had his black bag of medical supplies gripped in both hands.

"What's required?" he asked wearily. "Doctoring or burying?"

"Just dig the one hole deeper, feller. Be a family grave."

The middle-aged, ruddy-complexioned man who was not known to Edge showed a grimace. "Damn," he muttered. "Ed was the best friggin' shoemaker outside of St Louis."

"Well, some heel just backshot him and relieved him of his soul," the half-breed muttered.

Pollock scowled at the black humor, then looked startled. "Hey, what's Frankie's girl doing here?"

Edge glanced at Juanita who had emerged from the bedroom. "The kid's father knew about her. They were holding some kind of wake. Maybe you'll need to give her something to sleep."

The doctor deepened his scowl, as the unknown man turned and went back down the stairway, calling out the news that Ed Heller was dead.

"Anythin' for me to do, Mr. Edge?" Deed asked.

"Some diaries, letters and papers in the bedroom, feller. Obliged if you'd bring them down to the law office."

Deed nodded and followed Pollock into the room, allowing the half-breed space to go outside. The narrow street was empty of curious bystanders now. There was just Adam Steele, leaning against the wall in the shadows, Colt Hartford sloped to his shoulder.

"Talk is Frank Heller's father was just shot dead?" the Virginian said.

"Right. But Deed and me have it under control. You can go back to bed. Unless you play a bugle?"

The smaller man's expression was quizzical in the moonlight as he stepped out from the shadows.

"You and Ed Heller being in the same army a few years back, Reb. And him being the town shoemaker."

"You lost me, Yank."

Edge showed a quiet smile. "Figured that might put him in line for the Last Post."

Steele drew back his lips to show his boyish grin, and said, "Cobblers."

NINE

STEELE did not return to his rented bed in the Town House that night. Instead, he joined Edge and Deed in the law office and did his share of reading through the papers taken from the trunk in the Hellers' bedroom.

The letters were quickly dealt with for all of them were written to Ed Heller by his wife while she was living with Franklin in Richmond, Virginia and he was fighting in various theatres of the Civil War. Likewise, the diaries, which were also written in the hand of Amelia Heller, recording the trivia and the highlights of the nineteen years and three months from her marriage to her death by consumption.

She wrote in a neat hand in pen and ink and in the clear, concise style of a woman of some education. Not so her husband.

His account, based upon talking with witnesses, of a savage afternoon in a small Mississippi town in the year of 1864 required great patience to decipher. For it was written and printed in pencil—the form of the lettering almost illegible, the spelling bad and punctuation nonexistent.

But, by the time the first bright light of Sunday shafted over the ridges to the east of Southfields, the three men in the law office had gained a good impression of what Ed Heller had called the Masonville Massacre. And were able to rest their eyes from pained study of the discolored and curled sheets of paper on which the events had been recorded.

Masonville had been in sharecropper country on the banks of the Tombigbee River in the north of the state, close to the Alabama line, unaffected by war until a January morning in 1865. When, as Confederate held territory began to shrink before Union advances east and west of the

94

Big Muddy, a twenty-five strong band of Union irregulars rode into town.

They had styled themselves the Kansas Raiders and, if the accounts of the massacre given to Heller were to be believed, the events which took place on that late summer day left one of the greatest stains on the history of that blood-stained state.

The motley uniformed men rode into the one-street riverside town at eleven o'clock and demanded food and liquor. There was adequate food, but Masonville was dry. By noon the townspeople could be said to have been reluctantly co-operative with their disgruntled "liberators."

The first rape was at ten minutes after midday. The victim was an eleven-year-old simple-minded girl. Her protesting father was hung up by his wrists to a tree branch, castrated and forced to watch repeated sexual assaults on his daughter—on penalty of seeing his elderly mother disembowelled if he should close his eyes.

Shortly after one o'clock, the girl died from internal bleeding. Moments later her father's anguish and agony were ended by a sabre blade which split his skull—wielded by the leader of the raiders who took exception to being cursed for allowing the atrocity.

Then the old lady had her insides gouged out with the same sabre. As an example of what would happen to every person over the age of fifty if another insult was directed at the raiders.

For the next two hours, the force of Union irregulars got drunk on sex and violence as substitutes for the liquor they had craved. Raping the tight-lipped girls and young women. Beating up on unprotesting boys and men with fists, gun butts and even a bull whip. This savagery committed while the old people of Masonville were forced to stand in a line, bellies bared through the tears in their clothing, sabre points pressed to the flesh.

At 3:30, every building in the town was put to the torch. And as the flames leapt high and the smoke drifted out over the river, the people whose homes were burning were offered a brutal choice. For the raiders, astride their horses now, herded everyone into the Tombigee, like cowpunchers on the trail with a bunch of docile longhorns. And cut loose with a constant barrage of gunfire. Did not ride off until their leader was certain everyone had made the choice—to die by bullets or to drown in the red run waters of the river.

But a boy who was ten at the time survived without physical injury. So did a woman of fifty-two. Two ten-times-raped girls of eighteen and nineteen. A middle-aged man who had to have his right arm amputated because of infected bullet wounds. And a younger man driven blind by the shocks of that day.

Ed Heller's brother, mother and young niece were not among the survivors. For they were the first three victims of the Masonville Massacre.

"Guess that makes it certain it wasn't Steele the kid tried to kill at the restaurant," Charlie Deed said to end a long silence which followed the reading of the final page by the men. "Way you're always callin' him Reb, he—"

The half-breed did not alter his impassive expression as the man with the ugly teeth looked at him without rancor. He said, "He was sure enough fixing to kill me last night at the cantina, feller."

"He had just as much hate for me, Yank," Steele put in. "Happened to be turned toward you when he got his hands on the gun."

Edge nodded. "How I figured it."

The Virginian rose from behind his desk, went to the door and opened it. To let fresh morning air into the office which was layered with blue smoke from the many cigarettes smoked by the half-breed. "And I've got no reason to believe you weren't a regular cavalry captain."

There was a trace of tautly controlled anger in Steele's tone as he spoke, staring out at the deserted street etched with long shadows thrown by the just rising sun. The first sign of emotion revealed by any of the men since they had begun to learn of the events in Masonville more than ten years earlier.

"It was a lousy war, feller," Edge said evenly, and stretched in his chair to loosen bunched muscles. "I saw a few places hit by the likes of Quantrill. And had more than a taste of Andersonville."

"I was out in California lookin' for gold while the war was on," Deed muttered.

"So you have nothing to contribute to this conversation!" Steele snapped.

An angry scowl flashed across Deed's weathered face and was immediately gone when his eyes locked on the glittering stare of the half-breed. Edge nodded and shifted his attention back to the Virginian. "You saying it, feller, I figure that means you have a nagging doubt. Sure I was a regular in the Union cavalry. But I did a few irregular things. Never was in any town called Masonville, though. Never got into Mississippi."

Steele pursed his lips and vented a soft sigh as he turned and leaned a shoulder against the doorframe. "There wasn't any doubt, Yank," he drawled. "It was a lousy war. Reckon war always was and always will be. Most of the time, the worst parts are forgotten."

"Unless a man wants to remember them," Edge said.

Steele nodded. "For future reference."

"We're in the future now," Deed scowled. And poked a dirty-nailed finger at the papers on the half-breed's desk. "Far as this stuff goes."

"So?" the Virginian said.

"I can speak without gettin' my damn head bit off by you or my balls froze off by the look in Edge's eyes?"

"Reckon so."

"You got anything worthwhile to say."

"Reference for what in the future, I'd like to know. Heller wrote down what people told him happened. Ain't one damn thing in all this about who these Kansas Raiders were."

"Maybe some of the papers are missing," Steele said.

"Or hidden," Edge added, getting to his feet. "Could even be Heller didn't write down any descriptions he got. In case somebody else with an interest in what happened found them and beat him to the punch."

"Are we going to talk to Merritt, Yank?" the Virginian asked.

"Merritt?" Deed said, perplexed.

"You read what Heller wrote, " Steele said, with a tone

of impatience. "You want the Yank and me to draw you some pictures as well?"

"But that's crazy. Clinton Merritt and Ed Heller have lived in this town for years. Why hasn't nothin' happened before this?"

Edge shrugged as he went to the open door, passing Steele who came back into the office to get his rifle. "Maybe Heller wasn't sure, feller. Or maybe he was just waiting for the right time."

"Or the right kind of help," the Virginian added. "Like Chris Kelly."

"And the Heller kid went off half-cocked. Tried to kill the Reb and me before Kelly got back."

"The shot that killed Ed could have come from the rear of the Town House?" Steele asked Edge.

"Maybe, Reb. You were sleeping in the place."

"Sleeping real well, Yank. The shot woke me. I reckon. But I can't say how close to me it was fired."

The half-breed had moved out onto the sun-bright street and the Virginian joined him. As Deed moved into the law office doorway.

"You going to tackle Merritt about it?"

Edge swilled some saliva around in his mouth, then spat it out with some of the stale taste of a night's cigarette smoking. "Going to have me some breakfast," he told Deed. "Then carry on with the job I was hired to do. Which is protect this town from the unwelcome return of its former sheriff."

He started across the street in the direction of the still-shuttered Mexican restaurant.

"Without giving a damn about the kind of man who hired you?" Steele called after him.

The half-breed looked back over his shoulder without breaking his slow stride. "Same way I don't give a damn about the kind of fellers I work with. Long as they deliver what's expected of them, when it's expected, what they did in the past doesn't interest me."

"I think that was meant for you, not for me, Steele," Deed muttered. As Edge reached the front of the restaurant and banged a fist on the door. "Somethin' in particular?"

"I killed his horse."

Deed was surprised. "You killed his horse?"

"It was a mistake," the Virginian answered in the same taut tone. "I was aiming at him."

Deed whistled softly and watched as the half-breed was allowed into the restaurant by a sleepy-eyed Mexican woman. "Guess that explains somethin' he said last night about you and him once walkin' out together. He let you get away with tryin' to kill him?"

"Not yet," Steele replied, shifting his pensive gaze from the restaurant facade to Deed. "I owe him one more favor before we can part company."

The taller and older man gave it a few more moments thought, then shrugged. "You fellers beat me."

"We don't have to. We're all on the same side. Go get some sleep. I'll hold down the office for a while."

For more than an hour after Charlie Deed had ambled lazily off along the street in the direction of the Town House, Adam Steele sat alone behind his desk in the law office, listening to the Sunday morning sounds of the town coming awake and feeling the dry heat rise up the temperature scale. As his thoughts ran, unknown to him, along similar lines to those which had occupied Edge for a while last night.

Concerned as they were with the strangely similar patterns of their lives and the affinity this created, one with the other. An affinity which, on Steele's part, was regarded with an uneasy ambivalence: a respect for the other man's necessarily crude code—which was more or less the same as his own—and a repugnance for those traits in Edge's character and attitudes which went against his own grain. His view of the half-breed colored, he angrily admitted, by the incident of the dead horse and its outcome. An accident instigated by Steele—totally out of character—which had since placed him constantly on the defensive against this man who was so much like him.

Why had he taken a shot at the slow-riding stranger in a valley of the Sierra Madre foothills? Imitating, he now recalled, the actions of an army deserter up north. But that trooper had been in desperate straits after leaving the army post known to the men as Fort Despair.

Steele was in no such situation less than two days ago. He had food, water and stamina enough to reach on foot this town for which he was heading. But what he also had, he now acknowledged with a frown to show a degree of the same emotion, was a deep anger burning inside him.

Because of the long trail he had followed and was in danger of losing, which mattered not at all to anybody except him. Mattered because he wanted to be absolutely sure that no other murder charge could be leveled against him. For to know he had killed his old friend Jim Bishop and to accept his ruling fate's punishment for the cowardly crime was enough. To be in the shadow of the gallows for a murder he did not commit . . . there was only so much anguish even a man like Adam Steele could live with.

Thus, out of the frustration of being without a horse had erupted anger at Sven Karlsen for killing his wife, at himself for continuing the chase which everyone else concerned considered futile, and at everyone else for thinking the way they did.

And it was all this anger—which at the time he refused to admit to—that caused him to draw a bead on the stranger and squeeze the trigger. A fraction of a second too late. In the full knowledge that he was about to commit another cold-blooded murder. Justifying the act to himself by thinking that the man in the Colt Hartford sights was not at all like Bish.

The sonofabitch should have been a ten-dollar-a-head bounty hunter, lacking the talent and instinct to be anything else. Then he would have been just a buzzard-ravaged heap of bones down in Mexico by now. Instead of which, the . . . "sonofabitch . . . !"

The Virginian heard the word rasp between his own lips as a footfall sounded at the law-office doorway. And he looked up to see Edge standing there, a cloth-covered plate in one hand and a steaming mug of aromatic coffee in the other. There was a smile on the half-breed's mouth which did not reach up to the ice-blue slits of his eyes.

"Matter of degree of personal desire, ain't it, Reb?" Edge said as he came into the office and set down his burdens on Steele's desk.

"What is?"

100

"Those Kansas Raiders hitting the town in the war and you trying to kill me. Unless a man gives a full account of his motives, others got no right to judge him."

"I reckoned at the time I badly needed a horse," Steele supplied tautly as Edge swung to head back for the door.

"I've already bought that."

"You going to ask Merritt why he—"

"Eat your breakfast, feller. I'm going to get a shave. You told me without me asking. If Merritt has anything to say, maybe it'll be the same with him."

Then he was outside, turning right to walk along the sidewalk to the barber's shop next to the livery stable. Steele formed his lips into the shape of an obscenity, but then sighed into a scowl. Which changed into a smile as he became aware of the smells of coffee and food. He pulled the cover off the plate and saw two slices of thick ham, two eggs, a pile of grits and a hunk of bread with a knife and fork lying across the center. The meal was too greasy because it had been cooked in the kitchen of a Mexican restaurant. But it was welcome.

"Just the sight of it looks to have improved your mood, Reb," Edge called from where he had halted to peer into the office through the dusty window.

"Reckon I'll eat it while all I have to lose is my appetite, Yank. Grateful to you."

"We also serve who only stand and wait."

"Go get a shave."

"You'll be around if it turns to be another close one?"

Steele's expression and tone suddenly altered, replacing the good humor of the exchange with grimness. "I haven't forgotten the debt is only half-paid, Edge."

"If you want to go on flogging a dead horse, feller."

"That's the part that bothers me," the Virginian muttered as Edge continued on his way to the barber's shop. Recalling the first shootout at the Cantina Plata—Dave with a bullet in his belly and Jerry with one in his heart. Brad didn't count. "A dead man and a half was easy."

While he ate the breakfast, Steele heard the pace of Sunday morning life in Southfields quicken. Not by much. But with the rise in the volume of sounds as more and more people rose to undertake the chores of a new day, the tempo did increase.

But the citizens of the town and their business and pleasure did not touch Steele until he had eaten every scrap of food and was taking his last swallow from the coffee cup. Which was when the bulky form of the bald headed Chico Lopez, flanked by his two whores, blocked out most of the sunlight from the office doorway. All three of them were heavily burdened with armfuls of handguns and rifles.

"Hey, where do you want these, *hombre?*" Lopez asked.

"Back up for when your shotgun's not handy?" Steele asked.

"What?" Lopez growled, sweating with the effort of carrying more than a fair share of the weapons.

"The man who does not smoke or drink or go with women, he makes a joke," the shorter and fatter whore explained with a sneer.

"A man like that, he has to have some fun," the other woman muttered.

Lopez snarled a Spanish obscenity, shared a scowl between the women and had enough of it left to direct at the Virginian. "After you and the man Edge shoot so many people, my people—the Mexicans, you understand—they are quick to obey the law you make. Bring their guns to me as Mexican deputy. To bring to you. Where you want them?"

Steele jerked a gloved thumb toward the open-barred door giving onto the cells behind the law office. "Through there."

Lopez led the women across the office and into the back. Where all of them dumped the guns with a clatter into the cell which was now an arsenal.

"If more come, I bring them," the disgruntled and sweating fat man tossed over his shoulder as he left.

"Hey, you got any more jokes to make, *gringo?*" the slimmer of the two women said as she swayed out from the cell area.

"*Si*, but one to make us laugh this time," the second one said in the same taunting tone as the first.

Steele showed his boyish grin. "I reckon I could have you ladies splitting your sides," he said evenly, reached down and drew the knife from his boot sheath up into sight. He turned the knife so that its blade glinted in the morning sunlight.

"Hey, Maria, Isabella!" Chico Lopez yelled. "Come on out! Men are riding in! Maybe customers!"

Both whores, tight lipped and with sweat-sheened faces, had to tear their transfixed eyes away from the knife blade turning in the Virginian's hands.

"Back to the daily grind, ladies," Steele urged gently, and slid the knife back into its sheath as the women hurried out of the office.

Then he got to his feet, picking up the Colt Hartford from where it leaned against the desk, and going in the wake of Maria and Isabella. But without haste. As the bell in the tower of the Catholic church across the street began to ring out. To be joined after two mournful tolls by the sound of another bell at the Baptist chapel which was at the northern extreme of Southfields—built on a hill slope at the end of a winding pathway.

The ringing of the bells masked the clop of hooves as four travel-stained men steered their horses along the center of Main Street, entering town from the east.

From the doorway of the law office, the Virginian watched the quartet of riders as they eyed the street and the people on it with unconcealed distaste. And saw, also, the equally apparent apprehension with which the citizens of Southfields viewed the strangers. Citizens who, with the exception of Lopez and the two whores—already back on the threshold of the Cantina Plata—were spick and span in their Sunday best clothes as they converged on the town's two churches.

"Nice day," Steele greeted as the four men, riding abreast, were about to come level with the law-office doorway.

They reined in their horses and swung their heads to look at him, like cavalrymen executing a well-rehearsed drill. But in no other way did they resemble soldiers. All four were of medium height and build: unshaven and filthy dirty—their flesh and clothing. Clothing that was all dark-hued and stiff with old sweat. Made for riding rough country in all kinds of weather. The same as their Western-style saddles which were hung with all the necessary accoutrements. Including a boot into which was slotted a Winchester rifle.

Around each of the men's waists was a gunbelt with a low-slung holster holding a handgun.

"Can't argue with that," the man furthest away from Steele replied.

"Even for a funeral," the man who was closest growled, as the familiar black horses with black plumes jutting from their heads emerged from the alley beside the livery stables. "A nice day."

"Who's dead?" a third stranger asked dully.

Steele glanced along the street as the glass-sided hearse came into view, the high-hatted Harry Pollock up on the seat.

"The two fellers in the caskets," the Virginian supplied evenly.

The man at the far end of the line showed a scowl of irritation. "Names, mister. Lee would like to know the names."

"Heller. Edward and Frank. Father and son."

The man who had not yet spoken vented a low, short sigh. The others gave no response.

As the hearse trundled toward the western end of Main Street trailing disturbed dust, the church-bound citizens continued on their way. Having paid their mute respects to the Hellers and now eager to attain the sanctuary of their places of worship. Or perhaps anxious to get off the street where the four strangers sat weary horses and emanated an almost palpable aura of tension.

"Lookin' for three friends of ours, lawman. Gerald Follett, David Segal and Bradley King."

The churchgoers close enough to hear the enquiry quickened their pace still more. Others took the cue.

"They were here," Steele answered. "Now they've gone."

"They were supposed to wait for us." This again from the man at the far end of the line, as the street became empty of local citizens.

"They got the call."

"To go where, lawman?" His eyes, and those of his three

104

companions revealed that they had a strong suspicion what the answer would be.

"Depends what kind of lives they led," Steele supplied, holding each hard gaze without blinking.

"Shit, I knowed it," Lee growled.

Then his and the attention of the others was switched to the intersection of Main Street and Via de Bello. Attracted by raised voices, speaking Spanish.

A middle-aged couple were arguing with Juanita. Words failed to win against the young girl and they tried to get a grip on her slim shoulders. But she evaded their outstretched arms and lunged away from her parents. She had a two-handed grip on a rifle. A Henry repeater which she held by the muzzle and the stockplate.

"*Ojo!*" her mother called after her.

"*Loco!*" her father cried, anger turning to pleading in his eyes as he shifted his gaze from the girl to Steele.

Juanita slowed her pace as she crossed in front of the mounted men, determination faltering under the assault of fear as she cast apprehensive glances at them.

"Nice lookin' tail," the man beside Lee said flatly.

"Still got the crib marks on it, I reckon," the man to his left countered dully.

"Gives a man fine handholds."

Juanita stepped up onto the sidewalk and had to take a deep breath to say, "I was told to bring this to you."

She thrust out the rifle toward the Virginian, still holding it like it was something hot or bad smelling.

"Grateful to you," Steele said, and took the gun in one gloved hand, rested it against the front of the law office. As the bells were curtailed. "Now best you get on to church."

"Reckon I could give her a better service," The man next to Lee vented a harsh laugh as his leering face and slow-spoken words sent the girl scurrying back across the street. Behind the horsemen, as her parents hurried to meet her in front of the church.

"You got a mind like a sewer, McCloud," the obvious leader of the group growled. "Keep it on the business in hand. How did they die, lawman?"

With the street to themselves and only Steele, Chico Lopez and the two whores in sight, all four strangers chose to look at the Virginian.

"By mistake."

"An accident?" The leader's brow furrowed in a frown.

Steele shook his head. "No, we meant to kill them. They made the mistake of trying to kill me."

Lee, McCloud and the man beside the leader became tense in their saddles as their dirt-streaked, unshaven faces expressed mute snarls.

"*We*, lawman?" the impassive-faced man at the end said.

"Him and me, feller," Edge drawled. As he stepped onto the threshold of the barber shop next to the law office. He had his right thumb hooked over the buckle of his gunbelt. One side of his face was freshly shaven but there was still a layer of lather on the other side. And one half of the white cloth draped over his shoulder had been pulled clear so that the star on his shirt could be seen.

"And me, *hombres*," Chico Lopez called. As he shouldered between the two whores to step from the shadows of his cantina so that the morning sun glinted on his star. Then he replaced his grim expression with a beaming smile. "But if you cause no trouble, you are welcome to use my establishment and its facilities."

The four strangers had shifted their disconcerted eyes away from the Mexican before he began to make the sales pitch. Their attention drawn to the balcony above the Town House stoop by the sound of an opening window. To watch as Charlie Deed, clad in gray longjohns with a gunbelt slung around his hips, climbed over the sill.

"Wasn't on the team then, gents," the fourth deputy announced. He jerked a thumb over his shoulder to indicate the room behind him. "But now I got me a badge inside someplace."

"Jesus, Henry. The friggin' town's crawlin' with lawmen."

"Oughta make for peace and quiet, Clyde," the leader responded evenly.

Of the deputies, only Steele and Edge were close enough to see the struggle Henry had to regain and hold his composure.

"That's right," the Virginian agreed. "We only shoot at

people who shoot at us. No chance of that happening to you if you obey the new law."

"New law?" Lee asked.

"He has trouble readin'," Henry explained. "Seen the notices. On the way in. You want our guns?"

"That or for you men to ride on out."

"Somethin' else we could do, lawman."

Steele shook his head. "For the time being, we have enough men with badges."

Henry looked from the Virginian to the half-breed, to Deed and to the unarmed Mexican. And nodded. "Seems like," he agreed. "But if you need some extra help, we'll be around."

He started to unbuckle his gunbelt. McCloud, Clyde and Lee took their cues from him, but this time they scowled their reluctance to do so. Gunbelts and rifles were handed along the line and dropped in a heap on the street.

"Any other laws we oughta know about?" Lee growled.

"Just the ten Moses told the world about, feller," the Virginian answered.

Henry showed a tight-lipped grin as he shot a glance at the Cantina Plata. Where Lopez was now flanked by Isabella and Maria, the woman adopting seductive poses as they smiled at the strangers. "Figure the one about not screwin' a woman who ain't your wife could get broke, lawman," he drawled as Charlie Deed yawned and swung a leg back over the window sill to return to his room.

"My mistake, seven," Steele allowed.

"Seven?" Henry echoed as the other three heeled their horses forward.

And Lopez ushered his whores into the cantina and Edge turned to go back inside the barber shop. But halted the move.

"Blasphemy I'll let pass," the Virginian said. "So long as it's not in the hearing of decent women. And you can labor on the Sabbath if you need."

"Thanks a whole lot," Henry muttered as he set his horse moving in the wake of the others.

Edge showed a cold grin to Steele as he allowed the white cloth to fall back into place. "Turning out to be a peaceful Sunday, Reb," he said.

The more slightly built man stepped across the sidewalk and down onto the street to gather up the discarded weapons. "Reckon so, Yank," he answered. "Even without arrest."

TEN

SOUTHFIELDS was like any other small town in at least one respect—anything of note which happened in any part of it was quickly related elsewhere. And by noon that Sunday the cell allocated to the storage of surrendered weapons was piled high with them. Just the occasional man made it know that he was handing in his gun under protest—had been urged to do so by his wife or his boss. A few men expressed resentment at the way Frank Heller had been gunned down and the lack of interest the newly appointed lawmen were showing in tracking down the killer of Ed Heller. And a handful spoke appreciatively at the way the four potential troublemakers had been dealt with earlier in the day.

John Clements from the stage and telegraph office, Harry Pollock's dour-faced son Dave and the portly town druggist whose name was Barney Gehlen said they were prepared to be deputized—but only in an emergency. For the time being, they lodged their guns in the cell behind the law office. Leroy, the Negro jack-of-all-trades from the hotel offered his services immediately, provided he was given a gun. Despite a scowling protest from Deed, he was put on the short-list.

At midday, with the blisteringly hot air permeated with the appetizing aromas from countless cooking pots, the westbound stage rolled into town. The law office door was closed and locked and Edge and Steele watched from the stoop of the Town House as the Concord ran in off the east trail. While Charlie Deed patroled the back streets of the American section of town and Chico Lopez attended to the needs of his customers.

From the houses came the domestic sounds of meals

being prepared. And from the cantinas and the bar of the Town House other subdued noise as men drank, talked, played cards and kept movement to a minimum in the stifling interiors of the buildings.

"One of those fellers Pollock had to carry out of the cantina, Reb," Edge said from where he leaned against the hotel doorway, a smoking cigarette sloped from a corner of his mouth.

"What about him?" Steele asked from the rocker which he wasn't rocking.

"Said something about Clark would be glad to know you were dead."

"Has to mean Clark Ludlum. Kelly's boy deputy."

"Right. You figure that means Ludlum is the son of that feller you trailed all the way down from the north?"

"Could be."

There was a pause in the exchange as the stage rolled by, brakes applied, dust rising from under the wheelrims and the hooves of the four-horse team. Not too much dust, though, for the half-breed and the Virginian to see that the Concord was carrying six passengers.

"Follett, Segal and King," Edge went on, as both he and Edge shifted their eyes along narrowed sockets to watch the stage as it slowed to a halt outside the last building on the north side of Main Street. "In town to meet with Ludlum. And Kelly, it follows."

Steele nodded. "And the new bunch came to meet the others."

"Saturday's a long time from now."

"Guess Kelly's not honor-bound to stay with the schedule he announced. Reason we should talk with Merritt as soon as we can. I don't like surprises. Yank."

"Tell me what he says," Edge said, straightening from the doorway and moving along the stoop. Intent upon reaching the front of the stage-line office at about the same time as the man named Henry who had emerged from the Cantina Plata.

"If I reckon it's the truth," Steele called as he rose from the rocker. "I don't spread rumors."

Henry, who was as dishevelled as he had been when he reached town, walked with the wavering gait of a man with

110

a lot of liquor in his bloodstream. But when he became aware that the half-breed was heading for the same destination, the knowledge had a sobering effect on him. He straightened and quickened his pace, after directing a malevolent scowl toward Edge.

All the passengers had climbed out of the stage, but it was only mail and freight which the driver and guard lowered down from the roof and boot to John Clements.

"You want somethin', mister?" the blond-haired, round-faced Clements asked of Henry as Edge cast a cold-eyed look into the office.

"Espectin' a letter," the man snarled. "Name of Henry Sutton."

"Well, give me time to get the damn sack inside, will you?"

A youthful army lieutenant and a young woman sat just inside the door of the office, using handkerchiefs to wipe the sweat and dust of the trail off their faces. A much older woman was close to them, using a large hat as a fan. Across from these a preacher was reading a Bible.

"Two more usin' the facilities out back," Clements said in the same growling tone he had used to Sutton. "One's a drummer, looks like. The other one, I don't know. Nobody's scheduled to leave the stage here."

Edge nodded and stepped aside so that Clements could struggle into the office with a sack of mail. Followed by the grim-faced young guard and the tobacco-chewing middle-aged driver sharing the burden of a pile of wooden boxes.

"Are you expecting trouble here, sheriff?" the bearded preacher asked, looking up from his Bible and marking his place with a finger.

"Expect trouble everywhere, reverend," Edge answered. "Way to avoid unpleasant surprises."

"You're new," the elderly woman said, not altering her expression of discomfort as she continued to use the hat as a fan.

"Newer than you, ma'am. But old enough."

The woman sniffed. "The previous incumbent of your office was a real nice man. Polite to ladies. No one can avoid getting on in years."

"They can if they get on the wrong side of this guy,"

111

Sutton growled as he stepped onto the threshold, scowling at Edge from close range. "Way I hear it he kills people easy as other men swat flies. You found my letter yet?"

He halted just inside the doorway, his broad back to the half-breed. His breath and even the sweat beads on his flesh smelled of whiskey.

"Give me the damn time to sort them," Clements muttered irritably from behind the counter where he had upended the contents of the sack in front of him.

As the stage driver and guard helped themselves to cups of coffee from the pot on the stove. And a thin, city-suited man who did look like a drummer emerged from a door at the rear of the office. Followed by a pale-faced, paunchy old-timer attired in recently purchased Western-style garb which did not quite fit him. A tourist from the East, maybe, trying unsuccessfully to look a part of his unfamiliar surroundings.

"Dead folks don't get any older, do they, lawman?" Sutton said in the same growling tone. "Men like Jerry and Dave and Brad, they got no worries about losin' their hair or their joints stiffenin' or—"

The drummer had the kind of face that seemed to show anxiety all the time. But the man who looked like a tourist had started a friendly smile before Sutton took up again his verbal attack on the impassive half-breed. And then his frown expanded to an expression of fear as John Clements cut in with:

"Get out of my place if you're fixin' to cause trouble! I'll not have innocent travelers endangered by your personal feuds!"

Mere irritation had been displaced by anger in the eyes of the round-faced depot manager as he looked up from his mail-sorting chore to glare at Sutton, Edge, then Sutton again.

"Keep lookin' for my friggin' letter and your nose outta business that don't concern you, mailman!"

"Watch your language, mister!" the army lieutenant snapped, sitting up straighter. "There are ladies present."

"And a man of the cloth," the elderly woman added.

"Oh, my goodness," the man in the too-small clothes gasped.

A frown of worry creased the face of the stage driver, who shot an expectant glance at the guard.

"Ain't my responsibility here," the younger man responded with a shrug.

The driver's frown deepened, then he banged down his cup, slopping coffee, and strode toward the gap in the counter. "All aboard, folks," he announced. "Ready to leave."

The tourist sighed his relief and beat the driver to the gap. "Yes, I think it wise we be on our way," he said.

As the preacher closed his Bible and stood up, the sound of the book slapping shut triggering others to make the first moves of leaving the depot.

Although Edge could not see the face of Henry Sutton, he saw in the abrupt stiffening of the man's stance that he had become tense. It also showed in the way Sutton's head snapped from side to side, looking at everyone in turn—except the half-breed.

"Hey, folks," he growled suddenly. "Ain't nothin' to be afraid of. This here lawman with his shiny star ain't about to start nothin'. Not without his buddies to back him up. And I'm only here to get my letter."

"Get him out of here, Edge!" Clements demanded. "It's been a long haul and the passengers need the full hour rest stop."

"No, no, it's perfectly all right, sir," the tourist assured. "I'm sure we are all anxious to get to our destinations as soon as possible."

"Ah, shit to you," Sutton snarled. "So frig off!"

"I warned you, mister!" the young lieutenant yelled.

He was three feet away from the scowling Sutton, holding the woman's elbow to steer her toward the doorway. He did not begin to close on Sutton until after he had spat out the words. And the roundhouse punch he threw at the bigger man was telegraphed by the way he squared up to him.

Sutton's acting abilities, which had been tested and found wanting in the scene of contrived provocation, showed even greater shortcomings in the slow clumsiness of his attempt to defend himself. For the young officer's swinging right cross was lacking in power and off target.

The kind of punch a man like Sutton should have been able to evade with ease and counter with devastating effect. Instead of which, he jerked his jaw into line with and toward the bunched fist, not starting to raise his hands until after contact was made.

"Sonofabitch!" he croaked, and staggered away from the lieutenant, banged into the tourist who shrieked in fear and lunged past Edge on to the sidewalk, then sprawled to the floor.

"Bravo!" the elderly woman cried, jammed her hat back on her head and stalked out, treating the half-breed to a bright-eyed glare of disapproval.

"Cyrus, take care," the younger woman implored. As the uniformed man, pride in achievement replacing his former anger, massaged his damaged knuckles with the palm of his other hand, looking almost eager for Sutton to get to his feet.

But Sutton stayed down, rubbing his jaw and groaning. As the preacher crouched at his side and asked, "Are you all right, my son? Not that you did not invite punishment by your foul tongue."

"Get away from me!" Sutton snarled. "You all said you was goin'! Why the hell don't you all go!"

The woman tugged at the officer's sleeve and he submitted to her urgings. The man who looked like a drummer also went out of the office. Then the preacher. The driver. Finally, the guard, after emptying what was left in his cup with a single swallow.

"If I didn't have a good job," he said as he crossed the office, "I'd maybe apply to become a lawman in this town. Sure seems to be an easy number."

His eyes showed deep contempt for the tall, lean man who did not shift from his nonchalant stance against the doorframe until the smaller, more slightly built man was level with him, then he straightened up. And just this act caused the guard to come to a suspicious halt.

"How old are you, feller?" Edge asked.

"No more trouble!" Clements snapped, anxious about Sutton who was now getting to his feet, as scornful of Edge as the guard was.

"Twenty-five. Why?" The guard was belligerent and ready to get aggressive.

"I got better than ten years on you, feller. Lived that long because I learned early when to keep this closed." He raised a forefinger to touch his mouth. Moved the finger to indicate his eyes. "And to only close these when I'm asleep. You've had some luck."

"Get out here, Rex, we're all ready to roll!" the driver yelled.

"Twenty-five ain't too old to learn," Edge went on in the same even tone. "You do that, you won't need so much luck to keep your number from coming up."

"You want me to say thanks for the advice?" the guard asked, his voice heavy with sarcasm.

A shake of the head. "Everything I want right now, I can get from him."

He jerked a thumb at Sutton, who had got to his feet and suddenly stood like a statue.

"Rex, move it out here!"

The guard treated Edge to another scowl, then went over the threshold, across the sidewalk and clambered up on the Concord. The driver of which yelled his team into motion before Rex attained his seat.

"What d'you mean, lawman?" Sutton snarled, and moved his hand toward his holster before he realized it was empty.

John Clements had hurriedly riffled through the rest of the mail and now snapped, "There's nothin' here for anyone named Sutton. Try again at noon tomorrow."

"Hey, Henry!" McCloud yelled from out on the street. "Everythin' okay?"

Edge glanced over his shoulder and saw McCloud, Lee and Clyde Carter grouped in front of the Cantina Plata doorway. None of them looked so drunk as Sutton did when he emerged from the bar to cross to the stage depot.

"You want to tell him, feller?" the half-breed asked.

Sutton licked his dry lips. "I asked you what you mean about me giving you what you want, lawman."

Sutton's partners, able to see Edge framed in the doorway and not getting a response to Carter's question from

115

beyond the half-breed, started across the street. Edge could visualize their progress from the sound of their footfalls.

"Henry!" McCloud called.

"You want some help with the lawman?" Carter asked.

"Just give the word," Lee added.

Somewhere, a window banged open. Then a rifle shot cracked out. A puff of dust and a divot of hard-packed dirt rose from two feet in front of the advancing trio. And brought them to a sudden halt, caused them to swing their heads and look with a mixture of anger and fear at the window of Clinton Merritt's room on the second floor of the Town House. Where Adam Steele stood, the Colt Hartford aimed from his shoulder, smoke still wisping from the muzzle.

"Dammit, there's no need for more gunplay!" John Clements snarled, glaring at Edge.

"You're mighty damn brave, deputy!" Lee yelled. "With our guns locked in a friggin' cell!"

The Virginian triggered another shot down into the street. And the report sounded against two screams. One vented by a woman in the room behind Steele. Another by Lee as the tip of his finger—moving to point accusingly up at the rifleman—was blown off by the bullet.

"Cussing's much the same as blasphemy!" Steele called as all three men on the street stared down at the chunk of displaced flesh in the dust. "Also isn't nice to point."

This as Henry Sutton vented a low growl of rage and lunged forward.

"Yellow-backed bastards!" he roared, unable to see what had happened out on the street but convinced by what he heard that Steele had badly injured or maybe even killed Lee.

He had started to move before he yelled the insult, and Edge did not turn his head around until the whiskey-reeking Sutton was a few inches outside of arm's reach. And six of these inches were taken up by the blade of a knife.

"Edge!" John Clements yelled, too late to be of any help.

The half-breed had the disadvantage of being surprised. But the advantage of coolness in face of the other man's

116

blind rage. Fast, but without panic, he took a single stride across the stage depot threshold, his back coming away from the doorframe and his right arm lashing out behind him.

Sutton had opened the attack with the knife held low down, then started to swing it in an upward arc—aiming to drive the blade deep between Edge's ribs at the side. He saw the defensive counter but his forward momentum was too powerful and his mind was in too great a turmoil for him to fully adjust to it. He tried, but the backward movement of the half-breed's arm prevented it, as the wrist of Edge slammed into his forearm. And the thrust of the knife was deflected to the left instead of the right. To sink two inches of blade into the timber of the doorframe.

Sutton's cry was a mixture of pain from the jarring effect of the knife meeting solid wood and anguish at looking—from close range—into the mask of evil that in part of a second had taken command of Edge's features.

With fluid speed, the half-breed had swung around to face Sutton—the move completed before the knife had been jerked out of the wood. And not only had Edge whirled toward his attacker. He had also raised his right hand to the nape of his neck, delved it through his long hair, and brought it back into view again—fished around the handle of the straight razor.

In that sliver of time while Sutton was transfixed by the sight of the glinting threads of the man's eyes and the cruel twist of his mouthline with the teeth just visible between the lips, the blade of the razor made contact with flesh.

It would have been easier to kill Sutton. And, vaguely aware of gleaming metal closing on him, Sutton was certain from the set of Edge's features that death was only a moment away. But the half-breed stopped the swing of his arm. Skilfully ending the move with the honed metal of the razor resting on but not cutting into the skin at the center of Sutton's throat.

As the threatened man curtailed his cry, both he and Edge became absolutely still. Standing for a stretched second on the threshold of the stage depot like some two-figured carving. In that time, they held their breath, did not bat an eyelid and it was even between heartbeats, so no pulse throbbed in their throats. Then Edge said softly:

"Your buddy lost the top of a finger, feller. That worth dying for?"

He reached with his free hand to take hold of the knife blade with a finger and thumb. And tugged gently. Initially, there was resistence. But then, after Sutton had glanced outside—moving only his eyes—and seen that all three of his partners were still on their feet, he surrendered the knife. And swallowed hard. Edge allowed the razor to move with the flesh rather than cut into it. As the killer glint became subdued in his slitted eyes and his lips closed over his teeth.

"I thought—" Sutton began.

"What you thought doesn't interest me, feller," the half-breed cut in, and drew another cry from the man as he dropped the knife to the floor and slammed a knee into Sutton's crotch.

The injured man screamed. And would have died had not Edge jerked the razor away from his throat. For Sutton instinctively made to double up in an effort to ease his agony.

Lee stayed where he was, sucking the bleeding tip of his finger. But Carter and McCloud each took a pace forward. Then came to an abrupt halt when a third shot from Steele's rifle caused dirt and dust to kick up a few inches in front of them.

"This is madness!" Wanda Merritt shrieked. "Stop it! Please stop it!"

"Quiet, girl!" her father roared. And glee was stronger than anger in his voice.

"You need any more help, Yank?" the Virginian called.

"You hear me ask you a first time, Reb?" Edge answered.

And in response heard the window of Merritt's Town House room bang closed. But the three men in the center of the street, although no longer threatened by the Virginian's rifle, did not dare to advance further on the stage depot. For the straight razor was again endangering the life of Henry Sutton.

The man was down on his haunches, back rested against the doorframe and hands pressed to his pained groin. Head raised so that the sweat beads on his bristled face glistened in the early-afternoon sunlight. Edge had also dropped to his haunches, back sliding down the opposite doorframe, right arm pushed forward to bring the razor to within a half inch of Sutton's left eye. A menacing position of which the injured man was not aware until the intensity of his pain lessened sufficiently for him to ease up his eyelids.

He caught his breath and jerked his head away, banging the back of it against the doorframe.

Edge pushed the razor forward so that its point maintained the same distance from the vulnerable, staring target. "Don't know what the local preachers had to say today, feller," he murmured. "But let's take as our text what the Good Book has to say about an eye for an eye."

Sutton trembled.

John Clements had to clear his throat with a strangled sound before he could urge, "No, don't!"

"Attend to your work," the half breed ordered. "Leave me to do mine."

"I didn't do you no harm," Sutton croaked, saliva trickling over his lower lip and running down his chin. "Way it turned out."

"You aimed to, feller. But we'll get to that later. Or maybe sooner if you don't tell me what was in the note you slipped to the passing-through preacher."

"Note?"

The razor moved. In a blur of speed. So that it was back where it had been at the start before Sutton realized he had been cut—in the blinking of his eye his captor had slashed a shallow but long opening across his left cheek.

"Jesus!" McCloud gasped.

And Clements made a sound like he was about to be sick.

"To be a good liar you have to be a good actor," Edge said softly as Sutton winced in response to the spread of warm blood on his cheek and the sting of salt sweat beads seeping into the cut. "Way you set up that fight and left yourself open to that shavetail lieutenant's sucker punch . . ."
He shook his head but kept his slitted eyes under their

hooded lids fixed upon Sutton's bloodied face. "Well, if all the world's a stage, feller, you got no future on it."

Sutton squeezed his eyes closed and groaned. But Edge did not believe in the over-emphasized desperation of the attitude—for he saw the way the man tensed his hunched frame to prepare for a counter-attack.

And the half-breed's right hand and the razor it was fisted around moved again. In a different direction. Did more damage. Caused greater pain. Deeper shock.

"You vicious bastard!" Clyde Carter roared.

As Henry Sutton's left ear, neatly sliced from its roots, dropped to the shoulder of its owner. And balanced there for a moment, until the gush of blood from the side of his head dislodged it and it fell to the sidewalk. The man snapped open his eyes which were filled with agony. Then gaped his mouth to vent a scream.

But he managed to trap the sound in his throat as John Clement surrendered to the need to retch. But the self-control Sutton required was too great a strain on his system and he slumped into unconsciousness. Not acting, Edge saw, as the contents of Clements' stomach gouted to the floor behind the counter in a series of noisy splashes.

"You killed Henry!" Lee accused as Sutton's limp form toppled to the side and sprawled across the sidewalk.

Lee moved forward, going between Carter and McCloud, who fell in behind him. All three walking slowly. As Edge came erect at the same unhurried pace, after first wiping the razor clean of blood on the arm of Sutton's shirt.

"You fellers are nothing but a bunch of liars," the half-breed answered evenly as he slid the razor back in the neck pouch. "He's a long way from being dead. Yet."

He draped a hand over his holstered Colt and folded away from the doorframe to face the advancing men. Who came to a stop less than ten feet away. Clements ceased vomiting.

"Same as you three."

"We ain't armed, mister," McCloud said hoarsely.

"Neither was your partner after I took his knife away from him. Now he's even easier to handle."

Edge drew the Colt and aimed it across and down the

front of his frame at the senseless Sutton slumped on the sidewalk.

"The murderin' sonofabitch will do it, Lee," Carter gasped.

"There's a feller who speaks the truth," Edge drawled. "Unless Sutton wakes up and talks before. Or one of you people starts to talk. Before."

"Before what?" McCloud croaked.

"My patience runs out. Figure that'll be about when I get the hammer cocked." He rested a thumb on the Colt's hammer.

Carter swallowed hard. "He means it, Lee."

Edge held up his free hand with the fingers splayed. "Four times over I mean it. Figure four more of Kelly's men dead will cancel out me not knowing what was in the note Sutton gave to the preacher."

The hammer was thumbed back to half-cock.

"About the guns!" Lee said quickly. "Preacher Burns came through to check if everyone was supposed to be here was here. Henry guessed one of you lawmen would be watchin' the stage so he wrote the note. Told about Jerry Follett and the others being killed. And how you been makin' everyone turn in their guns. That's all there was in it."

"Much obliged," Edge acknowledged, eased the hammer forward and slid the Colt back in its holster. "Doc Pollock's office is in back of the Town House."

Then he raised a leg to step over the raggedly breathing form of Sutton and moved at an easy pace along the sidewalk. As Lee, Carter and McCloud hurried forward to gather around the tortured man.

"*Hombre!*" Chico Lopez called from the doorway of his cantina, a shrill note of urgent warning in his tone.

But Edge had already sensed danger and was halfway through a whirl, Colt clear of the holster and hammer cocked.

It was Lee who had started to come erect, Sutton's knife held over his shoulder in his good hand. The hand came forward but the fear crowding Lee's eyes showed he knew there was no chance of completing the throwing act.

The Colt's muzzle spat a bullet with a spurt of flame and

121

a puff of smoke. The lead took Lee in the chest, left of center. He staggered backwards for several feet, the knife sailing out into the center of the street as he threw his arms wide. Then he died, teetered on his feet for a moment, and fell sideways to drape himself over the stage-depot hitching rail.

"Pollock runs his undertaking business from out back of the livery stable," Edge said to the two shocked men still crouched beside Sutton. And pushed the Colt back in the holster.

Then, as the acrid taint of exploded powder became neutralized in the hot air, the half-breed's footfalls on the boarding of the sidewalk were the only sounds to be heard in Southfields. Until the fat Mexican on the threshold of the cantina called:

"Hey, *hombre!* The richer you make Harry Pollock, the poorer I become! Always it is the drinking men you kill! If this goes on, soon I and my *amigos* in the other cantinas will have no customers!"

Edge responded with a spit into the street as the paunchy, bow-legged Pollock came hurrying out of the Town House, a napkin still tucked in his collar. He was carrying his bag of medical instruments and supplies.

"Shooting all over, mister?" he asked in his squeaky voice. "More work for me, I guess?"

"One to fix up and one to make arrangements for," the half-breed confirmed, jerking a thumb over his shoulder to indicate the direction in which Pollock should go.

The doctor and mortician stopped close to the taller, leaner man so that he could whisper, "The injured gunman? Do you want him to recover, mister?"

Edge looked down into the upturned face of the man and his voice was as hard as the look in his ice-blue eyes when he replied, "You seen me digging any holes around here, feller?"

Pollock gulped and took a backward step from the half-breed. "All right, I'll mind my own business. I just thought—"

"They say it's what counts," Edge cut in. "I figure for most of the time for nothing."

Pollock turned and hurried along the street. As Wanda

Merritt appeared at the doorway of the Town House, eyeing the half-breed and the departing Pollock with deep contempt. "God, how I despise men like you!" she rasped. "Getting rich from other people's suffering!"

As Edge walked toward the angrily scowling woman, he replied, "You feel so bad about it on account of your pa's paying, lady?"

Her rage expanded, "I'll have you know my father's a self-made man—"

"Big of him to accept the responsibility," Steele drawled grimly as he eased by her to emerge from the hotel.

The Virginian fell in beside the half-breed and matched his slow progress along the Town House stoop.

"He never made a red cent out of killing people!" the woman shouted in their wake, her voice almost a scream. "Not like you two! Death! Death! Death! That's your business."

Edge vented a low sigh and murmured, "It's a living."

ELEVEN

"THAT wasn't just on accout of you shooting a feller's finger off, uh Reb?" the half-breed said as they reached the law office and Steele used his key to unlock the door.

"She was around when he admitted he was at Masonville," the Virginian answered. "And I reckon he was relieved to do it. You've just seen and heard how his daughter feels about it."

They went inside the stale-smelling office, leaving the door open to admit the hotter but slightly fresher air from the street. And sat behind the desks they had respectively chosen as their own.

Edge took out the makings and rolled a cigarette. While Steele spent a few moments gazing out of the doorway, not really seeing the scene on the sun-bright street as people began to move about again after the shooting. Instead, reviewed fragmented images of what he had recently experienced in Clinton Merritt's hotel room.

"She already knew?" Edge asked after striking a match on the desk top and lighting the cigarette.

Steele nodded absently then allowed this and other questions from the half-breed to occupy the forefront of his mind, while in answering them he relived vivid events from the past. Much, he guessed, as the man in the wheelchair had after his daughter opened the door to allow the Virginian inside.

"The name Masonville mean anything to you, Mr. Merritt?" Steele had asked across the front of the women's slender body as, after scowling at the caller, she turned to look toward her father.

She had gasped, then swung back to glare angrily at Steele, her cheeks coloring to match the hue of her hair.

124

Made to slam the door in the Virginian's face. An impassive face that transmitted nothing of what he intended. So that she was taken totally by surprise when he thrust out a splayed hand. And took a step forward. But it was not the closing door he reached for. Instead, the gloved palm and fingers made contact with her flat belly. Not as a blow. For a split second his hand rested against the silken fabric of her white dress. Then, with a short but powerful thrust he sent her staggering backwards into the room. With enough force to wrench her hand free of the doorknob and cause her to lean forward from the waist as she backed involuntarily away from him.

He took a further step, to cross the threshold, and pushed the door closed, leaned his back against it.

The woman's enforced retreat was halted painfully by the edge of a heavy table against her rump. She groaned, but kept the sound low.

Her father, who was eating a salad lunch off a tray resting across the arms of his wheelchair, wiped a fragment of food off the corner of his mouth with a napkin and said:

"Is that any way to treat a lady, sir?"

His voice was steady and the only signs of his tautly controlled anger were the patches of insipid pink which colored his fleshy gray cheeks.

Steele glanced briefly at Wanda Merritt who was now standing erect, her rump still against the table with her hands hooked over its edge. Her feet were slightly apart and she was breathing deeply as she struggled to recover from the shock of the attack. Her Sunday best dress was low cut at the neckline and tight fitting to the waist, contouring those areas of her torso which it did not reveal. As was so often the case with a woman, her face was at its most attractive when she displayed anger.

"I can see she's a woman," the Virginian answered. "She has yet to prove she's a lady. What about Masonville?"

"You—" Wanda began to hiss through teeth clenched between drawn back lips.

"Start proving what I've always tried to make you, girl!" her father cut in, allowing his anger more freedom, but directing it at her. Then he moderated his tone to add, "Pour our guest a cup of coffee . . . please, my dear."

She snapped her head around to glare at her father, but the power of his green-eyed stare through the lenses of his spectacles forced her to contain what she planned to snarl at him. Instead, she muttered:

"I said at the start it was crazy to hire them."

Then she went to a sideboard on which there was a silver tray laid with a silver coffee set and two china cups and saucers. The fine style of this representative of the furnishings and decorations of the room.

It was a large parlor designed for gracious living. Wood-panelled walls hung with classical oil paintings in gilt frames. Heavily carved and luxuriously upholstered furniture of oak and polished leather. A crystal chandelier hung from the center of the white-painted ceiling. One other door apart from that which gave onto the landing—presumably giving access to a bedroom. No carpets on the floor, probably because it was easier for Merritt to move his wheelchair across the polished boarding.

"There is little glory and precious little honor in any war, Mr. Steele," the cripple said as Wanda poured coffee from the pot to a cup and he lost his appetite for the food on his tray. "Opposing armies always feel they have right on their side and consider they may go to any lengths to triumph."

Wanda set the cup and saucer down on the centrally placed round table—forcefully enough to rattle the china and slop the coffee. Then she went to the window and stood, arms akimbo, staring into the street through the lace curtains.

Steele remained where he was at the door, Recalling that he and Edge had agreed this very point after reading Ed Heller's papers.

"Did Masonville help to win the war for the Union?" he asked evenly.

Merritt rolled his chair forward to the table, set his tray down on it and reversed to his previous position beside the ornately styled fireplace. "It helped my men and I to come to our senses after what the Rebels did at Providence. That's Providence, Kansas. In the November of '64."

Steele went to the table, pulled out a chair from beneath

it and sat down. He tried the coffee which tasted as good as it smelled. "A revenge raid, is that it!"

Merritt nodded. "We were regulars in the infantry at the time of the Providence attack. Harry and Dave Pollock. Gilbert Reade. John Clements. Barney Gehlen and some others. All from the same little town on the Kansas-Missouri border. Managed to keep all together in the same outfit for most of the war. Lost a few here and there, but gradually got to come to terms with that. Guess you lost friends, didn't you?"

Steele sipped his coffee.

Merritt shrugged. "All right, son. I'm not trying to justify what we did by accusing anyone else of doing the same thing. Except the bastards who hit Providence!" His voice had risen and a scowl of hatred had started to take command of his features. But he fought for control of his emotions. And sighed when he succeeded. "It was after Sterling Price lost the battle of Mine Creek and we were chasing what was left of his troops all over the damn country. Anxious to have done with it and spend some time with our families in Providence. We spent some time with them. Mr. Steele. Burying most of them and trying to console them that were left."

Wanda turned from the window and seemed to have regained her composure. Until she saw that Steele was showing no reaction to what her father had said. When she compressed her lips and hardly moved them at all to say:

"My mother was one of the dead, mister. And my twin brothers who were seven years old. I never saw them killed with sabres. I was kept too busy in a back room of our grocery store. By three men who took it in turns to take me. Two of them holding an arm and a leg while the third had his way. I was fifteen!"

"There was nothing we did at Masonville that wasn't done first at Providence," Clinton Merritt went on, undisturbed by the Virginian's calm acceptance of what he was listening to. "After we'd buried our dead, we went back to the war, son. But we didn't get to do any fighting. Confederacy was all but beat on the western front and we was left biding our time until they surrendered in the east and the south.

"Maybe if we'd got us into some battles—killed some Rebs in the heat of the moment—we'd have been able to get what happened at Providence out of our systems. But we didn't. We just sat around and felt the hate building up in our bellies. Until we couldn't take it no longer. And we took off on our own. Deserted. With me in command because I had sergeant's chevrons. Twenty-five of us. Called ourselves the Kansas Raiders and went looking for Reb soldiers."

Wanda had gone to the sideboard, poured a second cup of coffee and now she gave it to her father. He took it, but made no attempt to drink it as his daughter returned to the curtained window and her disinterested survey of the street.

"Trouble was, we didn't find any. Rode across Missouri, Arkansas and into Mississippi spending most of our time ducking Union regulars. Did a lot of drinking to keep our feelings from gnawing our insides out. But there were too many dry days before we rode into Masonville." He squeezed his eyes tight shut and swallowed hard. "Well, like I already said, what happened there was no worse than what happened at Providence, Kansas. Women, children and men too old or not fit enough to fight. Guess you know about that, uh?"

Steele nodded and replaced his empty coffee cup on the saucer. "Ed Heller had it all written down. His mother, his brother and his brother's daughter were among those you killed."

Merritt nodded now, the gesture slower and his eyes behind the spectacle lenses wise. "Always figured Ed had the goods on me, son. And that his boy was working here at the hotel to try to get something to make what his Pa knew stick. But we never knew the names of the people in Masonville. And after it was done, we all changed ours. Those that survived that is. Lost three-quarters of our number in a crossfire between Union and Rebel forces up in Georgia a month after Masonville. I was lucky, or unlucky, I sometimes think. Took a bullet in the base of my spine that lost me the use of my legs. But the boys that were left, they got me out of there. And they fixed up for Wanda to join us. Then we came out west and settled down here. Started

128

this town from nothing. Made a good job of it until the hard boys moved in. Did a good job, too, on forgetting about Providence and Masonville for most of the time. Until Chris Kelly found out about what happened. From Ed Heller, maybe? I don't know. What I do know is that Kelly won't figure the war's over until me and the others pay for the Masonville Massacre."

He drank his coffee now. It was tepid from being in the cup so long and he finished it at a single swallow, grimacing.

"Anything else you want to know, son? Before your ride out of Southfields?"

"Pa, there's going to be trouble out on the street," Wanda Merritt said dully.

"Hey, Henry!" one of the four new arrivals in town shouted. "Everythin' okay?"

Steele rose from the table and crossed slowly to the window. The woman shifted out of his way, eyeing him with contempt.

"Do you know who killed Ed Heller?"

Merrit shrugged. "Maybe Harry Pollock or his boy. Clements. Barney Gehlen. Not Gil Reade. He's had no use for the gun since he took to newspaper work. And certainly not me." He slapped the arms of his wheelchair. "I'm in no position to commit murder in the dead of night and duck out of sight. We're all that's left of the original bunch that survived the war and came out here to build Southfields. Couple of others died from natural causes in the early days."

Steele had his back to the room, looking out of the window at Lee, McCloud and Carter as they advanced on the stage depot from the Cantina Plata.

"Just give the word!" Lee yelled.

And the Virginian banged open the window, thudded the stock of the Colt Hartford to his shoulder and triggered a shot. Then another to take the tip off Lee's pointing finger, as Wanda Merritt screamed. A third to force the trio of men to halt yet again.

The woman implored him to cease the shooting. Her father snarled at her to be quiet. Edge turned down the offer to further help and Steele shouldered the rifle and closed the window. The dust of the stage's leaving had settled by then.

"What's Kelly's interest?" the Virginian asked calmly, as if the shooting had not interrupted the conversation. And, with the rifle still sloped to his shoulder, he swung out the loading gate and turned the cylinder to drop the spent shellcases from the chambers to the polished floor.

"He's from Texas and he fought for the Confederacy," Clinton Merritt replied as Steele pushed fresh rounds into his rifle. "But it goes deeper than that, I think. When we came out west at the end of the war, we needed money to start a town. I planned a robbery on the bank in Big Springs north of San Angelo, Texas. The men went in shooting and the banker and his wife who worked for him were killed. Place was called Kelly's Bank and Loan Company."

Down on the street, Chico Lopez yelled, *"Hombre!"*

A pistol shot cracked.

Other voices were raised.

"Kelly's a common enough name," Clinton Merritt said evenly as his daughter tried to stop him trembling— whether from a result of the shooting or hearing again of long ago events it was difficult to know. "But . . ."

He broke off and shrugged as Steele pulled open the door. "Thanks for the coffee and the story, feller."

"A true story, son," the cripple replied, and maybe it was his spectacle lenses rather than moisture at the corners of his eyes which glistened in the sunlight. "And it's I should thank you for listening. When a man's life is built on deceit and evil, it can ease his mind some to admit it."

"Stop it, Pa!" Wanda snarled. "You don't have to make excuses to the likes of him! He ain't nothing but a dirty little hired killer!"

"I ask you to overlook the girl's outburst, Mr. Steele," Merritt said to the Virginian after directing a withering look at his daughter. "I'm afraid she has not been herself since her expectations of Kelly proved groundless."

There was no doubt about the tears in the woman's eyes. For they spilled over the lids and ran down her cheeks. Tears of anger, humiliation and regret.

"It's a crying shame, feller," Steele muttered as he went

across the threshold and glanced back at the Merritts. "Seems like a lot of things in your life have been ill-conceived."

When he had finished replying to Edge's questions in the quiet, sunlight and tobacco-smoke-filled law office, the Virginian recalled another man in a wheelchair who lived in luxury in another hotel room far away from Southfields. A cripple named Justin Ford in Chicago. A city where Steele had made enough money from poker to make working for Clinton Merritt—or anybody else—totally unnecessary for some time to come.

Then, almost as if he had gained an insight into Steele's line of thinking, the half-breed said:

"Merritt figures you're going to quit, Reb?"

"Reckon so, Yank. But only because I was on the wrong side in the war. Don't think he has a much higher opinion of me than his daughter does."

"Are you?" Edge crushed out his cigarette on the desk top and brushed the resulting mess to the floor.

Steele pursed his lips. "I still owe you for the horse and we may never meet up again."

"No sweat, feller."

"For you."

"I can square it any time you like."

Steele shot a sidelong glance toward Edge, was certain it was seen, but drew no further explanation from the half-breed. And resisted the impulse to ask for one.

"What was the trouble about down at the stage depot?"

"Sutton slipped something to a preacher man. It didn't look like an offering and I wanted to know what it was."

"What was it?"

"A note. The preacher's with Kelly. Be able to tell the Texan we've got every gun in town locked in the jail. And he's three men short."

"Out-of-date information now."

Edge nodded. "Four men short."

"Sutton?"

"He'll be a little hard of hearing and if he ever needs to wear glasses he'll have a problem. No. Lee."

An easy silence fell over the law office, broken from time to time by some normal Sunday sound from the town outside. As both men thought their own thoughts—without revealing by the merest flicker of an expression what it was that concerned their minds.

"Reckon I'll stay for a while, Yank," the Virginian said eventually.

"Figured you would, Reb."

"Not just because I owe you a horse."

"That never was enough. You used to be rich. Means you can never have too much money."

Steele felt the stirring of anger at the pit of his stomach. But he kept the emotion cold. "There are some things I won't do for a buck, feller."

Edge heard the underlying tone in the other man's voice and gave a slight nod without looking at Steele. "Like bounty hunting—anymore."

The smaller man pursed his lips and sighed, the threat of hot temper subsiding. For he realized the half-breed was not setting out to needle him. Nor was he merely talking to fill in time. For this tall, lean, narrow eyed man was not the kind to do anything just for the sake of convention.

"I was one once, Yank. Just for a while. After almost a month of hard drinking didn't touch the memory I had of killing my best friend." He looked at Edge now. "And I didn't care much whether I brought them in dead or alive. Maybe I thought that working for the law would help more than drinking had. It didn't. But while I was doing it, I was good at the job. Same as I'll be good at this one. Answer your question, feller?"

Edge ran the back of a hand over his jaw and the action caused a rasping sound from the bristle which had sprouted since the early morning shave. "Need to be sure about you, Reb. I'm wearing this tin star for the money Merritt's paying. And when the shit starts to fly I'll be shooting to earn the money and to stay alive to spend it. Need to be sure my help ain't got part of its mind concerned with the rights and wrongs of what's being fought for."

"You want to be more specific, Yank?" the Virginian asked.

Edge rose from his desk and ambled across to the open doorway. The injured Henry Sutton and the corpse of Lee had been removed from in front of the stage depot, but the Sunday-afternoon strollers seemed to be steering clear of the area. Maybe because there was still a bloodstain on the sidewalk. Or perhaps simply because of knowing that a man was shot dead there less than an hour ago. With a few exceptions, the citizens of Southfields did not wish to be associated with death. Which was not unusual. But, in the current circumstances, was inconvenient.

"Figure you're staying in town to square things, one way or another, with Clark Ludlum. On account of he'll think you had something to do with killing his father."

"I'll ride easier knowing somebody isn't gunning for me for something I didn't do." Steele admitted.

"And after that business is done? It'll be just another part of the war, Reb. A few years later. No uniforms, but everyone'll know which side they're fighting for."

"War was over at Appomattox, Yank," Steele said flatly. "So happened I had a personal battle to fight after that. It didn't matter then that the men I killed were Southern sympathizers."

"You said it."

"What?"

"That was personal."

"What do you want, Yank?" the Virginian asked with a note of irritated impatience in his voice. "An affidavit written in my blood that I won't get an attack of conscience when Kelly and his men hit town?"

Edge turned just his head to look into the law office and show that his lips were drawn back from his teeth in a smile—an expression that was made ice cold by the fact that it did not extend to his slitted blue eyes.

"If you do, feller; there'll be blood enough to write your epitaph in letters six foot high."

Steele displayed his own brand of frosty smile—as hard and menacing as that of the half-breed. "Reckon it won't be anything on the lines of 'Deepest Sympathy,' Yank?"

Edge injected a trace of good humor into his smile as he replied, "Figure something like 'He Died of a Bleeding Heart,' Reb. And I'll have Harry Pollock mark your grave with a double-cross."

Having said this, the half-breed stepped out of the doorway onto the sidewalk. Then called back as he crossed in front of the window, "Figure we know where we stand now, feller. You want out, you tell me in good time."

Steele started to develop his expression from the hard-eyed smile into a scowl. But then reversed the process to show a grin of satisfaction as the footfalls of Edge administed along the boarding. For he reflected, it was better to have trust in and understanding of a man on whom your life might depend than to base such a partnership on mere mutual need. And, out of the probing questions and veiled threats of their conversation had resulted trust and understanding between them.

Each had already proved his abilities to the other.

More footfalls sounded outside and Steele saw Charlie Deed amble across the window and then turn into the law office. The man was freshly washed up and shaved, alert-eyed following his rest period:

"You wanna go get yourself some sleep?" Deed asked, using a finger to wipe come crumbs of food off his moustache. "Some grub and maybe a hot bath. Makes a man feel good."

"And good men are hard to find," Steele replied pensively as he stood up from the desk, suddenly aware of how weary he was. And dirty with the sweat and dust which had oozed from and clung to his flesh since the luxury of yesterday's bath.

"One here you can depend on, Mr. Steele," Deed said as he dropped into the chair recently vacated by Edge. And showed his ugly teeth in a cunning grin as he added, "So long as the price is right, you understand?"

As he stepped outside and started along the sidewalk toward the Town House, the Virginian's sense of well-being improved still further, his thoughts running along a line suggested by Deed's parting comment.

It was said that every man had his price, and for a man who lived by the gun, cash money was the only form of payment that was acceptable. It was a trade made necessary by the times in which men lived, but it was not an honorable one. Few men who practiced it—in Steele's experience—ever paused to consider it in such terms. Those who did—like Edge and himself—could maintain their self-respect only by holding on to the bottom rung of honor. By remaining loyal to the man who made the first acceptable offer for their skills—no matter who made a later, higher bid.

Steele had always assumed the half-breed to be this kind. And he now thought Edge had been convinced of his integrity in this respect. In the light of the circumstances under which they met, it had been foolish to resent the man's need to be sure. Better to acknowledge a sound basis for his doubt and be content it was removed.

Hooves clopped along the alley between the hotel and the livery and the half-breed halted Sven Karlsen's gray gelding in the gap between the sidewalk and the Town House stoop.

"Be back in a while, Reb," Edge said. "We know the country to the south well enough. Going to take a look around elsewhere."

Steele nodded. "You'll let me know anything I need to know, Yank?"

Edge raked his hooded eyes along the length of Main Street and the Virginian made a similar survey. There were more people out strolling now. Most of them in family groups, interspersed with a few young couples, enjoying the less harsh sunshine of late afternoon closing with evening. This enjoyment marred by the sight of two gunmen with tin stars watching them.

"Guess you don't need to be told not to trust anyone in this town, feller?" the half-breed muttered.

"Way I feel now I was born a hundred years ago," Steele answered. "Sure wasn't yesterday."

"I'll try to remember that," Edge growled as he heeled his horse out of the alley and tugged on the reins to head west along the street.

"That's one murdering sonofabitch on his way," Wanda Merritt rasped as Steele turned in through the hotel entrance. "You going to pack up and leave now?"

She was seated in one of the lobby's comfortable armchairs, gazing out at the dust raised by the hooves of the half-breed's mount.

"Leroy!" Steele called, and waited for the Negro to

show behind the desk to ask, "Be grateful if you would run me a tub."

"Right away, sir," Leory responded and retreated into the back again.

"Figured it was wishful thinking on my part," the woman said with a sigh as Steele started up the stairway. "Both of you are staying?"

"Yes, Miss Merritt."

She rose from the chair and turned to look up at him as he reached the head of the stairs. An expression of helpless pleading on her almost pretty face. "Please, Mr. Steele," she implored. "Take what Pa paid you and leave. You and Edge and Deed. If you don't, you'll only end up destroying what he's paying you to protect."

"That's his risk."

"And everyone else's in this town!" she came back, her temper rising again. "But they don't have any say in the matter. Have you bothered to ask them how they feel about their town being turned into a battlefield?"

"No, Miss Merritt," he answered and moved out of her sight along the hallway, heard her vent a throaty sound of exasperation and then her footfalls crossing the lobby and coming up the stairs.

He went past the door to his room and into the bathroom at the end. He left the door open for when Leroy came up with the pails of hot water. But it was the woman who appeared on the threshold first, making an obvious effort to control her emotions.

"But you've seen them," she said tautly. "You've seen the kind of people who live here. Simple, hard-working people most of them. In a town Chris Kelly made safe for them to live in.

"All right, Chris and some other men feel that after what they did, Pa and the Pollocks and Mr. Gehlen and Mr. Clements don't deserve to have what they do. But I know Chris. He'll see reason. I know I can make him see reason. But there won't be any time for that if you and the rest start shooting the moment he returns to Southfields."

Steele began to undress slowly while the woman put her case—put it so strongly and with such fervor that she did not realize what was happening in front of her until, stripped to the waist, the Virginian began to unbutton his pants. When she gasped and shrieked:

"What are you doing?"

"Getting ready to take a bath," he answered evenly.

The anger she had contained down in the lobby suddenly surfaced to neutralize her shock. "You haven't been listening to a single word I've been saying!"

"Been listening," he said.

"But I'm not getting through to you!" she accused.

He pushed his pants down over his hips and drawled, "Looks like you haven't made much of an impression on me, Miss Merritt."

Her green eyes were drawn open to their full extent as she stared for a stretched second at his nakedness. Then she croaked, "Oh, my God!" whirled around and lunged along the landing. Not seeing the Negro with a pail of water in each hand who had to press himself to the wall to avoid being bowled over by her.

"Golly, Mr. Steele sir," Leroy muttered as he entered the bathroom. "I don't think I ever saw Miss Wanda move so mighty fast. Like a bat out of hell."

The Virginian lowered himself into the empty tub and gestured for the black man to tip the steaming water over him. Then showed his boyish grin as he said, "Or maybe as quick as a flash?"

TWELVE

STEELE had Leroy make him a sandwich and he ate this in his room after bathing and shaving. Then he slept for the remainder of the afternoon and throughout the evening, not waking until full night enveloped Southfields. Because the town was so quiet, he thought the night was well advanced toward the morning until he went down into the Town House lobby and saw from the clock above the unattended reception desk that it was not yet ten.

The street was illuminated by a high, bright moon, this supplemented only by lamplight from the hotel lobby, the law office and the Cantina Plata windows.

The only sounds to be heard came from in back of the newspaper office two doors down from the Town House. Until the rocker on the hotel stoop creaked and Shep Mallison said:

"Ain't exactly what can be called rip-roarin' is it, mister?"

The old-timer spoke without a slur in his voice. Just misery.

"All good things have to come to an end, feller," the Virginian replied as he turned out of the Town House doorway.

"Weekends sure do. Too damn quick. On account of workin' folk havin' to be early Mondays."

"Except for Gilbert Reade, seems like."

"Special edition of the *Reporter*, mister. Paper don't normally come out until Wednesdays. But seems like Mr. Reade can't bear to wait that long to tell folks what he thinks about you and them other fellers that got the deputy badges on your shirts."

"So long as he spells our names right," Steele said as he continued on past the liquor-reeking Mallison.

"Guess it ain't no use me asking you for the price of a drink, mister?" the old-timer called after him. "Before Chico closes up?"

"If it's more than fifteen cents it's too much," the Virginian answered.

"Mean bastard!" Mallison rasped, and spat to score a hit on the hotel hitching rail. Then stood up to go to the front of the sidewalk and peer eastwards along the street and out onto the trail.

Where Steele was already looking, toward a lone rider who was approaching Southfields at an easy pace.

"He a stranger, mister?" the old-timer asked, abruptly ingratiating. "My eyes ain't what they used to be."

"Looks like it's going to be a dry night, feller," Steele answered. "Reckon Edge is as sparing with money as he is with words."

"You'll both die rich and you can't take it with you," Mallison growled as he sank again into the rocker and stared malevolently across the street, in time to see the lights of the Cantina Plata go out.

"Even if we could," Steele muttered to himself as he stepped down onto the street, "I reckon where we're going it would melt."

He waited at the mouth of the alley for the half-breed to rein the gelding to a halt and swing down from the saddle.

"All quiet, Reb?"

"As the friggin' grave," Shep Mallison growled from the moon shadowed stoop.

"Out in the hills, Yank?" Steele asked.

"There's no army there now, but there could be if Kelly wanted to play it that way. Have to cross fenced range to the west and north. Thick pine forest beyond the ridges to the east. If they came that way, you can see how close they could get before we saw them."

"On every side," the Virginian acknowledged with a bleak-eyed glance along each length of Main Street toward the high ground into which the trails led.

To the south and north the rocky ridges were higher.

"Best you boys beat it," the old timer advised. "Only

help you're gonna get is from a bunch of has-beens and never-wases near as ancient and creaky as me. 'Ceptin' for Dave Pollock and as a gunslinger he's a fine liveryman. Kelly'll make mincemeat outta you. Then just for the hell of it he'll maybe cook the rawness of you in the ashes of this town."

"That what he told you he'd do, feller?" Edge asked.

"Sure enough did," Mallison came back quickly, warming to his subject, eager to hold the attention that was not normally paid to him. "Didn't mention you boys, of course. On account of he didn't know about you. But he said that anybody livin' in this town come Saturday mornin' wouldn't still be alive by nightfall. But it'll be kinda hard to know when night comes on account of it bein' so light from the fires burnin' in Southfields. That's what he told me, boys. Before him and the kid and then two ranch hands rode outta town."

Mallison grinned his enjoyment of having an audience. And his words were accompanied by a rhythmic creaking as he rocked the chair back and forth with increasing speed. This noise and the sound of his own voice masked to his ears the progress of a wagon and two-horse team approaching town from the west. And, as Edge and Steele watched the rig, the old-timer gazed with a bright, glassy stare across the intersection—seeing against the backdrop of Via de Bello a vision of the future or an image of the past.

"Them boys'll come back here. Them plus a lot more good old boys from Texas. And there ain't nothin' nor nobody who'll stop them. Be like it was at the Alamo, but this time it'll be the boys from the Lone Star State doin' the hittin'. And any damn fools who stay here tryin' to fight them off. And when they're through the rich bastards'll be all wiped out. And the decent folk can rebuild on their own land plots."

Mallison continued to stare and to rock and to talk. So enrapt in what he was saying that he was unaware when his audience shrank to a weary, doleful-eyed gelding. After Edge and Steele, satisfied the old-timer could give them no further hard information, started along the street to close with the slow-moving covered wagon.

It was an ancient rig, with sign writing on the patched and stained sides of the canvas cover. Drawn by two trail-weary grays. Driven by a man with a woman seated beside him. Both of them tall and thin and in their early thirties. He dressed in a frock coat and high hat. She in a high-necked ankle-length dress. All their clothing black, which emphasized the unhealthy looking paleness of their faces.

The man reined his team to a halt outside the bank, so that the front of the wagon was level with where the lawmen of contrasting statures stood on the street.

"Evening to you, gentlemen," he greeted, thrusting the reins into the hands of the woman and raising his hat.

He had a booming voice, which cut across the ecstatic chatter of Shep Mallison—and caused the old-timer to be jerked back into reality. Surprising him so much that he snapped his head around to search for the source of the unexpected interruption—and lost co-ordination. To the extent that a forward tilt of the chair sent him sprawling across the shadowed sidewalk and then on to the moonlit street.

"Sonofabitch!" he rasped through toothless gums clenched in a grimace of pain.

"What's that?" the woman on the wagon asked nervously.

Steele glanced at Mallison and then back at the woman, touched the brim of his hat as he replied, "Feller just went off his rocker, ma'am. But he's harmless."

While he read the sign on the wagon canvas, Edge added, "Most of the time legless."

The red and blue lettering was faded, but still legible:

PHINEAS FARROW
PATENT MEDICINES, OINTMENTS AND SALVES
FOR ALL THAT AILS YOU
FAMOUS FROM COAST TO COAST
MONEY BACK GUARANTEE.

"You're Farrow?" the half-breed said.

"That I am, sir. And this here is Mrs. Farrow. Come to your fair city to do some business. And anxious to abide by your laws. Here, sir."

141

He reached in through the gap in the front canvas and drew out a Winchester rifle—holding it around the barrel to push the stock toward Edge.

"Read the notice. I trust there is no ordinance against honest men carrying on honest business?"

Shep Mallison had got painfully to his feet, dusted off his ragged clothing and wove along the street to squint up at the sign-writing on the wagon.

This as the woman asked about accommodation in town and Steele suggested the Town House. While Edge, the rifle canted to his shoulder, went to the rear of the wagon and looked over the tailgate—watched with perturbed curiosity by Farrow.

"Hey, mister, you ain't givin' out no free samples of the snake bite cure, are you?" the old-timer wanted to know.

"You've been bitten by a snake?" the patent-medicine salesman countered absently, still concerned by the half-breed's interest in the contents of his wagon.

"No, I aint. But it's my experience that the snake-bite cure can be fine for keepin' out the night chills. When the places that sells liquor ain't open. Ain't got any free samples, have you?"

"No. No, I haven't!" Farrows's demeanor was suddenly lacking its previous amicability. But he hurriedly repaired the damage when Edge emerged from behind the wagon, as impassive as before. "I'm sorry, sir. What you doubtless were given for snake bite was a weak alcohol solution with a coloring agent. The concoction of an unqualified charlatan posing as a pharmacist. I make up my medicants only from recognized—"

"All right, all right, mister!" Mallison muttered as he turned away from the wagon. "I just gotta hope you got somethin' to take care of the pneumonia I could get from sleepin' with nothin' inside to warm my belly."

As the old man headed across the street toward the scant comfort of the Cantina Plata's doorway, Edge went to his horse and led it down the alley to the side door of the livery.

"Strong drink is an instrument of the devil," Mrs. Farrow announced as she climbed down from the wagon after watching Mallison settled himself for the night. "I'll see about a room, dear, while you attend to the horses."

"You'll give an eye to my wagon if I leave it here?" her husband asked Steele.

"Sure thing," the Virginian answered, and headed along the street as Farrow climbed down from the seat and began to take the team out of the traces.

"Give it a real close look, Reb," Edge advised softly from the darkness of the alley. "Make sure it's not bad medicine they've brought to town."

Steele acknowledged that he had heard the words with an almost imperceptible movement of his head. Then continued on down to the law office, where Charlie Deed was asleep in the chair behind the desk, hat tipped forward over his face, snoring softly, chest rising and falling evenly under his folded arms.

The Virginian frowned in at the sleeping man then continued on along Main Street, to turn left between the seed merchants and the boarding house. Preferring to make a patrol of the town's streets rather than kill time in the office while the Farrows bedded down.

He did not resent the half-breed's instruction couched in the terms and spoken in the tone of a suggestion. For Edge had filled the afternoon and evening with useful work by circuit-riding the town. But just maybe the irritation he felt towards Charlie Deed for sleeping on the job had been triggered by the half-breed's assumption that he would not check out the wagon of his own accord.

Then he pursed his lips and shook his head. The tall, taciturn man had obviously seen nothing in the rear of the wagon—at a casual glance—to arouse his suspicion. And perhaps he had not been aware of the way Farrow had allowed his composure to slip while his stock in trade was being examined.

Steele found his thoughts turning to another matter after he passed the dark, empty premises of the dead Heller and his son. On the surface, Clinton Merritt or somebody working for him, was the obvious prime suspect as Ed Heller's killer, with the motive of stopping the sick shoemaker from telling what he knew of the Masonville Massacre. Also in line were the other surviving members of the Kansas Raiders. Less likely, because they seemed less inclined to stand against the threatened revenge attack by Chris Kelly.

Because they did not have so much to lose? What posed another question—why didn't they? The robbery at the Big Springs' bank had been a joint effort by what was left of the Union deserters at the end of the war. And they had founded Southfields together. Yet Shep Mallison had said—and his story had not been refuted—that Clinton Merritt owned the town and collected rent on every piece of real estate in it. How had he done that?"

The Virginian shook his head again as he strolled across the path which lead up to the Baptist Chapel, curving through a turfed area featured with neatly cut and expertly lettered headstones. Beyond which, as he continued at the same easy pace around the back lots of some crudely built frame houses, was a wire-fenced meadow of scrub grass, dotted with weathered and leaning wooden crosses. With, on one side, a row of fresh graves. And a newly dug hole awaiting the pine-coffined corpse of the gunman named Lee.

"Nice evenin', lawman."

"End of all your days."

"Save the undertaker a trip out here."

They rose in unison from out of a patch of the tallest yellow grass beyond the recently dug grave. Forty feet from where the Virginian came to a tense halt, head snapping around to look at the three men aiming Winchesters at him.

Henry Sutton was the first to speak. The easiest to see in the brightly moonlit night because of the clean white bandage that was wound around his head at an angle to cover the dressing on the wound where his left ear had been sliced off.

Then McCloud.

Finally Clyde Carter.

Each man pumping the action of his rifle as he made the comment.

"Not from the jailhouse, I reckon," Steele said.

"Cool little runt, ain't he?" Carter snarled, as if he was disappointed.

144

"Not from the jailhouse," McCloud confirmed.

"We got ways and means, lawman," Sutton supplied. "Come on in, unless you're scared of graveyards at night."

"You got reason to be friggin' scared!" Carter rasped.

There was a gap in the wire fencing, the iron gate sagging open on one hinge, twisted and rusted. Steele turned and went through the opening, treading on grass flattened by the recent frequent passages of Harry Pollock's hearse. Just for a fraction of a second, when Sutton had spoken the first word, the Virginian had revealed the tension which gripped him. Since then, to the obvious irritation of Clyde Carter, he had seemed to be as nonchalant as before. Giving no clue to the trio of riflemen that beneath his surface attitude his body and limbs were poised for smooth action—the muscles coiled to power whatever move his coolly working brain decided offered him the best chance of survival.

"Keep comin', lawman," Sutton urged. "Over here by the hole that's been dug for poor old Lee. So as our dear departed buddy will have company into the hereafter."

Steele was afraid. Since those opening days of the war his life had been on the line so many times and always he was afraid. But he had long ago learned to control the emotion—and to use it. Channel it into caution before it could expand to panic.

He came to a halt on the far side of the hole from where the three men stood. And they moved forward, out of the tall grass and onto that which had been trampled by the gravediggers—stopped short of the elongated mound of displaced earth.

Steele was close enough to see the depth of Carter's hatred for him, the lines of pain inscribed deeply into Sutton's skin and the relish with which McCloud viewed the scene.

"Gonna kill you, lawman," Sutton announced. "Like for you to drop the rifle and get down in the hole. Then plan to kick the dirt down over you. Make for a nice quiet funeral, if you don't start screamin'."

"Or we can blast you where you stand, punk," Carter threatened venomously. "Noisy. Bring some people runnin'."

145

"And only your buddies with badges will have guns," McCloud added. "We'll be well hid again by then."

"And quiet as mice, " Carter put in.

"Until we start blastin'," Sutton elaborated. "Your choice, lawman."

There had never been a chance of survival by using the Colt Hartford. Maybe he could have put down one or even two of them. But it would have cost him his life.

"Heads you win, tails I lose," he drawled, allowing the rifle to drop to the trampled grass.

Sutton grinned through his pain. "Doin' it this way, you could save a few lives, lawman. Edge and Deed are goin' to die anyway. But if other people leave the way Chris Kelly told them, they'll live beyond next Saturday. Get in the hole!"

He snarled the order. As he, then the others, canted the Winchesters up to their shoulders.

"Dirt into dirt!" Carter growled. "Friggin' lawmen!"

"Don't let Chris hear you talkin' like that!" Sutton snapped, not taking his eyes off the Virginian as his order was complied with.

First Steele went down onto his haunches, then pushed his legs over the edge of the grave, eased forward and dropped into the earth. It was arid soil and dust rose up around him, to cling to the sweat of fear on his face. The dust combined with the darkness of moon shadow to conceal his action of drawing the knife from his boot sheath.

The grave was some five feet deep, six long and four wide. As he stood in it, with just his head above ground level, Steele had to fight the urge to panic. Something which had not been necessary in very many years. His gloved hand fisted around the knife was shaking and he had an almost irresistible urge to make his move too soon. To strike out from terror with the certainty of killing one of the three. But he beat it. Just as he had earlier kept from swinging the Colt Hartford toward them on the chance of killing two.

Three was the number he wanted.

"Down, lawman. On your back. Pray if it'll help."

"It friggin' won't," Carter snarled.

Steele half-turned and lowered himself until he was completely below ground-level. In a crouch, his right hand around the knife easing backwards, his left going to his throat to check that the scarf with the weighted corners was unfastened.

He squeezed his eyes tightly closed for just a moment, then opened them, tilting his head back. Grinned with the relief of fast-draining tension. For there had always been a chance that Sutton was lying—had tricked his victim into the grave so that he could indulge some twisted desire to pour bullets down upon the trapped and helpless Virginian.

But the three men, as they stood tall upon the mound of dry earth, showing brutal grins of anticipation, still held the Winchesters canted to their shoulders.

"Goodbye, good guy," Sutton hissed between his clenched teeth.

And used the side of a booted foot to scrape the first pound or so of dusty soil back into the grave.

Then started to die.

The knife came free of Steele's gloved fist at the end of an underarm throw, unseen until it spun out of the falling dirt and its blade glinted in the moonlight. A split second later was buried to the hilt in Henry Sutton's flesh. It went in under his chin, into his mouth and then pierced his palate, skewering his tongue on the way. As he staggered backwards and fell to the ground, his feet losing their hold on the treacherous surface of the loose soil, the scream that burst from his throat was swamped by the warm, salt blood that filled his mouth. He hurled away the rifle to use both hands in a vain attempt to wrench the knife out of his flesh.

Even before the fatally injured Sutton began to reel off the mound of earth, Steele's right hand had grasped one weighted corner of the scarf. Then he powered to his feet and punched his hand forward and upward. Sending the opposite corner curving toward the right ankle of Clyde Carter.

For a stretched second, neither Carter nor McCloud were aware that the Virginian was attacking them. For they were half-turned toward Sutton, staring in amazement at the man's antics—for which there seemed no reason. Then, as Sutton threw down his rifle and reached for his

147

throat, they saw the knife. And snapped their attention back to the grave. Began to swing the rifles down from their shoulders.

Too late.

The scarf had taken a turn-and-a-half around Carter's ankle, was fastened securely enough for Steele's purpose.

He jerked on it.

To pull Carter's leg out from under him. The man gave a strangled cry of alarm as he was forced off balance. Tried to maintain it on one leg. Failed. Yelled, "McCloud!" and dropped his rifle to reach for the support of his partner.

"Sonofabitch!" McCloud gasped. Then lunged backwards, away from Carter's clawed hands.

Carter screamed in naked terror as he tumbled into the ground, amid a shower of dirt which shifted from under his feet. He fell sideways, arms flailing and hands still clawed to grasp at something—anything—to keep him out of the hole. There was nothing. And in his screaming panic he was defenseless against Steele's next move. Which was a double-fisted punch, started low down between his knees bent in a crouch. He whiplashed erect and swung his arms, the blow given greater impact by the momentum of Carter's fall.

The shrill sound of the man's terror was abruptly curtailed. The crack of fists against jawbone immediately followed by the sharper snap of Carter's neck breaking.

His body thudded to the bottom of the grave and Steele went down onto his haunches again, reached forward and wrenched the man's discarded rifle from under him.

The dust of frenetic action rose up out of the hole.

Steele held his breath and after a stretched second felt as if his lungs were going to burst. Every pore of his body was oozing sweat and he was gripped by the nightmarish sensation that he was melting. And that the rectangle of star-pricked sky he could see above the grave was coming down upon him.

"Clyde?" McCloud called. Soft and fearful.

The single word triggered Steele out the private world of dangerous fantasy that had enclosed him in the bottom of the grave he shared with a dead man. And transformed terror into anger. A cold anger that caused the beads of sweat on his flesh to feel like droplets of ice. Heightened his awareness of his surroundings. Made him as tensely ready to react as when he had entered the gap in the fence to advance on the grave.

"Clyde?" the last of the three called again. Louder.

A cold and ugly killer's grin took command of the Virginian's features. Although he had heard McCloud the first time, he had been too deeply drawn into the fantasy world created by a mind gone out of control to do more than fasten on the spoken name as a step back toward reality.

This time he was able to get a bearing on the man's position. Beyond the mound of earth, halfway between the long grass where he and the others had been hiding and the edge of the grave. To Steele's right. No more than ten feet away.

Steele half rose, stepped up onto the slumped form of Clyde Carter, and powered erect. The unfamiliar Winchester leveled from his shoulder.

He had to swing the rifle from lengthwise along the grave to aim it up and out to the side.

McCloud wasted a fatal part of a second in indecision. Maybe not sure whether it was Steele or Carter who appeared so suddenly.

Both men squeezed their triggers simultaneously. But McCloud's Winchester was still tracking toward a target and the bullet which blasted from the muzzle smashed into the remaining hinge on the gate.

The gate collapsed completely into the long, dry grass. As McCloud splayed his legs and thrust both arms high into the air, his right hand still fisted around the frame of the rifle. Blood fountained from his back, through the exit hole made by Steele's bullet. And spread an ugly dark stain across the front of his shirt, around the entry wound. It was a heart shot that killed him instantly, his straining attitude of stretched limbs caused by a shocked nervous system.

Steele pumped the action of the repeater while the sound of the double report still rang in his ears and McCloud teetered, dead on his feet. Then the dead man's limbs and body became limp and he crumpled to the ground—sprawling across the already inert form of Henry Sutton.

A breeze wafted across Potter's Field, rustling the long

grass, stirring the dust and taking away the acrid taint of burnt powder smoke. The impact of his body against the ground caused the last breath to rattle in the throat of the final man to die.

"Well there you go, McCloud," the Virginian drawled. Retrieved his scarf but left the Winchester down in the grave as he climbed up off the yielding flesh of Carter. Picked up his Colt Hartford and then crossed to wrench the knife out of the head of Sutton.

The town was as quiet now as it had been before the double blast of the rifle shots. And as dark under the moonlight. The citizens of Southfields having learned over two days to remain detached from the violence which strangers had brought here.

But, as he started away from the grave with its dead occupant and the heaped bodies of the two men beyond it, Steele sensed eyes watching him from some of the darkened windows of the houses overlooking Potter's Field. Then became aware that he was under surveillance from closer at hand. Pin-pointed the position of the watcher—in the deep moon shadow beside an outhouse on one of the back lots—before a match was struck on timber and a face was illuminated in the flame.

"Been there long, Yank?" he asked as Edge lighted his cigarette, blew out the match and flicked it away.

"Long enough."

"For what?"

"To have gotten you out of trouble if it was needed."

"Grateful to you," the Virginian said as he came through the gap in the fence. His gloved hand fisted around the frame of the rifle canted to his shoulder shook one more time. Not enough for the half-breed to see the movement.

"No sweat, feller," Edge answered, stepping out of the shadows.

He was carrying his own Winchester. Wore no gunbelt and his shirt was unbuttoned to the waist over his red longjohns. Had obviously been getting ready to bed down when his attention had been diverted to other things.

"Where did they get the rifles?" Steele asked.

"The Farrows' wagon."

"Was on my way back to check it over. Reckoned I'd let them get settled into the hotel first."

"I ain't criticizing, feller." This as they fell in beside each other on the pathway that curved toward an alley which reached to Main Street between the tailor's store and the stage line depot.

"And I'm not making excuses."

Edge nodded and Steele's new resentment of the half-breed's negative attitude toward trouble diminished. The tall, lean man had trusted him to handle Sutton, Carter and McCloud without help. And the Virginian felt bound to trust Edge's word that he would have intervened if it had been necessary.

"You figure Deed will try to make one, Reb?"

"Or Lopez, Yank. He wears a star, too. And he isn't exactly coming running is he?"

"Looks like it's just you and me, feller."

Steele showed his boyish grin. "Not much of a combination to make a town safe."

"At the latest count we closed the door on seven of Kelly's men."

"But we have to reckon on there being plenty more where they came from."

"Plus those that are already here."

The Virginian nodded. "Or why else would the Farrows smuggle guns into town?"

They emerged from the alley on to the street, stepped up on to the sidewalk and moved across the front of the stores toward the center of town, where the wagon was still parked outside the bank and the lights were still on in the lobby of the hotel. Beyond the intersection, the street was unlit—the lamp in the law office out.

"We know all the right questions, feller," Edge muttered. "But we seem to be running out of people who could give us the answers."

"Phineas Farrow seemed to like to hear the sound of his own voice," Steele drawled and, when the half-breed nodded, made to turn into the Town House doorway.

But Edge went on by and glanced back to say, "Figure we've done our share of keeping the peace today, Reb. About time Deed started to earn his keep."

151

Steele saw in the light from the hotel entrance that weariness had deepened the countless lines which harsh times had engraved into the lean face of Edge. Although the slits of his blue eyes under the hooded lids looked as alert as ever.

Then he faced front again, to continue on toward the law office and Steele trailed him, his own coal-black eyes raking over the façades of the buildings flanking Main Street.

Buildings, and others behind them, in which people remained as hidden and as quiet as those in the houses which backed onto Potter's Field. Content to let hired guns paid for with Merritt money protect them and their town? Or resentful of the presence in Southfields of such men? Did he—or Edge—care enough about the truth to ask questions of more people than Phineas Farrow?

They went into the law office and knew from the pungent odor of burnt kerosene that it had not been long since the lamp ran dry and guttered out after the flame destroyed the wick. In the darkness, Charlie Deed was still behind the desk in the same attitude as when Steele last saw him.

Back along the street, it had been impossible to tell whether the half-breed's eyes were expressing anger or if the hard glint in them was caused by reflected light from the Town House lobby. But here, on the threshold of the darkened office, the slivers of ice cold light had to be generated from within.

And, recalling the unaccustomed terror which had gripped him in the new grave as the three men looked down at him, Adam Steele had to struggle to contain his own rage. Found this more difficult to do with each soft snore which came from beneath Deed's tipped forward hat.

He moved into the office and tapped a gloved forefinger against the stock of the canted Colt Hartford. Edge nodded and stepped forward to join the Virginian in front of the desk where Deed slept. Neither man took pains to set his feet down lightly. The cocking of the Colt Hartford's hammer and the pumping of the Winchester's action were loud within the confines of the room.

Much louder were the reports of the rifles as they exploded shots in unison. To blast bullets into the floor-boards. From muzzles held no more than an inch to either side of Charlie Deed's ears.

The man came awake with a scream of pain—from the noise assaulting his eardrums and the powder burns searing his skin. Then tipped backwards in the chair and sprawled to the floor, pressing both hands to the sides of his head.

For long moments he remained like this. Then pulled himself up into a sitting posture with his back against the wall, moved his hands and seemed surprised not to see blood on them. Next showed his big and ugly teeth in a scowl as he raised his eyes to meet the cold gazes of Steele and Edge.

"You friggin' shot me, you bastards!" he accused.

"Fired our rifles is all, feller," Edge said evenly, and turned to go to where the lamp stood on the side table.

"Missed you," Steele added. "Like you were missed out at Potter's Field a while back."

"Find you sleeping on the job again, it'll be you that's fired," Edge said as he refilled the lamp from a can of kerosene beneath the table.

"Shit, how the hell am I supposed to know what you guys are up to?" Deed complained, as he got shakily to his feet, massaging his ears now. "You never tell me a friggin' thing about—"

"Couple called Farrow staying at the hotel," Edge cut in as he struck a match, touched it to the lamp wick and filled the law office with light. "Go get them and bring them here. That plain enough?"

He replaced the glass funnel on the lamp.

"No need, Yank," Steele said as footfalls sounded on the sidewalk outside. And all three men in the office looked toward the doorway as Phineas and Mrs. Farrow halted on the threshold—fear clouding their eyes and etched deeply into the flesh of their faces.

"Maybe I'd say good evening, but it looks like it ain't," the half-breed said.

"For me it is, *hombre*," Chico Lopez announced cheerfully and showed his grinning face between the shaking shoulders of the Farrows. "I think these people they hear what you *hombres* are saying on the street a few minutes ago. And they not like it, so they try to leave town. I think you not like that. I am right, *hombres*?"

Phineas Farrow's Adam's apple bobbed with every third word Lopez spoke. While his wife kept clenching and unclenching her fists at her sides.

"You're not wrong, Chico," Steele replied.

The grin broadened still further across the Mexican's fleshy face.

"What is the meaning of this?" Farrow managed to force out around his frenetically active Adam's apple. "Ernestine and I heard shooting and left the hotel to see—"

"Good you've found your voice, Mr. Farrow," Steele interrupted. "Because talk is what we want to hear from you?"

"Inside, *hombre, mi bien,*" Lopez instructed, and touched the twin muzzles of his shotgun to the shoulder of Phineas and then Ernestine Farrow. And beamed at Edge as the couple complied. "I know you would want them held. The people around here, they think I know damn nothing. But Chico Lopez he know damn all!"

The half-breed responded to the fat Mexican's misuse of the English language with a quiet grin that revealed a trace of humor at the sides of his mouth.

But there was no mirth in the way Steele's lips curled back and he rasped at the Farrows, "Reckon you have to know better than that."

THIRTEEN

LOPEZ stood on the threshold of the law office, shoulder leaning against the doorframe, shotgun held in the crook of an arm, picking at his teeth with a thumbnail.

Charlie Deed rested his rump on the side of the table with the lamp on it, still resentful of the way he had been roused from sleep.

Edge and Steele sat behind their respective desks, the half-breed smoking a cigarette and the Virginian with his gloved hands clasped, every now and then cracking his knuckles.

Each time the pulled joints made a snapping sound in the otherwise silent room, a tremor shook the woman's thin frame and her husband blinked. They stood in the center of the office, facing the seated men, their misery and fear expanding with each moment that passed and nobody spoke.

For a full minute it was like this, after everyone had taken their positions, until Edge said:

"You gave me one rifle when you came to town, feller. A while after that, I saw three men go to your rig and take out three more. Just like they knew what they were looking for. And just where to look. Took those rifles and tried to kill the Reb, here. Told him that afterwards they planned to kill me and sleepytime Charlie Deed."

"What about me?" Lopez asked. "Didn't they say anything about—"

"Shut up, feller," Edge cut in evenly without shifting his narrow-eyed gaze from the Farrows. "Like for you to explain that."

"Sir, I am a reputable pharmaceutical manufacturer and salesman—"

"What's he talking about, *hombre*?" Lopez growled.

"Means he's a druggist," Deed supplied.

"And since we already have one in town, he isn't indispensible," Steele added.

"Phineas, we have been tricked!" the woman said suddenly, her anxiety replaced by a frown of anger. "If what these men are saying is true, our wagon has been used for a nefarious purpose without our knowledge!" She shifted her intent gaze away from the perplexed face of her husband to switch it between the impassive faces of Edge and Steele. "We had dinner at a stage stop some miles west of here. There was another wagon there, in the charge of two most disreputable looking men. And a stagecoach. From the driver of which we learned of the existence of this town. And of certain trouble here. The other wagon and the stage left while Phineas and I were eating our meal. If we brought guns to Southfields, I can assure you we knew nothing about them. And I can only assume there was some kind of chicanery at the stage stop."

She spoke more quickly with each sentence, and was breathless when the explanation was finished. While it was being given, her husband began to nod as his eyes expressed enlightenment. Then both of them looked expectantly at the seated men, eager to see a reaction from them.

"Could've been that way," Charlie Deed said, and drew flickering smiles of relief from the Farrows.

"Hard to disprove," Steele allowed, and the smiles took a firmer hold.

"Or prove," Edge added, and the smiles faded as fast as the glow of tobacco leaves when he crushed out the cigarette on the desk top. Then he gave a weary sigh and stood up, brushing the mangled stub of the cigarette to the floor. "Figure like me you people are anxious to get back to the hotel?"

The Farrows exchanged frowning glances. And the man elected to speak. "Sir, if we are not under arrest, I think Ernestine and I would prefer to leave Southfields as soon as possible. We did not realize the extent of the trouble here and since it is none of our concern, it would be foolish of us to endanger ourselves by remaining here."

Edge nodded. "You're not under arrest, feller," he confirmed. "Because there ain't no case against you. But you'll be safer here than leaving."

"How can that be?" the woman asked.

"Have to reckon flight as an admission of guilt, ma'am," Steele answered.

"But that is ridiculous—" Phineas Farrow blurted.

"Quit while you're ahead, feller," Edge interrupted.

"And while you both still have one, *hombre*," Lopez added, aiming his shotgun high at the Farrows as they responded to the half-breed's finger gesture and turned toward the door.

Edge led the way out, followed by Farrow. The woman halted for a moment, nervous to be so close to the twin muzzles of the Mexican's shotgun. Asked of Steele, "What about our wagon? It contains our entire stock in trade."

"Seems to be, ma'am," the Virginian replied, "it also contains the locks, stocks and barrels of another trade. So I reckon we'll impound it for a while. See that what's yours is taken good care of."

"This is insufferable!" Ernestine Farrow snapped as she flounced out of the office. "I intend to see that the territorial authorities hear of this!"

"Fine, lady," Edge growled, waving his Winchester to urge the woman and her husband toward the hotel. "They got the time and the men and maybe the inclination to check out your story." He raised his voice. "Deed, get the team out of the livery and drive the wagon over to the barn next to the shoemaker's shop. And guard it."

"Me, *hombre*? What will I do?"

"Get some sleep. And meet the Reb and me over at the restaurant for breakfast at sun up."

Lopez spat noisily into the dust. "I do not eat slop, *hombre*. You want to eat with me, you come to my cantina. Maria and Isabella, if they ever marry, their husbands will be very fat. They are fine cooks, both of them."

"You hear that, Reb?" the half-breed called.

"Reckon the whole town did, Yank!" Steele answered as Charlie Deed emerged from the law office, his expression suggesting that he was still nursing a grudge about his rude awakening.

But Edge was already moving away along the sidewalk,

trailing the Farrows, as Chico Lopez angled across the street toward the Cantina Plata. While Deed brought up the rear, walking even more slowly than usual.

The Farrows and Edge went into the hotel. Lopez entered his premises, causing Shep Mallison to grunt in his sleep as he kicked the old-timer sleeping in his doorway. Charlie Deed made no attempt to work quietly in getting the horses from the livery, hitching them to the wagon and then driving the rig along Main Street and off to the side to the barn.

But after this, peace descended upon Southfields. And those of its citizens without cause to be awake could, if their consciences allowed them, go back to sleep as the early hours of the new day passed darkly to give way to the first light of Monday morning.

The cocks crowed, dogs barked, babies cried, women rattled pots and pans and men grunted their irritation with the start of a new working week. The sun rose to dispel the coolness from the air and began to climb up a cloudless sky which promised another long day of rainless heat.

Edge, freshly washed up and shaved, emerged from the Town House on to the stoop and lit a cigarette as the Virginian—weary-eyed and with thick bristles on his face—came along the sidewalk from the law office. The smell of tobacco smoke was quickly masked by the aromas of frying food and brewing coffee which rose from many of the town's chimneys.

The pot-bellied and bandy-legged Harry Pollock came out of the hotel as the two lawmen nodded to each other. He was attired in his mourning suit.

"Heard shooting last night, didn't I?"

"Right, feller," Edge answered.

"North side of town, wasn't it?"

"You lost your patient. And another two more need burying."

"Figured something of the sort. North side they wouldn't bother anybody. And keep just as well in the open at night as in the morgue. Someone would have called me if doctoring was what was needed."

"You put in a hard day yesterday," Steele allowed.

158

"Appreciate it if today is a slow one," Pollock said. "Three, you say? Leave me fresh out of caskets."

"We all have our problems," Edge replied as he and Steele stepped down from the stoop.

Across the intersection, Chico Lopez pulled open the doors of his cantina and launched a vicious kick at Shep Mallison, the old-timer's growling responses lost amid a barrage of Spanish invective the Mexican spat at him.

"Hey, Shep!" Pollock called. "Three more graves to dig! Build a thirst and earn enough money to satisfy it!"

"Sonofabitch knows I don't need to build no thirst," Mallison grumbled as he staggered out into the sunlight, blinking.

The air inside the cantina was still fetid with the odors of last night. But morning freshness from the open doorway and unshuttered windows and the aromas of breakfast coffee and food from in back of the place quickly neutralized the staleness.

"Sit, sit, *hombres*!" Lopez invited with expansive hand gestures toward chairs at a table close to the doorway, where he was already seated. Then he clapped his hands and yelled, "*Camarera!*"

Maria and Isabella, with shining clean faces, neatly brushed hair and attired in crisply laundered white dresses emerged from the rear. Looking not in the least like whores, each carried a tray. Maria with the coffee and Isabella the breakfast of American-style ham and eggs and beans.

Their dispositions as they served the meal to the three men were as cheerful as that of Chico Lopez—who was also cleanly turned out this morning.

"Eat, then we talk," the Mexican urged. And set about the meal with noisy relish as the women left the cantina bar—one to stand outside on the street and one going into the back.

While Edge and Steele ate with less speed but equal enjoyment.

There was no talk until Lopez rattled his fork down on his empty plate, belched and asked, "They cook good, do they not, *hombres*? My daughters?"

"Real good," Steele allowed, the food in his belly increasing the feeling of lethargy which had been building throughout the long night. "But if I have a heart, the way to it isn't through my stomach."

"You sure are acting like a feller trying to impress," Edge added. "But I figure it ain't your daughters you want to get off your hands."

Lopez laughed. "*Si*. My daughters they are not even my daughters. I have always called them that since I found them like orphans in a storm in Mexicali on the Baja." He winked. "And trained them for a trade in a way no real father could do. Many would not approve, but since then, they have never gone hungry."

"And now I'm not hungry anymore, feller," Steele said as he finished his breakfast and glanced out of the open doorway.

Edge and Lopez looked in the same direction—at the familiar sight of Harry Pollock driving his hearse along Main Street. But this time the scrawny old Shep Mallison was up on the seat with him. And four coffins were stacked in the glass-sided rear, only one of them occupied as yet.

The grim expression which spread across the fleshy face of the Mexican obviously had nothing to do with the mournerless funeral. "Sir we get down to the business. I wish it to be known—to you *hombres* and to all in this town— that I am with you. At first when you come here, I did not like you. Because I have had much trouble in my life and I wanted no more. Even after those three other men make trouble for you in my place. I take this—" he stabbed a thumb at the star pinned to his clean white shirt "—only because I must admit to myself this is just the beginning. And I do not wish to be unarmed if my daughters are in need of protection."

Lopez looked briefly toward the two doors through which the women had gone. And neither Edge nor Steele could doubt the sincerity which sounded in the Mexican's tone and showed in his dark eyes.

"Have you changed sides or just come down off the fence?" Steele asked.

Lopez scowled. "Isabella and Maria have never gone hungry, *hombre.* I already tell you this. But times, they got lean for them—and for me—Kelly was here. For many months, I sell small beer and sometimes a tequila to local *hombres*. One time a farmer who has wife who leaves him come here and have my daughters for whole week. But my trade, it go all to hell. I have no reason to be with Kelly."

"Ain't our aim to make this town wide open again, feller," Edge said.

The Mexican nodded vigorously. "*Sí, sí,* I know this. And nor is it that *hombre's* intention to become sheriff again. For a reason I do not know—and do not wish to know—Kelly hates this town. I am not stupid, *hombres*. A town is just buildings and a man he does not hate just buildings. It is the people in them that causes him the great anger. And not all the people. Kelly, he gives fair warning to everyone. And many will take heed, and I do not say they are wrong. Kelly I say is wrong. To take revenge against the innocent as well as the guilty. If there are any guilty even."

"There are guilty ones, Chico," Steele replied softly.

Lopez nodded again, less emphatically. "You tell me this, *hombre*, and I believe you. For you know more of this than I do." He sighed. "Once when I was very young, I was a Federale. I had ideals then. Concerned with protecting the innocent against the guilty. But they were dashed. Many times I saw wrong repaid with wrong and soon this sickened me so much I deserted. Came to this country to escape the firing squad. And to make a new life. It took many years to get what I wanted which if you look around you is not very much. Now I have it, I will keep it or I will die losing it, *hombres*. I think, maybe, it will be wrong against wrong yet again. But in such a situation a man who sits on the fence, all he can do is fall off. Better, I think, to step off. To the side of his choice."

"Grateful for the breakfast," Steele said as he pushed back his chair, picked up his rifle and got to his feet. "And for your confidence that we're the lesser of two evils."

"Not only I, *hombre*," Lopez said quickly. "Isabella and Maria are with me. If there is anything they can do to help, you have only to ask. You may place your trust in them."

"Or anything else, I guess, Reb," Edge said lightly and

flicked a finger at the underside of his hat brim. "Sleep well."

The Virginian showed a fleeting smile. "Intend to, Yank. Been on the job all night and all I want to lay right now is down."

Lopez expressed irritated concern as he watched Steele move wearily out of the cantina and cross the intersection toward the Town House. Then, when Edge's hooded eyes returned their impassive gaze on him, he complained, "I do not like that you *hombres* do not take seriously what I say."

"The man told you he was grateful, feller," the half-breed said flatly. "And now I'll tell you I'm obliged to you. For your help with the Farrows last night and for making your position clear."

The Mexican nodded his satisfaction with this. Then stabbed his thumb at the star again. "I want no money for wearing this. My daughters and I do what we do because we—"

"You've already covered that," Edge cut in. "But Steele and I have nothing to lose in this town except our lives. So we'll take the Merritt money or there ain't no point in us being on his side of the fence. Reason I wanted to see you this morning—anyone else in this town the Reb and I can trust to be in the same mind as you. So far had offers from the Pollocks, Clements, Gehlen and the Negro."

Lopez nodded sagely. "The black *hombre,* he has a good life here for one of his skin. And Kelly, he did not treat him good. I think you can trust him, though I don't know if he can handle a gun. The others? With Clinton Merritt, the founders of this town. The ones Kelly has reason to hate, maybe?"

"You asking?"

A shake of the head. "I know. As much as I want to know."

"So do I, feller. About those. It's other men I'm interested in. Like you. Also people like Merritt's daughter."

"Ah, I like her. I tell you, *hombre,* Chris Kelly had no need of the services of my daughters while he lived in Southfields. And she is to be much pitied because of this. Never did I see a woman so much in love." He shook his

162

head, as if it required such a physical action to dislodge this line of thought from his mind. "Since Kelly left and gave the message to the drunk, there has been much talk. I hear it here in my place and out on the street. Talk of the respect people have for Kelly. And of the opportunity he offers for them to own their own homes and land."

"They knew when they came here that Merritt and his partners held the reins."

"*Sí*. Except that Merritt, he has no partners. Much brains for the business. So that those who shared his good fortune at the start were one by one bought out. For a long time now, he has owned all." A deep sigh. "And if a man must have a landlord, Clinton Merritt is not so bad. But if a man can become his own master by leaving town for just one day . . . well, *hombre*." A shrug now of his flabby shoulders. "It is not their fight, but they will be on the winning side if they do as Kelly has asked." Bitterness took a grip of his features and sound bitingly in his tone. "Like the vultures who wait high out of danger until the time comes to descend and feast on the remains of the fallen!"

Edge stood up.

"You are leaving, *hombre*?"

"Just the cantina, feller. Got what I came for."

Lopez grinned. "It is good to know I am not the only fool around here. Your partner, he should know what I have told you."

"Figure he already thinks he does. I'll tell him he's not wrong. Obliged."

Outside, the sun was much brighter and hotter than when the half-breed had entered the cantina. Isabella was leaning against the whitened adobe wall, her face sheened with sweat and her white dress stained dark under the armpits. She had unbuttoned it from the modestly high neckline so that now the upper slopes of her breasts were bared to take advantage of whatever slight cool breeze might waft along Main Street.

"I have been keeping watch, *señor*," she reported. "But have seen nothing worthy of note." She smiled and from habit it was the provocative smile of a woman who traded in lust. "Chico, he has told you we are with you?"

"He's been keeping me abreast of the situation, lady,"

Edge answered, and reached out a hand as if to pat her on the jaw. But instead he went lower, to clutch the two sides of the plunging dress neckline and close them. "Ain't none of us in this are bosom companions, though. Best all of us keep our minds on the job in hand. Wouldn't you say?"

Fear had swept the alluring smile off her face. And now she swallowed hard as she nodded.

Edge released his grip and said, "First like you to go get Maria. Then bring her down to the wagon repairer's barn."

"Sí, señor."

She went quickly into the cantina as Edge ambled out across the street which as yet was still deserted, every business establishment except for the Town House and Lopez's place not yet open. As he moved on the intersection, he sensed watching eyes from just one direction and when he glanced up and to his left he saw a lace curtain fall back into place. At the window of Clinton Merritt's suite. But it was not the grayness of the cripple's hair he glimpsed before the fabric concealed the watcher. Instead, the long red tresses of Wanda.

The side street was as deserted as Main. But the domestic sounds of rising and the preparations of breakfasts came from behind the closed doors of the houses on the east side. And something made a noise inside the premises of the wagon repairer. Not Charlie Deed, for the man was not there.

There was just the Farrows' wagon, a half dozen other rigs in various stages of disrepair, and one of the Farrows' two horses. Attached to one canvas side of the covered wagon was a piece of card bearing the crudely scrawled message:

I've had enough of this lawman crap. And taking crap from your lawmen. Maybe I'll see you in hell.

Deed had used the pin on the star to fix his goodbye note to the canvas.

"Señor, what is it you want of us?" Maria asked as she and Isabella came into the barn.

Edge crooked a finger at them and led them to the rear of the wagon, dropped the tailgate and had to move a couple of cardboard cartons before he located a case of brand new Winchester rifles. The hinged lid of the case was not locked.

He took out a rifle and showed the whores what he required. They watched intently, but then looked blankly at him when he shot an inquiring glance at them. So, patiently, he showed them twice more. Then gave each of them a Winchester and nodded approvingly as he watched them imitate his actions.

"You then put them all back on the wagon the way you found them."

Maria nodded.

Isabella asked, "What will happen when Mr. Carlton comes, *señor*? This is his place."

"Bar the door from the inside and when he tries to get in, you tell him to come find me. If he won't listen, scream rape."

Maria laughed. "Whores accusing a man of rape, *señor*?"

Edge grinned coldly. "Yesterday you were whores, ladies. Today you're deputy sheriffs."

Isabella grimaced into the rear of the wagon. "I think I liked it better what I was yesterday, *señor*."

"Forget about that for a while," the half-breed answered. "I don't want you lying down on the job."

He went outside and closed the big doors, heard footfalls, then the sound of a plank being dropped into brackets to bar entry to the place.

Then, instead of back tracking to Main Street, he went in the direction Steele had taken last night toward the unexpected appointment in Potter's Field. At the end of the side street started along a pathway that curved around the back lots of the houses on the northern fringe of Southfields. And became aware that, as he was seen from each building, the sounds from within were subdued or curtailed altogether. As if the occupants of the houses were indulging in some activity which they did not want the tall, lean impassive faced half-breed to know about.

The pathway toward the Baptist chapel was on a constant upgrade and as he reached the highest point, he could see across both the American and Mexican sections of

165

town—to the shacks and fields of the dirt farmers on the south slope of the valley. No one had yet taken advantage of this coolest part of the morning to start work on the plots.

Beyond the neat graveyard in front of the chapel, Shep Mallison was hard at work, sweating and cursing softly as he enlarged the grave which had been dug for Lee. Working up a greater thirst than usual and working for the money to slake it.

The pot-bellied Harry Pollock had done as much as was needed for a while and he sat in the shade of the hearse, leaning back against the pile of four coffins which were now all occupied.

The old-timer eyed Edge malevolently as he came through the gap in the wire fence. Harry Pollock stubbed out his cheroot on the side of one of the coffins and groaned as he got to his feet.

"Seen this yet?" the high-hatted man asked, and thrust a copy of Gilbert Reade's newspaper toward the half-breed. "Guess it explains all this."

As Edge took the folded broadsheet, Pollock waved his free hand to encompass the town spread out below them.

The newspaper had just four pages, with the title "Southfields Reporter" across the top of the first one with Special Edition printed diagonally in the lower-right-hand corner. The top headline proclaimed in large type: THE TRUTH ABOUT OUR TROUBLES and underneath was the rhetorical question: WHY DO HIRED GUNMEN STALK OUR STREETS?

In the story beneath, Gilbert Reade answered the query. Coldly and boldly, fulfilling the headline's promise that it would be the truth. He told the facts about the Masonville Massacre, the bank robbery in Big Springs, Edward Heller's record keeping and Chris Kelly's connection with the victims of the Texas raid.

The story was written clearly and concisely, with Reade making no attempt to excuse his own involvement in the wrongdoings of many years ago.

It was across the two center pages of the newspaper that the editor of *The Southfields Reporter* became emotive. In an editorial in which he urged his readers to take heed of

166

Kelly's warning. And to do so before the deadline which had been set:

For the former sheriff of our fair town cannot now be expected to adhere to the time limit he set. A time limit which this newspaper is certain he intended to honor. But the situation has changed. The vested interests in this town have used their wealth to engage professional gunmen who take human life with the same lack of compunction as decent people tread on a roach or swat a fly.

Do not be impressed or provoked by these men who kill for blood money. For their presence in our town will surely be regretted by those who pay them and those who support them.

This town was built by evil men who committed evil deeds and they deserve the retribution which faces them. The man who has taken it upon himself to make them pay for what they did has given the honest, decent and innocent citizens of Southfields fair warning. But he is only human.

The men he sent here in advance, doubtless to ensure that the innocent did not suffer, have been ruthlessly gunned down. And we did nothing.

Chris Kelly's patience must surely be being tried. And it is the opinion of this newspaper that the day of retribution will be advanced.

Go. Go now!

For today could be the day. And who could lay blame at the feet of the avenging angels if, when they come, they consider that every person remaining in Southfields is there to thwart their purpose?

There was more in the same vein, the editorial set in large type. But the largest type in Reade's printroom had been reserved for the back page of *The Southfields Reporter*. In capital letters, with one word a line, was the legend:

YOU
HAVE
BEEN
WARNED —

Edge refolded the newspaper and gave it back to Pollock.
"I don't subscribe," he said evenly, and looked out over the
town to where there was now movement around some of
the dirt farmers' shacks. As people carried items out of
their homes to load onto buckboards. Valises, bundles,
sacks, cartons and in some cases pieces of furniture. Toted
by men, women and even children.

"Neither do I, mister," Pollock answered. "But Gil
Reade left a copy in the grave."

"Leavin', are they?" Shep Mallison muttered as he
rested for a few moments, to lean on his shovel, rub a forearm over his sweaty forehead and squint across the rooftops to the far side of the valley. "Be kinda interestin' to
see how many smart people there are in this town."

"You going to leave, old man?" Pollock asked.

Mallison showed his teethless gums in a grin. "Depends
how long it'll take me to drink through the money you're
gonna pay me, Mr. Pollock. Long ways to the next wa-
terin' hole of the kind I drinks from. And if Chris Kelly and
his good old boys get here while I still got money for liquor. Well, I guess I'll be happy to die with a bottle in my
hand." He started to dig again, but paused to laugh and
look up at Pollock and Edge as he added, "Provided it's
best part empty, of course!"

"You're a fool, old man!" Pollock rasped. "Leave with
the others. There's sense in what Gil Reade printed and
this ain't going to be your fight."

The composure of the doctor-mortician was cracking
and it was obvious to the half-breed that the man had been
under great strain while trying to conceal how much the
special edition of the newspaper had affected him.

Mallison took another pause from his labors. And shook
his head. "Sure ain't my fight, Mr. Pollock. But a man who
ain't got no score to settle can have his sympathies. And he
can root for them that he wants to win. Never have made
no secret that I'm for Chris Kelly and his brave boys.

Won't be able to root for them and see them win from way out in the hills."

"Crazy," Pollock muttered.

"Already said the folks that are leavin' are smart," the old-timer growled. "So I'm admittin' I'm a fool."

The half-breed had rolled a cigarette during the exchange. Now he struck a match on the top coffin in the pile and lit the tobacco. Shifted his narrow-eyed gaze from the activity on the south slope of the valley to something that was moving far out on the west trail. A billowing dust cloud that showed on the ridge and then advanced toward town. Raised by two or maybe three horses ridden at a gallop, Edge guessed.

Pollock saw the direction in which the tall, lean, glinting-eyed man was looking and stiffened when he saw the object of his interest.

"Coming fast," he said tensely. "Them, you think? Is it starting?"

Edge raked his gaze around the other ridges which encircled Southfields. And paid particular attention to the dark line of pine trees which etched the top of the high ground beneath the fully risen sun.

"Maybe it's starting, feller," he murmured, allowing smoke to trickle out of the corner of his mouth as Shep Mallison clambered up from the mass grave to peer toward the approaching riders. "But there ain't enough of them to start anything yet."

"There'll be more, there'll be more!" the old-timer blurted excitedly. "Remember the Alamo!"

"I ain't old enough," Edge growled. And turned away from the graveside to amble out through the broken-down gateway.

"Anything I can do, mister?" Pollock called after him, using a handkerchief to mop the sweat of fear off his brow and chin. "And my boy? John Clements and Barney Gehlen?"

"Could be all the help you're gonna get, mister!" Shep Mallison taunted. "Against them brave good old boys from Texas Chris Kelly's gonna bring here."

Edge paused, ignoring the toothless old man to say to Pollock, "Obliged if you and your people would fix a schedule to keep watch from up here." He nodded toward the chapel with an exposed bell in the stumpy tower above the arched entrance.

"If you see anything that bothers you, give me a ring."

"Sure, I'll do that."

"You ain't got a chance!" Mallison put in gleefully. "Way the country is around here, them avenging angels like Reade called them will be able to hit you from all over."

Edge jerked a thumb toward the tree-topped ridge. "Pay particular attention to that direction, feller," he said.

"You know something?"

The half-breed shrugged. "No, feller. Just a feeling I got. That Kelly's heroes will show up from out of the east wood."

FOURTEEN

ADAM STEELE had been asleep for less than an hour when the clatter of wagon wheels and the clop of hooves roused him. Although he had drawn the heavy-drape curtains across the window the strength of the bright morning sunlight penetrated the fabric to lance painfully into his eyes as he snapped up the lids.

He groaned his irritation at being awakened after such a short period of rest. Then cursed at the sluggishness of his weary muscles as he swung his feet to the floor and stood up. He had sprawled out on the bed, fully dressed except for his hat and boots, and had not even splashed water on his bristled face. And he was distastefully conscious of the smell of stale sweat on his body and clothing as he padded across the room, drew aside the drapes and blinked while opening the window.

Louder noise came into the room along with the brighter sunlight. But he frowned in mild perplexity for just a moment as he looked down on the reason for the din.

A line of heavily laden wagons, all heading west. The convoy growing longer as other rigs pulled away from in front of the buildings on both sides of Main Street or made the turn from Via de Bello. Buckboards, flatbeds, one or two ancient Conestogas and even a few buggies. Loaded with the personal belongings of the families or couples who rode on the seats. Some with milk cows on lead ropes at the rear. Others with cages of fowl lashed on the tailboards. An occasional dog trotted along beside the turning wheels.

The dogs barked, the hens and cocks clucked and crowed and every now and then the cows lowed. But no human voices contributed to the sounds of the mass exodus from town, the smallest child as grim-faced and tight-lipped as the most elderly of the departing throng. Even babies were silent in the arms of their mothers.

Directly across the street from where the Virginian stood at the window, Chico Lopez was in the doorway of his cantina, a scowl of contempt on his fleshy face as he watched the wagons roll by. Further along the street, outside the store of the Mexican gunsmith, two men sat astride horses. Riders and mounts alike were covered with trail dust which was pasted to them by their sweat. Hard-faced men who viewed the convoy with satisfaction, nodding from time to time. But not in response to any gestures from the people aboard the wagons, who all peered directly ahead at the hurriedly loaded freight on the rig which preceded them.

The two strangers were dressed Western-style and sat saddles fitted with all the necessary accoutrements for trail-riding across dangerous country. But their holsters were empty. So were their rifle boots.

"Power of the press, Reb," the unmistakable voice of the half-breed said from the Town House stoop below where Steele stood.

As Charlie Deed had done the previous morning, the Virginian swung a leg out over the windowsill and stepped outside onto the railed balcony. The Colt Hartford remained canted to his shoulder, but the two men on horseback along and across the street saw him and looked pointedly down at their empty holsters.

Steele went to the rail and looked over it. "Saw the newspaperman out delivering in the early hours. Didn't drop a copy by at the law office."

"Here."

He glanced along the balcony and saw Wanda Merritt at the open window of her father's parlor, thrusting a rolled newspaper through. Her voice had carried to Edge, who called up:

"Lot of reading, Reb. All about Masonville and Big Springs. And how Gilbert Reade thinks the local people should go while the going's good."

Steele made to touch the brim of his hat toward the woman before he realized he was not wearing it. So he shook his head and asked, "That say it all, ma'am?"

She shrugged. "Most of it. Except for some not very nice things about you and the rest of the trigger-happy men with tin stars pinned to your shirts."

"Girl, come help me with my pants!" her father bellowed from the bedroom of his suite.

The woman grimaced and withdrew from the window.

Steele surveyed the line of slow-moving wagons again, recognizing a face here and there from when he had patrolled the town on Saturday night.

"We have the founding fathers, feller," Edge called up. "Lost Deed. Left a note that he'll see us in hell."

"And me if you'll have me, sir," Leroy offered, his voice sounding from in the hotel lobby. "Though all I know about guns is that you points them and presses the trigger."

"You squeeze the trigger, feller," Edge corrected. "But you've got the general idea. Here's the keys, go down to the law office and get a rifle out of the cell."

"Who are the strangers, Yank?" Steele asked as keys rattled together on a ring.

"You two gents are more strangers than they are," the Negro said. "Them are Hoyt Shaw and Lester Noon. The two hands from the Bar-M spread that left town with Kelly and Ludlum."

"You take their guns, Yank?" the Virginian asked as the final wagon clattered along the street, tagging on to the line after swinging out of Via de Bello.

"No, they rode in like that."

"Seems word about the new ordinance has spread pretty far."

The two men they were discussing waited for the last wagon to pass, then clucked their horses away from the store-front to the center of the street and tugged at the reins to head them toward the intersection. Against the regular clop of slow-moving hooves, Steele could hear movement in the hallway beyond his room door. The turning wheels of Merritt's chair, the footfalls of his daughter as she pushed him, then the mechanism of the rope elevator.

Down below, Edge stepped off the stoop and Chico Lopez advanced a few paces out from his cantina doorway.

"We're obeyin' the new law," the shorter, broader, more

swarthy of the ranch hands said quickly. "We ain't carryin'."

As they reined their mounts to a halt ten feet in front of where the half-breed stood, both of them briefly raised their hands, fingers splayed, in a gesture of confirmation of what had been said. As the man who had said it flicked his small, bright blue eyes from Edge to Steele, to Lopez and back again.

The second man, who was in the same late-twenties age group as the first, was of medium height and build, with red hair and warts on his jaw. He also had blue eyes, but they were large and round. And they did not move from the impassive features of Edge.

"This here is Shaw," he introduced dully. "And I'm Noon."

"How are you Shaw," Steele greeted flatly. "Hi, Noon."

"Sure smells like it," Edge said.

Shaw blinked. "What?"

Edge spat the dead stub of a cigarette off his bottom lip. And wrinkled his nostrils. "High noon, feller."

Chico Lopez laughed.

Steele said, "Reckon the Yank means he can smell a rat."

"Or two," the Mexican added, and vented another harsh laugh.

The exchange increased the nervousness of Hoyt Shaw, but did no more than try the patience of Lester Noon.

The sounds of the wheelchair and the woman pushing it now came from the Town House lobby. And drew the attention of both mounted newcomers as they were curtailed at the hotel entrance.

"What the hell do you sonsofbitches want?" Clinton Merritt snarled.

"Whatever it is, it ain't to talk to you and what's left of the Kansas Raiders," Noon rasped, with venom dripping from every word.

"Why you—" Merritt started.

"Shut up for once, Pa!" his daughter snarled. "And listen to them. It looks like they've come a long way. And it wasn't just for the ride."

"Right, Miss Merritt," Noon growled, and touched the

brim of his hat. Obviously having trouble in curbing his impatience and his anger. "Brought a message from Chris."

"Yes?" Wanda asked eagerly, her grip tightening around the handles of her father's wheelchair.

"Ain't no billet-doux, Miss Wanda," Hoyt Shaw said.

"For him and him," Noon said, stabbing a finger at Edge and then at Steele. "And him too, I guess." A head gesture toward Chico Lopez. Then a double-take along the street which caused everyone to glance in the same direction. And see Leroy standing out front of the law office, leaning against the hitching rail with a Winchester rifle held diagonally across his chest. "Jesus Christ, the nigger!" Noon blurted. And vented a short, harsh, contemptuous laugh. "Merritt, you're really scraping the bottom of the barrel."

He shook his head in disbelief, as the man in the wheelchair showed a scowl which was probably due as much to his feelings about Leroy being a deputy as his hatred for Noon.

"Guess the message is for the nigra, too, Lester," Shaw said.

"Reckon the message isn't urgent," Steele drawled from the balcony.

"Uh?" Shaw grunted.

"The feller's saying your boss should have used Western Union," Edge explained. "Hell of a lot quicker."

"Yes, man!" Merritt snarled. "Spit it out then get out!"

Noon tightened his mouthline and seemed to snap an angry retort. But he bit back on it and although his features remained hard set, he kept his tone even.

"Chris don't like what your hired guns done to Follett and Segal and Brad King. And to Henry Sutton and his boys. But he ain't got room to carry no more grudges. Says that if you people get out like everyone else, he'll overlook the killin's."

"How you feel about that, Reb?" Edge asked.

"Real grateful," Steele replied, "And you, Yank?"

"Figure it shows Kelly has a big heart. And the bigger the target, the easier it is to hit."

Chico Lopez laughed and Clinton Merritt showed a grin that held more than a grain of relief.

175

Noon leaned to the side and spat down at the street. Then pasted a grin across his face to growl, "Kinda glad to hear that, mister. On account of me and Hoyt hired on for a real fight. And it wouldn't have been nothin' if it was us and the rest of Kelly's boys up against just a cripple and a bunch of hasbeens."

He tugged on the reins to turn his horse and Shaw was just a moment behind him. But both men froze as the bell on the Baptist chapel tolled once.

"What the hell?" Merritt asked, as his daughter stiffened.

"Another message," Edge said and looked up at Steele when Harry Pollock yelled:

"Rider to the east!"

Without a hat, the Virginian used a hand to shade his eyes from the glare of the sun. Staring hard into the heat shimmer that hung in a sheened veil in front of the distant ridge. For a few moments, the man and horse which Pollock had seen were merged as a blurred, dark blob at the fringe of the haze. Then they could be seen in sharp focus, but only as silhouettes. Against the undulating shimmer which closed in behind them to conceal everything more than a mile distant from town.

"On his own, coming fast," Steele reported as dust began to show, rising from beneath the pumping hooves of the galloping horse. Then he looked out along the west trail and was in time to see the last of the line of wagons become distorted by and then disappear into the shimmering heat haze in that direction.

"Maybe Deed is coming back, *hombre?*" Lopez suggested as the Virginian checked the terrain to the south before shifting his gaze back to the approaching rider.

"Charlie left town?" Merritt asked, startled.

"Said he'd see us in hell, Yank," Steele reminded.

"And this is one hell of a situation, feller," Edge muttered, his eyes closing to the narrowest of glittering slits as he shifted his gaze to the gray complexioned face of the man in the wheelchair.

For a stretched second, Clinton Merritt was afraid, sitting rigid in his chair as if forced hard against its seat and back by the power in the ice-blue eyes of the half-breed.

But then his green eyes behind their spectacle lenses became ignited by hot anger.

"All right, mister!" he snarled. "I admit it. I gave Charlie Deed a bonus to take care of Ed Heller for me! He was supposed to do it before Heller told you and your partner about Masonville! Because I thought you wouldn't work for me if you knew about the massacre! And I didn't say anything about hiring Deed for the killing because I thought it would go against your grains!

"Now you do know! And if it does go against your grains, you can take up the offer Kelly's made you! This is a fine town! A good place to live in! It don't matter it got built because a lot of innocent people got slaughtered! It don't matter, because a good many of the dead were ours! Tit for tat! Eye for an eye and a tooth for a tooth! It ain't ever been a perfect world and it never will be!

"Here it could have been as near perfect as it can get! If Heller hadn't stirred the shit so Kelly could smell the stink! So now it's gotta be another eye for an eye!

"Heller deserved what he got and I ain't ashamed of my part in it! Because I ain't got any more room for shame in my heart! It's too full up with that I carry for Masonville and Big Springs! And I'll carry it to the grave!"

He was still rigid, but sitting forward in his chair now, raking his glazing eyes across the faces of Edge, Lopez, Noon and Shaw. Sweat oozed from every pore on his face which had become crimson and then purple. And saliva spilled from his mouth and ran down his chin. Abruptly, he could sustain the high pitch of his emotions no longer. And he sagged back into the trap of his wheelchair. The fires died in his eyes and his voice became weak.

"Carry it to the grave because there ain't no way for a man like me to absolve himself from the weight of guilt I have." He moved his hands from the chair arms to his wasted thighs. "I accepted infirmity as punishment and did so gladly. But it was not enough. So I built this town as a place where people could come and settle and live happily and peacefully. It was still not enough, but I could do no more."

He had been staring down at his big gnarled hands clutched tightly to his emaciated thighs. Now he lifted his head to look up, and realized he had lost the attention of his audience. For all eyes were turned toward the man riding on to Main Street from the east trail.

The animal was no longer galloping. Entered town at an exhausted, staggering walk, nostrils flared, eyes bulging and coat covered with the dust-stained lather of sweat.

The rider was dead. Held erect in the saddle by lengths of rope lashed to a crude wooden framework fixed to the cantle. The ropes did not go around him. Instead, they went through him. At his belly, chest and throat. Double-thickness lariat ropes with knots tied at the front, crusted with black congealed blood where they were pulled half into the gaping holes which tunnelled through the man's body. The crotch of his pants was also caked with dried and discolored blood where his genitals had been hacked off. And the displaced flesh had been thrust into his mouth.

As the mutilated corpse, the rider was nobody. Before he died he had been Gilbert Reade.

"Oh, my dear God!" Wanda Merritt blurted, and threw her hands up to her mouth. As the exhausted horse staggered to a snorting halt directly in front of the Town House entrance. But the power of the vomit erupted from her stomach forced a way through her fingers and gushed to the sidewalk as she spun around and lunged into the hotel lobby.

"He deserved it, I think," Lopez said flatly. "For trying to buy his life with the printed word. He was a traitor to those who—"

"Shut your filthy mouth!" Clinton Merritt snarled, his mouth set in a line of disgust which did not alter as he shifted his magnified eyes from the corpse to the Mexican. "He shared the shame of the rest of us who were at Masonville! And sought to make amends by what he wrote in the newspaper."

Hoyt Shaw and even Lester Noon were visibly shaken by the barbarity with which Reade had been killed and mutilated. Noon recovered first.

"We didn't know this was gonna happen," he said hoarsely and although he had set his features into a hard expression, his small eyes pleaded to be believed. "But I guess it's Chris's way of warnin' you people what'll happen if you stay in this town. Them that he's given the go-ahead to leave if they want."

"His message is as plain as the one you delivered; feller," Steele said flatly.

"We can go?" Noon asked.

"Ain't nobody keeping you," Edge answered.

"You and your partner are gonna stay?"

"Like you wanted," the half-breed said.

"It's a fine town, like Mr. Merritt says," Steele added when Noon looked up at him. "Worth fighting for, I reckon. And the pay's good."

"You mind if we go that way?" Noon asked, turning in the saddle to nod toward the east.

As Hoyt Shaw did a histrionic double-take out along the west trail and then rasped, "What the frig?"

The bell in the chapel on the hill tolled again. And Pollock shouted, "West! A whole bunch of men."

"How you see it, Reb?" Edge asked, glancing up at Steele, then gesturing for Noon and Shaw to leave town in the direction requested.

"Something between twenty and thirty," the Virginian answered. "On foot. Unarmed, I reckon."

"Sheep returning to the fold maybe, *hombre?*" Lopez suggested eagerly.

"You're crazy letting Noon and Hoyt go, mister!" Merritt growled, his glee at the prospect of help from townspeople with a change of heart clouded by the knowledge that the two ranch hands would be able to report the new situation to Kelly.

"They came with empty holsters and rifle boots, feller!" Steele rasped from the balcony as he interrupted his survey of the men on the west trail to look in the wake of the two horsemen.

"Good as a flag of truce the way things are," Edge added, watching Noon and Hoyt as they rode past Leroy—the black man responding with a contemptuous expression to whatever one of the riders snarled at him.

Wanda Merritt, her pallid face wiped clean of vomit but with dark stains on the bodice of her dress, moved shakily onto the threshold of the hotel and rasped, "How can you expect a man like him to respect any code of honor?"

Her father snapped his head around, his face coloring with anger. But the depth of revulsion he saw in her eyes penetrated and shattered his rage.

"A leopard can't change its spots!" she hurled at him.

And the words of the trite phrase acted like missiles which beat against him and forced him to slump low in the wheelchair. He faced front again, then his head dropped forward and he cradled his face in his hands.

"Gil Reade hasn't carried a gun since the day we rode out of Big Springs," the cripple offered, a weak excuse spoken in a weak tone. "And just look what they did to him."

"I'm looking," his daughter came back, staring fixedly at the brutally mutilated corpse lashed to the sweat lathered horse. But with hatred instead of horror in her eyes now.

Noon and Shaw rode clear of town and out onto the open east trail. Where they heeled their mounts into a gallop that raised a dust cloud in which they were quickly hidden. This as the returning townspeople came in off the west trail. Perhaps twenty-five of them. Mexicans and Americans. Dirt farmers, storekeepers and clerks. All men. The youngest and most able-bodied of those who had earlier in the morning ridden out aboard the wagon line.

John Clements, Dave Pollock and Barney Gehlen emerged from the stage depot, each with a rifle. The guns were aimed at the ground but acted to bring the bunch of men to an anxious halt at the western fringe of Southfields. Where one of them began to speak rapidly to the men with rifles.

Ignoring everything that was happening around her, the woman continued to stare at the fly-infested corpse of Gilbert Reade and to speak her piece.

"I'm looking at what was done to him, Pa! And I know that Chris Kelly either ordered it done or did it himself! Which is what made me sick to my stomach, Pa! Chris Kelly, who was the first man I was able to give myself to after what was done to me at Providence. A man who said he loved me and who I loved. Who I hoped I would be able to talk to. Who I could make see he would be just as bad as you and the rest if he did what he threatened. Yes, I'm looking, Pa. And I've seen enough now."

She tore her gaze away from the corpse to rake her eyes

to her father, to Edge, to Chico Lopez, to Leroy, to the three men with rifles and the spokesman for the returning townspeople who were coming up Main Street. She even rolled her eyes to glance up at the underside of the hotel balcony on which Steele stood.

"Seen enough and had enough!"

Then she whirled and strode back into the shade of the hotel lobby. As her father, an expression of despair etched deep into his gray face, made to turn his wheelchair and follow her. But Clements called:

"Clinton!"

And the cripple stayed his hands on the wheelgrips. To look toward the blond-haired Clements, the grim-faced Pollock and the stockily built, pipe-smoking Barney Gehlen.

"We got us some help, Clinton," the stage and telegraph man blurted and jerked a thumb toward the broad-shouldered, square-headed man of about forty-five who stood at his side—staring in horrified fascination at the corpse astride the horse. "Jack Carlton here and a bunch of others have come back. Figure they got a duty to defend the town."

"Others wanted to come, Mr. Merritt," the wagon repairer added, finally able to wrench his attention away from the remains of Reade. "But we said no to anyone over sixty and under twenty."

"That's fine, just fine," the cripple said absently, obviously still concerned with what his daughter had blurted out. "Mr. Edge and Mr. Steele will tell you what's necessary. Tell all of you."

Then he completed the move he had started earlier; turning his chair and rolling it through the doorway into his hotel.

Up on the balcony, Steele pursed his lips and gazed impassively down at Edge. And the half-breed's lean features were just as inscrutable in their response.

"Well, Yank?" the Virginian asked at length.

"I'm fine, Reb. You?"

"Same as I was when I woke up. No change."

"Me neither. Can you stay awake? Long enough to make plans at least?"

181

"You should be making plans to leave," Wanda Merritt said dully from the window of her father's parlor.

When Steele looked at her he saw sunlight glint on the tears which teetered in the corners of her green eyes.

"Wanda, work the car ropes for me!" Clinton Merritt yelled from the lobby. Then added, in a pleading tone, "Please, girl."

"Thought about it a while back," the Virginian told the woman and flexed his muscles to try to ease their weariness. "But I didn't."

"Why not?" she craned her head through the window to stare eastwards. Where the two riders had gone from sight through the heat shimmer. When she looked back at Steele, some tears had spilled and were coursing down her cheeks.

"Reckon you could say my conscience pricked me, ma'am," he replied.

"Makes two of us, Reb," the half-breed growled.

"What's this I hear?" Lopez rasped. "Two *hombres* like you with consciences?"

"Could be, Chico," Steele allowed, shifting his gaze from the eastern horizon to the men scattered below along Main Street. "Or maybe two pricks."

FIFTEEN

WHEN Harry Pollock had said he was out of stock of coffins, he meant those of plain pine which he used for burials in Potter's Field. He still had some heavy-oak caskets with brass handles and silken linings. And after he had done the best he could with the remains of Gilbert Reade he dressed the corpse in fresh clothing and placed the body in such a casket.

While his grim-faced son and John Clements dug a grave in the cemetery of the Baptist Chapel. The sweating labors of these two men ignored by Barney Gehlen who had climbed up onto the roof of the chapel where, pipe clenched in his teeth, he kept constant watch over the terrain on all sides of Southfields. His ancient Henry carbine held in such a way that, at the first sign of movement against the shimmering heat haze, he could clang the metal stockplate against the chapel bell.

Shep Mallison had purchased three bottles of the cheapest tequila from Chico Lopez's cantina and was taking his time with the second after gulping down the first. Seated on the rocker in the partial shade of the Town House stoop.

Up in her room at the rear of the hotel, Wanda Merritt was making preparations to leave town on the noon stage. Her father, who had spent several desperate minutes begging, pleading and then berating her to stay, was now in the parlor of his suite. Staring blindly out through the lace curtains at the windows, regretting the past and dreading the future.

Lopez, on instructions from Edge, was at the premises of the wagon repairer, issuing each unarmed man with a rifle and thirty rounds of ammunition. This after he had silenced the soft-spoken protests of Maria and Isabella by telling them the half-breed knew what he was doing.

The two whores had then gone to the mission church on Main Street. Where, with no priest to listen to their confessions and give absolution, they could only pray.

Leroy put water on to heat for a bath for Steele and then ran some errands for him.

While the Virginian and Edge held a brief, tersely worded discussion in the law office. After which the half-breed remained smoking at his desk and Steele returned to the hotel.

The tactical plan for defending the town against Chris Kelly and his men had occupied little time. For the most part, the two loners made partners by accident or by decrees of their respective ruling fates had talked guardedly of their attitudes toward the situation in which they found themselves.

"I've been on the wrong side before," Steele had said. "And I'm not talking about the war, Yank. I mean the morally wrong side."

"If we didn't make mistakes, Reb, how would we know how good it is to be right?"

"Merritt was for gunning down Noon and Shaw. But you know that."

"Harry Pollock would have given Sutton something to kill him instead of to kill his pain. You didn't know that."

"Reckon we know all we need to."

Edge nodded. "Mortician's in process of burying the clincher, uh Reb?"

"And Merritt's money is as good as Kelly's. A man has to make a living at what he does best, Yank."

"And we do what we do best when we don't have to keep looking over our shoulders."

Now Steele nodded. "Sure. I want the money but I don't need it. What I need is to talk to Clark Ludlum."

"Or kill him, feller," Edge said as the Virginian rose wearily from behind his desk and ran a gloved hand over his stubbled jaw.

"I haven't looked for a fight," Steele said as he went toward the open doorway, "since that time after I cut my father's body down from a beam in a Washington saloon."

"With me, it was before I buried my wife in the Dakotas," Edge said, taking the makings from his shirt pocket.

The Virginian stood on the threshold of the law office, his back to the room, the harsh glare of the sun almost painful to his red-rimmed, weary eyes. While Edge rolled and lit a cigarette.

"Doesn't make it any easier though, does it, Yank?"

"Killing the men who pick the fight?"

"No, feller. Living."

He looked back over his shoulder and, just for part of a second as the slitted blue eyes met the coal black ones, the impassiveness of both men was displaced by something akin to deep sadness. Compassion? Pity from understanding? A yearning for the impossible? Or maybe utter hopelessness.

Then the half-breed's lips drew back to reveal his teeth in a wry grin as he said, "Best way I know to do that is to shoot first, Steele."

The Virginian's tired face dropped years as he responded with his boyish smile, "And straight, Edge."

"Secret of our success."

"If we're so successful, what are we doing here, Yank?"

"What we do best, Reb."

Steele raised the hand that was not canting the Colt Hartford to his shoulder and said, "Reckon there's no answer to that, feller. Stay a straight shooter, uh."

Then, as the Virginian moved out on to the sidewalk, Edge called after him, "Keep cheating." And, as Steele made to come to a rigid halt, added, "Death, feller."

The morning slid quietly into history. While the half-breed sat in the law office. The Virginian bathed and shaved and caught up on lost sleep in his hotel room. Wanda Merritt waited with two bulging valises at the stage depot. Gilbert Reade was buried in the cemetery with the two Pollocks, Clements and Clinton Merritt at the graveside—Barney Gehlen mourning the deceased from his vantage point on the chapel roof. Leroy, his chores for Steele completed, carried out tasks assigned by Edge. Shep Mallison, the half-empty third bottle of tequila clutched in both hands, slept off a drunken stupor in the rocking chair. Chico Lopez drank beer and the two whores prepared and

185

started to cook lunch in the Cantina Plata. And the men with the brand-new Winchester rifles selected their own places to watch and wait. And watched and waited, contented solely with the explanation given by Lopez on orders from Edge that it was easier to issue them with new rifles than to go to the trouble of sorting out their own from the heap in the jailhouse.

Everyone sweated. All because of the Arizona heat. But some sweated more than others. From tension which mounted with each quiet second that entered from the unknown future, hovered in the uneasy present and disappeared into the new memories of the past. Few words were spoken but many thoughts were pondered. Mostly, the men and women waiting in the town where the peace was broken only by the constant buzzing of flies sought to mask their line of thought behind masks of impassiveness.

It was ten minutes to midday when Gehlen, alone now in the vicinity of the chapel, clenched his teeth more tightly to the stem of his unlit pipe and clanged his carbine stock against the bell.

The sudden sound roused Shep Mallison from his drunken sleep and jerked many other men out of mental reveries. Steele came awake with total recall and was instantly alert should danger threaten. Edge unfolded lazily from behind the desk, picked up his Winchester from beside his chair and went to the law office doorway.

"It's okay!" The town druggist called, and an apologetic note could be heard in his raised voice. "Just the stage."

Steele dressed slowly in the new clothes which he had asked Leroy to get him from the tailor's store—giving the Negro money to leave in the owner's cash drawer.

Edge turned right at the law office doorway and ambled along the sidewalk toward the stage depot at the far end of Main Street.

"It gettin' started, son?" Mallison asked, rubbing his eyes and scratching his chest as the half-breed stepped up onto the hotel stoop.

"Maybe," Edge answered. "When it does, this won't be a good place to watch from, feller."

"You tellin' me or what?" the old-timer asked tightly.

"Figure you're old enough not to need telling anything."

186

Mallison nodded his satisfaction with the answer, took a swig at his depleted supply of tequila and showed his toothless gums in a grin. "And old enough to know when there ain't no point in gettin' any older, son. Without the guts to do anythin' about it myself."

Edge went on by him, as the stage rolled close enough to town for the sound of rolling wheels and pumping hooves to be heard along Main Street.

"Deputy," a man said from inside the Town House lobby.

Edge halted and glanced across the threshold. Saw the Farrows advance into the doorway, anxiety etched deeply into the flesh of their thin faces. The man held a grip in one hand.

"My wife and I . . . well, this trouble isn't any of our business. Not at all. We think—"

"We wish to leave on the stage, sir," his wife cut in sharply, letting go of his arm and somehow seeming stronger without the contact.

"No sweat," the half-breed allowed.

Farrow licked his lips. "Our wagon? We can come back for it? Later?"

"Suit yourself. But you've only got the one horse now. Feller named Charlie Deed stole the other one."

"It doesn't matter, sir," came the fast reply. Then the man took hold of his wife's elbow and hurried her outside, steering her toward the stage depot.

As Adam Steele came down the stairway, attired in his new gray suit, lace-trimmed white shirt, red vest, black stetson and boots. But the stained kerchief with the weighted corners still hung around his neck and the well-worn black buckskin gloves continued to contour his hands.

"You look like a real smart dude, Reb," Edge muttered as the stage rolled in off the east trail and along the street.

"Money can't buy happiness, Yank," the Virginian drawled as he crossed the lobby. "But it can give a man a little joy to spend it on wants instead of needs sometimes."

He joined the half-breed on the stoop and glanced along the street in both directions and then down the Via de Bello. After the stage had crossed the intersection, the driver and guard looking rigidly intense, apparently concerned with the lack of activity in Southfields on this Monday noon.

Wanda Merritt had emerged from the depot, followed by John Clements who was carrying her valises.

Chico Lopez showed himself at the entrance of his cantina, holding his shotgun one handed, low down.

The Farrows were half-running toward the stage stop, as if anxious the Concord would leave without them if they were not there to board it immediately it came to a halt.

Here and there along the streets, there were traces of movement behind sun glinting windows. Or curtains swayed.

A second storey window of the Town House opened and Clinton Merritt vented a soft, strangled word. Just, "Wanda."

Shep Mallison stared fixedly at Edge and Steele, taking meager sips from his final tequila bottle. While the two men he was watching concentrated their attention on the stage.

"With me it's tobacco and liquor," the half-breed said.

"What about women?" the old-timer in the rocker said, his voice slurred as the few sips of fresh tequila induced new drunkenness when it merged with the old in his belly and bloodstream. "Fellers young as you two are oughta get a lotta joy outta women."

"Women have to come for free, old man," Steele answered.

"And I don't ever pay to," Edge added.

As the driver and guard of the stage began to toss packages down from the roof of the Concord. While Wanda Merritt and the Farrows waited impatiently to climb aboard.

Then the man in the wheelchair shrieked, "Girl! Daughter! Look here! It don't mean nothing without you!"

Merritt's words, high-pitched close to the point of hysteria, resounded between the façades of the buildings along the otherwise quiet Main Street. As the unloading of the stage freight was curtailed and everyone at the depot snapped their heads around to stare at the hotel.

"All I've worked for. Everything, Wanda! This town!

188

This money! You're the only decent thing in my life! All I ever wanted and all I ever got was for you!"

The Virginian and the half-breed stepped across the stoop and down into the street to look up at where the cripple was making his plea. Sitting in his wheelchair and leaning as far out of the window as his infirmity would allow, elbows hooked over the sill. A thick wad of bills in his left hand and a knife with a serrated blade in the right. Spectacle lenses and sweat beads glinting in the sun's glare.

Then his pleading tone was displaced by snarling anger as only silence greeted his words.

"All right, girl! You want me to show you? You want to see what it means to me if you're not around? This much! This is what it means!"

He began to saw at the stack of banknotes with the knife. Slicing a half inch off one end, then another half inch. And although there was not a breath of breeze in the stifling heat of midday, the shreds of paper were caught in warm air currents and fluttered across the balcony and down into the street.

"Sonofabitch, the crazy galoot is cuttin' up money!" Shep Mallison cried, and came out of the rocker so fast that he pitched into the street again under the gently falling shower of paper strips. He clawed at the worthless pieces of bills and gasped. "What the frig is happenin'?"

"Appears the lady has made her father a little crusty, old man," Steele drawled, fanning his free hand to clear the falling paper from in front of his face.

"And all you got is sliced bread, feller," Edge added.

"Which doesn't look to me like the greatest thing in the world," Steele said.

As the chapel bell tolled once.

A bugle sounded in the east.

And a shotgun blasted death from two barrels. To send the virtually headless corpse of Phineas Farrow across six feet of street and sidewalk, where it collapsed in the stage-depot doorway.

SIXTEEN

ERNESTINE FARROW began to scream. With her hands covering her face and her head tipped toward the glaring orb of the midday sun. And for a stretched second the shrillness of her grief seemed to be the only sound in the entire world.

Then the stage team bolted in panic, the sudden jerk of the Concord from a stand-still pitching the driver and guard to the street.

The brakes were still on and the skidding wheelrims spewed up more dust than the pumping hooves of the four horses.

The men shrieked in alarm as they tumbled through the dust, then yelled their pain as they thudded onto the unloaded freight and rolled to the ground.

"In the coach!" John Clements roared. "The bastards are in the coach!"

"Not again, not again!" Wanda Merritt cried.

"Inside! Get inside the damn depot!" This from Clements.

All this happening amid the billowing cloud of dust which veiled the western end of Main Street. The voices heard against a background of the constantly clanging bell from the chapel to the north. And the rising notes of the bugle sounding a cavalry charge which reached into town from the east.

"Wanda!" Clinton Merritt cried despairingly from the window. As he hurled what was left of the bills and the destructive knife out across the balcony and down on to the street.

Shep Mallison, up on all fours now, scampered to capture the largest shreds of paper, like a starving dog foraging among the contents of a spilled garbage pail.

As Steele, Colt Hartford leveled from the hip, peered at the veil of dust and tried to penetrate it. Seeking the whereabouts of the stage which had caused it.

And Edge, having whirled to face in the opposite direction, gazed through narrowed eyes at a second dust cloud. This one moving faster, in a wider band. Its cause plain to see by the half-breed and everyone else who stared toward it.

A line of horsemen. At least twenty. Strung out thirty feet to either side of the trail. Still a half mile from the town limit, but closing at a gallop. One man close to the center blasting at a bugle. Another at his side brandishing a sabre. Sunlight glinting on the instrument and the weapon. And striking with less intensity the polished buttons on every rider's tunic. The tunics were gray, matching the men's pants, which had yellow stripes down them.

"You know something, Reb," Edge muttered to the smaller man who stood beside him but facing the other way.

"Lots of things, Yank," Steele replied, now able to see the stage. Which had come to a halt only some thirty yards west of town when a lead horse dropped in the traces, a fetlock joint shattered by a well-aimed revolver shot. "But I've no idea where the fellers off the stage went to."

"I got a feeling I've been here before," Edge said. "If you were color blind, maybe you too?"

Each of them glanced over their shoulders.

The Virginian to frown toward the line of advancing riders. The half-breed to rake his eyes over the stalled and empty Concord, the doorway of the stage depot with the body of Farrow sprawled across it and the area of street littered with freight and the unconscious forms of the driver and guard.

"I'm not color-blind—or prejudiced," Steele drawled.

"Tell you something."

"Never too old to learn."

"If we don't get off the street pretty soon, we're both going to be dead."

The sound of the bugle was abruptly curtailed and for several moments all that could be heard was the thunder of hooves. And this on a diminishing note as the uniformed riders reined their mounts down to a canter, then to a walk. Finally a stop. Perhaps a quarter mile from town.

The dust began to settle behind them.

The man with the sabre thrust it into the scabbard.

Shep Mallison cursed softly as, seated with his legs splayed at the side of the street, he tried unsuccessfully with trembling hands to match up pieces of mutilated bills. Only his voice punctured the tense silence that was suddenly clamped over the stiflingly hot town and the surrounding countryside.

Despite what Edge had said, both he and Steele remained exposed on the street in front of the Town House stoop, the half-breed again watching the uniformed mounted men and the Virginian searching for a sight of those who had abandoned the stalled stage.

"Now!" the man with the sabre bellowed.

"Kelly!" Clinton Merritt rasped from the window, his anger toward, and then concern for, his daughter now subdued. Back in his wheelchair and not able to see the line of men to the east of town. But recognizing the voice of the vengeance-bent leader of the group. He added in a hoarse whisper, "Kill him!"

"All right, drop them guns!"

Elsewhere in Southfields, similar orders were barked.

Edge, Steele and Chico Lopez who was still in the doorway of his cantina, ignored the command directed at them. Did not even look at the man who growled it. Or the man backing him.

"Can see why he turned your daughter's head, feller," the half-breed said, with the briefest flick of his eyes up toward Merritt.

Chris Kelly was about forty-five. A tall, broadly built man with wide shoulders and a narrow waist. His hair was long and blond and he had an evenly tanned, clean-shaven face, the features almost classically handsome. He was smiling now, showing perfectly matched teeth. On a face such as his, no smile could look evil. This one was of pure pleasure.

192

Some of the men flanking him were also smiling. Others were grim-faced. A mixture of ages from the mid-thirties to the early-fifties. Which meant that all of them could be veterans of the War Between the States. And certainly the stained and patched uniforms they wore looked to have seen active duty—some of them now ill-fitted to frames which had thickened over the intervening years.

There was lieutenant's insignia on Kelly's tunic. Lester Noon had sergeant's chevrons on his sleeve. Hoyt Shaw had been a private. There were two other sergeants and four corporals in the line. A mixture of infantrymen, cavalry, artillery and even two from the medical corp. Who had served in a variety of two different regiments and companies. Just Kelly and six other men wore the Lone Star symbol of Texas on the front of their hats.

"Drop them, the man said!"

As four men showed themselves at the west end of Main Street. Two from the side of the stage depot and two appearing at the corner of the Golden Guitar Cantina. One of them still in process of taking off his duster to show that, like the others, he was attired in a Confederate uniform. It was he who had the shotgun. The others carried Winchester rifles in the crooks of their arms. All of the men smiling. One of them young enough, blond enough and with a sufficiently Nordic look about him to be son of Sven Karlsen.

When his pale-blue eyes met the coal-black gaze of Steele, the brief exchange of expression between two strangers revealed that each knew who the other was.

Just one second had elapsed between the order being given and then augmented. By men with brand new Winchesters. Who aimed them at Edge and Steele from the doorway and window of the bank. At Lopez from in front of the store next to his cantina. At Leroy on the threshold of the law office from the alley between the restaurant and mission church across the street. At Barney Gehlen on the chapel roof from the outhouses behind the houses backing-on to Potter's Field. At the Pollock father and son who were in the livery. And at John Clements who was with the grief-stricken Mrs. Farrow and strangely silent Wanda Merritt in the stage depot.

"The double-crossing bastards!" Clinton Merritt snarled with a vicious scowl at the rifle-toting turncoats within his field of vision.

Shep Mallison abandoned the hopeless task of fitting bills together and began to chuckle his delight as he returned to the rocker on the stoop.

"You want to tell them, Yank?" Steele said, continuing to keep his gaze locked on the now hate dripping features of the youngster who had to be Clark Ludlum.

Edge spat a globule of saliva at the ground and sighed. "Aim those rifles away from me or squeeze the triggers," he said evenly. "Always try to give people the one warning."

It was Carlton, the big-built wagon repairer, who had barked the initial order from the end of Via de Bello. And who now vented an animalistic growl, raised his rifle from the hip to the shoulder, drew a bead on the unmoving, impassive half-breed. Squeezed the trigger.

Blew half the flesh away from the bone on one side of his face. As the bullet left the cartridge and traveled no more than two inches along the rifled barrel before it smashed into another cartridge. Bulletless. Forced down through the Winchester muzzle by either Maria or Isabella. A cartridge packed with a double load of powder. Which exploded and showered Carlton's face with a hail of twisted gun metal shards. To gouge out an eye, blast away his jawbone and rip the flesh from his cheek so that his teeth and gums were bared in their entirety at one side of his face.

Two other men suffered similar fates. One aiming at Gehlen and another at Dave Pollock. Before witnesses to the gruesome sight of flesh-shredded and blood-run faces hurled down their Winchesters and screamed:

"Don't shoot!"

"Don't fire the rifles!"

"They been rigged!"

"We been tricked!"

Carlton lived for perhaps three seconds, writhing on the dusty street and thrashing his arms and legs. Then he became still. By which time the men with unfired Winchesters had flung them aside and lunged back into cover. Allowed to do so by those with the capability of gunning them down.

194

Shep Mallison sat rigid in the rocker, his laughter ended. And now Clinton Merritt began to cackle, as drunk with glee as the old-timer had been with liquor.

"Oh, Jesus!" one of the men at the western end of Main Street cried as all the previously smiling men expressed a gamut of emotions from shock to abject terror.

And, as Edge and Steele lunged for cover the blasphemous man died. Taking a bullet in the heart. From the rifle of John Clements exploding the shot across the headless corpse of Phineas Farrow in the depot doorway.

"Charge dammit, charge!" Kelly roared. And thudded in his heels to urge his mount into an immediate gallop, as he drew a rifle from its boot.

The bugler responded to the order and the men were just a second or so behind their leader in answering the call.

Lopez whirled back into his cantina with his shotgun.

The man at the end of the street with a similar weapon blasted both barrels at the stage-depot doorway to cover his own and the retreat of his companions—into the cover of facing buildings.

Barney Gehlen, empty pipe still clenched in his teeth, slid down the chapel roof and leapt to the ground. Then raced for the cover of the long grass in Potter's Field.

Dave Pollock moved to the front window of his livery as his father covered the back lot from the morgue doorway.

Edge went into the alley dividing the hotel from the livery and Steele entered that between the Town House and the bank.

Leroy remained where he was on the threshold of the law office.

Just as Merritt stayed at the window of his parlor.

Mallison made to rise from the rocker, but as the bugle ceased to sound and a fusillade of rifle fire sprayed the town with bullets, the trembling old-timer stayed the move.

The bullets exploded by the galloping horsemen shattered windows, splintered timber, powdered adobe and ricocheted off metal. The shots fired only as cover for the attackers, their former feelings changed to anger at the trick which had topped their own ruse.

A second fusillade cracked out as Edge turned from the

broad alley into the narrower one that ran behind the back lots of the buildings on the north side of Main Street.

"Fine start, mister!" Harry Pollock called in high excitement.

"Stay bright, feller," Edge replied as he passed the man in the doorway. "It's a good finish we need."

He ran across the rear of the blacksmith's forge and the barber shop, pulled up short and swung his Winchester to the aim as two men appeared at the far corner of the jailhouse. One ducked back out of sight, but the other became rooted to the spot and flung his arms high in the air.

"Don't shoot, mister!" he pleaded. "We're out of it! We're gonna go to the chapel for sanctuary!"

He looked like a dirt farmer.

"Beat it and say one for the feller that let you go," Edge growled, gesturing with the rifle. Then struck a match on the rear wall of the jailhouse.

The man dropped his arms, waved frantically to the other one who had got back into cover and the both of them leapt over a garden fence and raced out of sight. As Edge glanced in through the only barred window in the jailhouse—saw that Leroy had done as instructed and heaped kerosene soaked rags over the pile of surrendered guns. He tossed the match in through the bars and checked that the rags had begun to burn before he whirled and ran back along the alley.

Leroy should have been clear of the law office by then, having run along the sidewalk to the Town House.

Just as Maria and Isabella should have made a fast retreat from the flames after setting fire to the oily rags which the Negro had spread around the Mexican gunsmith's store.

Thus, the only sources of supply of reliable weapons in town would soon be unapproachable in the event that the men issued with defective rifles sought to rearm themselves. Or others who had left town came back to aid the attackers.

Attackers who exploded another hail of bullets from horseback before they reached the town's eastern limits and leapt from their saddles. To race into the cover of buildings on both the Mexican and American sides of Main Street.

Making their objectives without a single shot being fired at them. Their only casualties being three sympathetic townspeople, the uniformed man Clements had shot and Phineas Farrow—a non-combatant probably killed by accident in the heat of the moment.

For several stretched seconds, in the wake of the final volley of rifle fire, the only discernible sounds to be heard in the town were made by the hurriedly dismounted horses as they snorted and pawed at the dusty ground. Then, as the animals became quiet, there was the crackle of flames. Which those unaware of the two fires did not recognize until they smelled and then saw smoke.

For a while, other slight sounds could be heard, but soon the volume of noise from the spreading flames rose to cover these—and men moved faster, not so concerned with the heaviness of their footfalls as they sought to attain their various destinations.

As the others remained as still as the cover which protected them. Sweating with heat and tension. Some of them hearing their own heartbeats loud in their ears. Others holding their breath for fear of revealing their positions with the noise of inhalation and exhalation of the hot, smoky air.

The chapel on the hill and the mission church on the south side of Main Street were where many of the men went. Defenseless men, like the two Edge had seen, withdrawing to the sidelines. The religious to pray and the non-believers to hope that evil men would have some respect for the sanctity of the houses of God.

But those clad in gray regarded nothing in Clinton Merritt's town as inviolable. And after they had set fire to the Estella Cantina at the eastern end of Main Street, they put torches to the Mexican church.

The men who had taken refuge there plunged out through the smoke, hands clasped to their heads, screaming their allegiance to Kelly. Some pleading for weapons to fight with. These were knocked aside, with fists, back-handed blows or even rifle stocks. And snarled at for their stupidity in not checking the guns they were given in the first place.

After which, the men could only run. For the open country to the east. Racing for the clear sunlit air beyond the choking smoke that billowed from the cantina and the church on one side of the street. And the boarding house, seed merchants and law office and jailhouse on the other.

While, at the far end of the town's Main Street, the Golden Guitar Cantina, the gunsmith's store and the stage depot and two other stores were in flames.

So that two palls of black smoke hung above Southfields, moving in slow billows on gentle air currents. Blotting out the blueness of the sky.

But the bright, harsh sun—a little beyond its midday peak—continued to blaze down on the center of town.

Steele was by turns in the sunlight and the short shadows it cast. Backtracking toward the Town House behind the stores, newspaper office and bank after going to the stage depot.

Initially, his motive had been a selfish one, for he was intent upon finding Clark Ludlum and letting the youngster decide upon the alternatives—talking or killing.

But when he reached the side of the depot, he was forced to abandon the plan. For John Clements needed help.

The frame building was already alight and it was the heat and smoke which had driven Wanda Merritt and Ernestine Farrow outside. But now they were able to breathe freely, the women were deaf to the sweating Clements' entreaties that they must continue to move. As the older woman's body was wracked with dry sobs of mourning for her newly dead husband. And the younger one showed a vacant expression—her mind behind the blankly staring eyes recalling another day when a town had burned. Far back in time and many miles distant from this one.

Clements had whirled toward Steele, bringing up his rifle. Then had opened his mouth to say something, but seen that the Virginian required no explanation.

Steele merely grunted, and the grimace that etched into his face was as much due to the need to abandon his initial plan as to the conditions of the women. He stepped forward and Clements backed away. And his gloved fist smashed first into the jaw of the older woman. For she was obviously the more aware of her surroundings.

Clements gasped, then cursed when a second punch connected with the jaw of Wanda Merritt and she crumpled to the ground beside Mrs. Farrow.

"Look like a couple of easy pickups, feller," Steele muttered as he stooped, lifted the younger woman smoothly onto his shoulder and straightened. Then he showed a brief grin as he added, "Don't think much of yours."

He started back for the mid-town area then. Casting frequent glances over his unburdened shoulder. To check that the heavily breathing Clements was following and that there were no gray-uniformed figures in sight.

But the attackers were still intent upon putting the town to the torch. And with only three of Kelly's men advancing from the west, the destructive progress through this area of Southfields was slow. For it was not only the buildings on Main Street that attracted the men. They swung to the north and to the south. Their senses of victory expanding with each new building which burned.

The shock and anger they had experienced when Kelly's plan for taking the town with ease had been thwarted was now forgotten. For, apart from the single shot exploded from the stage depot, they had met with no resistence. And none of the men they had come to kill had escaped. Kelly had made certain of this—by sending Noon to the north and Shaw to the south. The former to occupy the roof of the chapel in the same way that Barney Gehlen had done. The latter to watch from one of the dirt-farm shacks beyond the end of the Via de Bello.

So, encircled by a closing ring of fire, the helpless defenders had to be huddling together in the center of town.

That was what Kelly thought—basing the assumption on the known facts. And acknowledging that in the same position himself—commanding a small group of men faced with a numerically superior force—he would have done the same thing.

"All right, Mr. Edge," Barney Gehlen said sourly from where he stood in the center of the Town House lobby. "Your figuring about the guns being smuggled into town was on the button. There was no point Kelly fixing that unless he counted on Jack Carlton and the others using them. Against us. But I don't like the way things are here."

The way things were was much as Chris Kelly expected

199

them to be. With everyone in the hotel. Gathered in the lobby. Steele and Clements returned from the stage depot with the unconscious women who were slumped uncomfortably in armchairs. Leroy from the law office. The Pollock father and son from the livery and morgue. Barney Gehlen coming in from Potter's Field. Chico Lopez and the two whores having raced across the intersection through the drifting, insubstantial cover of smoke. Clinton Merritt lowered down in the elevator by Edge.

"*Si, hombre,*" the fat Mexican said grimly. "It sure looks like we are the rats in the trap." He looked out through a window and grimaced as smoke began to wisp from the open doorway of his cantina. "And our goose, it will soon be cooked, I think."

"I don't know about that," the Virginian drawled as he raked his eyes over the frightened faces of the Southfields citizens. Saw all of them flinch as bullets began to explode in the jailhouse and the gunsmith's. Waited until the crackling sound diminished before he added, "Seems to me that Kelly's bunch could be in for a big helping of fried chicken."

Edge directed a globule of saliva into a spittoon and lit the cigarette he had just rolled. Then looked as bleakly as Steele around the nervous faces as he growled, "Unless we see to it that they've bitten off more than they can chew."

SEVENTEEN

THE BUGLER sounded a single, very long note. Eerie to hear for it was a disembodied sound that came out of the black, drifting smoke. Impossible to tell from which direction. Then, when it came to an abrupt end, a man shouted:

"Hey, you people in the hotel! I know you're in there! You don't have a chance. We have you surrounded!"

The man was bellowing the words against a background of crackling flames and cracking timber, shattering glass and crumbing adobe, as every building in Southfields except for the Town House and the flanking bank and livery stable was in process of being devoured by flames. But the voice was easily recognizable as that of Chris Kelly.

Ten minutes had elapsed since the citizens of the town had made known their feelings about gathering together in the hotel. And it was obvious from the haunted looks in their eyes and the sweat of tension sheening their faces that the terse assurances offered by the half-breed and the Virginian had served little purpose.

Assurances albeit based upon a guess, that Chris Kelly and his latterday rebels would want a more satisfying finale to their raid than simply to burn their victims alive in the hotel. Or to gun them down if they attempted to escape the flames. For in the first instance they would not be able to see the trapped men suffer. And in the second the end would be too mercifully quick.

The voice of Kelly, yelling triumphantly from the smoke-veiled Via de Bello, ignited a faint spark of hope in the minds of some of the doubters.

As the two unconscious women groaned their readiness to recover, stirred by the bugle call.

Wanda Merritt and Ernestine Farrow were still sprawled

awkwardly in the chairs where Steele and Clements had dumped them.

The Virginian and the stage depot and telegraph man were flat to the wall at the side of the windows in the hotel restaurant.

Barney Gehlen and Leroy stood in similar attitudes in the barroom.

Harry Pollock was at the window in Clinton Merritt's parlor with Isabella crouched beside him. While Dave Pollock was in Wanda Merritt's room, in company with Maria. The men with Winchesters and the whores holding Frontier Colts.

Edge and Chico Lopez flanked the hotel's open doorway.

The crippled Merritt sat, shoulders hunched and head tipped forward, in a corner of the lobby, his joy at seeing his daughter safe now negated by his inability to take a hand in the fight.

"Not me, Chris!" Shep Mallison called hoarsely. "I ain't with them! I always been with you, you know that!"

"The crazy old drunk, I forgot about him," Lopez growled.

As the rocker creaked, the old-timer's feet thudded to the stoop, then down on to the street.

Edge glimpsed Mallison moving at a staggering run across the intersection. Heard the blast of a shotgun. Saw the scrawny old man come to an abrupt halt, toothless mouth gaping wide in a silent scream, arms flung to the side. Right hand still fisted around the neck of the almost-empty tequila bottle.

Then Mallison fell out onto his back, spreadeagled. Still did not loosen his grip on the bottle.

Upstairs, Harry Pollock rasped, "Well, old man, you died the way you wanted."

But Mallison was not quite dead. Had enough breath left in his skinny frame to cry, "It's gettin' dark, dammit!"

It was, but the old man was not referring to the smoke which now completely obliterated the sun.

Edge looked with glinting eyes at the ghastly wound in Mallison's belly. A wide, deep hole, from which his stomach and intestines spilled on a swell of blood. And growled, "On account of your lights being out, feller."

The old-timer lay still.

"Anybody who wasn't with us at the start is against us!" Chris Kelly yelled. "'And every last one of you is gonna die! Fast, like the old man! Or slow! You people that weren't at Masonville and Big Springs, you got the choice! Come out now and take it! And you won't know what's hit you. You don't do that, you'll share in what's coming to the others!"

"How you figure to take us alive, *hombre*?" Lopez bellowed.

And showed no regret for the retort when Edge looked coldly across the doorway at him.

"My men have been soldiers! And they're soldiers again! They know their objective and they'll take it! Whatever the cost! With honor!"

"How can you speak of honor, you bastard!" Wanda Merritt shrieked as she moved shakily into the doorway.

Only Ernestine Farrow had seen the woman get unsteadily up from the chair. And no one heard her walk across the lobby carpet, her feet bare after her shoes had fallen off while Steele carried her to the hotel.

And when she spoke she was too exposed to the guns of Kelly and his men for either Edge or Lopez to reach her and drag her into cover.

"After what we meant to each other for so long and—"

"Wanda!" her father cried and a whole lifetime of despair sounded in his voice.

She was out on the stoop by then. Her mind in the present now and her green eyes peering through the smoke for a sight of the man she had loved.

"—all the time you were using me to—"

A single rifle shot cracked. The bullet blasted into the woman's left breast, tunneled through her heart and burst clear of her back in a spray of bright crimson. Then entered the doorway and left a trail of blood on the carpet before it smashed into the clock above the reception desk. Stopped it with the hands showing forty-four minutes after noon. Thus marked the time Wanda Merritt died, sprawling out on her back, half on the stoop and half in the street.

"Wanda!" Clinton Merritt cried again, and the sound of his voice was virtually a scream.

"Seems like romance is dead," Steele drawled to the sick-looking John Clements.

The cold-blooded murder of the woman had not figured in Edge's plans. But her death and her father's hysterical reaction to it served a purpose.

"Now!" he roared.

And all those at the front of the building—except himself—swung away from the walls and blasted shots across the street. Then ducked back into cover as the fusillade invited a counter blast from the men outside.

"Wanda!" Clinton Merritt screamed a third time.

As the half-breed gave the cripple's wheelchair a powerful shove. Across the lobby and through the doorway. Into the hail of rifle fire that was being poured at the entrance.

"No!" Chris Kelly bellowed. "No, no, no!"

As bullets smashed into the flesh of the figure in the chair. The men with the rifles, firing instinctively, unable to stay their fingers on the triggers until it was too late—the wheelchair had bounced over the unfeeling body of the dead woman, tilted to the side, tipped its bullet-riddled occupant onto the street and fallen on top of him.

For just a second the only sounds in Southfields were made by the raging fires. As the men and women in the hotel held their breath, waiting in high tension to see if the prediction of Edge and Steele would prove to be correct. And the gray-uniformed men behind the smokescreen outside came to terms with the fact that they had lost their greatest prize.

"Get the frigging bastards!" Kelly shrieked, rage sending his voice to an almost girlish pitch. "Slaughter the stinking sonsofbitches!"

They came out of the smoke with guns blazing. On the run. White-hot anger blinding them to the dangers of the wild charge.

From the restaurant and barroom windows downstairs and the parlor and bedroom windows upstairs, more rifles spat death. And from the hotel entrance, Edge's Winchester and the Mexican's shotgun blasted.

Gray uniforms were splashed with blood as the wearers were stopped in their tracks and sent sprawling to the street. And two died on the hotel's back lot, brought down by rapid-fire shots from Dave Pollock's rifle.

Barney Gehlen was not fast enough in ducking back after firing his first shot and took a bullet in the shoulder that sent him staggering across the barroom and sprawling over a table.

Every other man survived to swing into the open again and trigger another shot at the attackers.

"The back!" Dave Pollock yelled. "Three in at the back!"

One of those who had made it into the rear of the hotel lunged into the restaurant from the kitchen. His rifle was aimed at Clements, but Steele put a bullet in the man's head before he could squeeze the trigger of the Winchester.

There was a killer's grin pasted across the face of the Virginian. As Clements gulped and expressed tacit gratitude, he wrenched his gaze away from the sight of the falling man's blood curtained face.

And Steele rasped through his clenched teeth, "Serve the meat in here a little rare, don't they?"

Seven of the attackers had made the stoop and two reached the alley on the bank side of the hotel.

The two other men who had evaded Dave Pollock's rifle got no further than the archway behind the reception desk. When Ernestine Farrow shrieked:

"Murderers! You killed Phineas!"

And Edge whirled to blast a shot toward one of them. And from where he sat in a high-backed armchair in a corner, Clinton Merritt fanned an Army Model Colt to spray both intruders with bullets.

Both men died with looks of incredulity as their death masks. And were dead before Kelly roared:

"It's not him! It' ain't Merritt!"

"Life sure is full of surprises, ain't it, feller," Edge said flatly as he stepped on to the hotel threshold. His rifle aimed down at the handsome Kelly. Who was squatting on his haunches, staring at the corpse of the man who had died when he tried to kill Harry Pollock in the livery stable.

"But death is the greatest unknown of all," Steele added as he leaned out of the shattered window of the restaurant.

All the men on the stoop had been frozen into immobility by Kelly's revelation. Then tensed to move but became stockstill again. Like automatons programmed to react to a signal. In this case the two gunshots merged into one. As the Colt Hartford of Steele and the Winchester of Edge exploded bullets into the chest of Kelly. Killing the handsome Texan before he could translate the powerful emotion shown on his face into fast and violent action.

He dropped his rifle, came erect to his full height, took a backward step and incredibly managed to maintain his balance as he half-fell off the stoop and onto the street. The dark stain on his uniform tunic spread like the speeded-up blossoming of a flower. He did not have enough strength to form his features into a deeper expression of hatred.

"You—" he was able to force out.

But then he died, and fell forward on to the sprawled corpse of Wanda Merritt.

"Looks like the message on the back page of the newspaper finally reached him," Steele said, tracking his rifle back and forth over the unmoving men in a variety of frozen attitudes on the stoop. Seven of them in all, one of them with a blood-soaked coat sleeve.

Edge did the same thing. As did Leroy from the barroom window.

"Shouldn't do it on the street, though," Edge countered in the same even tone. "It could frighten the horses. You fellers want to drop your guns?"

"You know why we came?" a gravel-voiced man snarled. "A time in the war when some—"

"Not all of us," Lester Noon broke in as he and Hoyt Shaw—and a scared-looking Charlie Deed—emerged from the alley between the hotel and the bank, without rifles and with their army-issue holsters empty.

The grim-faced Dave Pollock was behind them, covering them with his Winchester. "Found they tryin' to break in the bank," he reported.

Edge nodded. "The killing at Masonville never was enough. For this many. Had to be a reward on the end of it for some of them."

"The guns," Steele reminded.

From their expressions as they allowed their rifles to clatter to the stoop, it was perhaps possible to tell which of the men had come for revenge and which for stolen money.

Already, the smoke drifting slowly across the intersection was losing its acrid taint of exploded powder. And the flies were winging in to feed on the blood-stained corpses which littered the dusty streets. As shafts of sunlight penetrated the darkness.

"Hey, you guys? Is the shootin' all over?"

"We're comin' with hands up!" a second man yelled. As nervous as the first.

Then emerged from the smoke-filled western stretch of Main Street. The driver and guard off the stage, both still stunned from the unsteadiness of the gaits.

"We didn't know we was bringin' trouble to town," the driver added hurriedly when he saw which side had won.

"No sweat," Edge said, moving out on to the stoop and yanking the wheelchair from among the three corpses heaped there.

"A man has to take the rough with the smooth," Steele added, and swung a leg over the glass-sharded window frame. Then stepped down onto the street to check over the dead.

He found Clark Ludlum, the youngster's blond hair stained crimson by the blood which had pumped from two bullet holes in his forehead. And experienced just a slight pang of regret that he was unable to tell the boy that he had not killed his father.

This while, inside the lobby, Edge lifted the sadly thoughtful Clinton Merritt out of the armchair and into his wheelchair.

"Thanks, son," the cripple said. "For everythin'. You did a fine job. You and your partner both."

"Never could have saved your town, feller."

"Even if you had wanted to?" Merritt countered without rancor.

As Steele entered the lobby in time to say, "We didn't count on you losing your daughter."

"What'll we do with them that aren't dead, Clinton?" the elder Pollock called from the balcony above the stoop.

Bitterness etched deep lines into the gray flesh of the cripple's face.

"Wanda dead and your town all but burned to the ground," the Virginian reminded.

"So maybe those that didn't come for the money will figure that the score's settled," the half-breed added.

Merritt sighed, then nodded and called, "Turn them loose, Harry!" Then lowered his voice to say, "I owe you men the second part of the payment."

He took two envelopes from an inside pocket of his jacket and extended them toward Edge and Steele.

"For saving your worthless life and the lives of the other monsters who raided Masonville?" Ernestine Farrow spat out.

"In war, mistakes are made," Merritt said dully.

"And not only in war," John Clements rasped as he emerged from the hotel restaurant. "Wasn't us blasted off your husband's head, lady."

She began to weep again. As hooves beat on the street ouside, the horses heeled into gallops by the survivors of Kelly's men.

"The people deserve to lose their homes and livelihoods," Merritt said in the same unemotional tone. "They are either traitors or cowards. And my daughter lost her life by committing suicide." He shifted his lens-magnified eyes from the recent widow to the two men who took the envelopes from his gnarled hands, "Like I said before, you did a fine job. When I came here first, I had only remorse and a dream. I now have grief and at least the beginnings of a new dream."

He gestured with his hands to encompass the hotel which was still standing intact. And drew for a response impassive nods from both Steele and Edge before the two men turned and left the lobby.

Less than thirty minutes later, when all the flames were out and the only smoke to show came from glowing embers beneath gray ash, it could be seen that there was just a little more than the mere nucleus of a town left standing. For, in addition to the hotel, the bank and the livery stable, the Baptist chapel on the hill was unscathed. And Chico Lopez and the two whores had managed to put out the flames in the Cantina Plata before the walls cracked and the roof caved in. While, here and there in both the American and Mexican sections of town, the shells of some other buildings stood.

The half-breed and the Virginian surveyed the ruined town with unemotional eyes as they halted their horses on the intersection after riding them out of the livery. The intersection which had been cleared of corpses, although several patches of dried blood showed where the dead had fallen.

Far to the west of town, a large group of people were gathered. Waiting for some men—the survivors of those who had come with Carlton—to reach them. There was no way of knowing if they would return to Southfields or stay away.

Closer to where the two riders sat their mounts, the stage was preparing to leave. A fresh horse in the traces to replace the one which had been shot. As soon as Ernestine Farrow was helped aboard by John Clements, the Concord pulled out.

"I think she was right, Yank," Steele said as he tugged on the reins to head his newly purchased mount westwards. "We shouldn't have taken his money."

The half-breed turned the gelding which had once been Sven Karlsen's so that he was facing east. "We did our best, Reb," he answered. "No one can be expected to do better than that."

"It's always the losers say they did their best."

A nod. "Then maybe he should have figured us for born losers."

Steele pursed his lips. "Reckon so. But it was a bad play we got into from the start."

"Yeah, Reb, with a real lousy . . .

". . . Last act."

"Hey, Yank, I'm supposed to have the . . .

". . . Final line.

"That's your story, feller. In my book I always get the . . .

    . . . *Last laugh.*"

Steele sighed, shrugged and heeled his horse forward. At a slow walk. While Edge sat easily in his saddle, rolling a cigarette. As he struck a match on the stock of the booted Winchester and lit the tobacco, the Virginian called:

"If we ever run into each other again, I'll remember I still owe you!"

The half-breed turned fast in the saddle, sliding the Winchester from the boot. An act which drew gasps and squeals from the hotel and the Cantina Plata where the remaining citizens of Southfields were watching.

But Steele did not need the vocal sounds to warn him of a threat. He sensed it. And powered off his gelding, taking the Colt Hartford with him.

The horse reared in panic at the sudden move. And Edge squeezed the rifle trigger. To blast a bullet into the animal's bulging right eye.

Steele had the half-breed covered by then—sprawling prone on the ground with the Colt Hartford hammer cocked and a gloved finger curled to the trigger. Lost him for a moment in the cloud of dust raised by the fallen horse.

Edge did not work the action of his repeater before he slid it into the boot, his back to the Virginian.

"We're even on the horses now, Reb," he said as he heeled his own mount into a slow walk. "Nothing owed." Then, too softly for words to carry to Steele, he murmured, "I'll even make an exception about a man who aims a gun at me twice."

The Virginian maintained his rock steady aim on the back of the half-breed for perhaps three seconds after the dust had settled. Then, as all eyes except those of Edge watched him, he eased the hammer forward, got to his feet and muttered:

"Agreed, Yank." He glanced down at the dead horse. "Let's just say it was a . . .

    . . . *Parting shot.*

PREVIEW

The savage saga of a heroic Indian warrior—
and his relentless battle against the
ruthless white man.

by William M. James

Apache

In the following pages, excerpted from the gripping Apache* series, you will meet Cuchillo Oro—a fictional character of heroic dimension and power. Cuchillo's strength as an Indian warrior, inspired by such notorious Indian leaders as Cochise and Geronimo, and his knowledge of the white man's ways aids him in his search for a just revenge upon the "White Eyes" for the crimes committed against his people. And though Cuchillo faces death at every turn, the Apache credo of living with honor and dignity gives him the inner strength to carry out his destiny. Here, then, is the often shocking and cruel realism of the Indian-wars—and some of the most exciting reading ever to come out of the West!

In the past, before an Indian-hating horsesoldier had lit the fires of mindless rage in the heart of Cuchillo, the Apache had been just another brave, living in dejected squalor—but peacefully—on the Borderline Rancheria of the Arizona territory, with his gentle wife and their newborn baby.

The threat of an uprising against the White Eyes was always in the air at Borderline, almost as tangible as the smoke from the cooking fires. But Cuchillo, even though he was descended from the great chief Mangas Coloradas, could never be persuaded by the hotheads to take up arms against the oppressors of the Apaches. He elected, instead, to put into practice only the peaceful tenets of his renowned ancestor. . . .

And he shared in the belief of the only White Eyes he called friend—the schoolteacher John Hedges—that the time would come when men of different races would cover tolerance of each other without resort to war.

Much blood would still be coursing through living veins instead of congealing on the dirt of countless battlefields if the evil Lieutenant Cyrus Pinner had not shattered the dream composed of an Indian's teachings and the belief of a White Eyes.

Cuchillo had been falsely accused of stealing an ornate and valuable dagger belonging to Pinner. A man less bigoted than the horsesoldier officer would have examined the facts more closely before taking action. But Pinner, unable to contain his hatred for all Indians, could not even think of giving the benefit of the doubt to one.

A knife and then a gun hacked and blasted the young brave's right hand into virtual uselessness, leaving him with just the third and fourth finger and the thumb, and these almost paralyzed.

Such a punishment would have been cruel enough to a White Eyes victim. To a full-blooded Apache it was utterly barbaric. For it was written that a brave not bodily whole was barred entry to the Land of the Great Spirits when it came his turn to die.

Cuchillo—given his second name of Oro following the incident involving the golden knife—set little store by such tales. After long periods of study in the schoolroom of John Hedges, he had learned to accept and reject by the art of reason those aspects of both the Indian and the White Eyes cultures that either did or did not appeal to him.

So, perhaps, he had never been just another Apache brave when Borderline had been an oasis of uneasy peace. Whatever he had been served to spur his violent response to the torture he suffered. And, for the purely personal purpose of taking his revenge against Pinner, Cuchillo Oro was the fuse that ignited Borderline into an uprising. A man alone in the midst of a bloody battle, he was also alone in experiencing the acid bitterness of personal defeat. The fort from which Borderline had been ruled was reduced to burning rubble. The Apaches won a small triumph at great cost. Pinner was one of the horsesoldiers who survived, to strut in personal victory before the crumpled and blood-run bodies of Cuchillo's wife and baby son.

In grief-striken defeat, Cuchillo had claimed one of the spoils of victory—the golden knife for which he was named and which was the cause of his suffering—claimed by the act of drawing its blade from the still-warm flesh of his dead baby son.

But he could not use it against Pinner, nor could he use any other weapon. His right hand was mutilated and his left had never been trained to work alone. So he had retreated into the mountains of Mexico, there to spend countless hours, days and weeks in schooling himself to become as skilled with his left hand as he had always been with his right. Only when he was completely satisfied that he could gain nothing more from his period of isolation did he return north across the border, to find and to kill Pinner.

He had found him, time and time again. And Pinner had found Cuchillo just as often. Both men were engaged on a bitter vengeance hunt, each for the other. One sought to kill in order to settle an old score, the other because he did not consider the lives of an Apache squaw and child payment enough for a golden knife.

Now, many moons later, it was winter, and even when the sun shone, the air was viciously cold. When the sky was leaden with clouds, when it rained, when there was sleet and this turned to snow, a man alone in the mountains was doomed to die. . . . Unless that man was Cuchillo Oro, the Apache brave wise in the ways of the White Eyes, a brave in his early twenties and extraordinarily tall for one of his race. He stood six-feet-two and was impressively built, with a massive chest and muscular limbs. Deprivation and his chosen life-style had never allowed an ounce of excess fat to form on his body. He was handsome as only an Indian can be, his features fashioned into proud lines. He had narrow, coal-black eyes, a nose with flared nostrils, high cheekbones, a wide mouth and a resolute jaw. Thick hair, as black as his eyes, flowed down to brush at his broad shoulders. His complexion was an even bronze, the taut skin of his face scoured with aging lines before its time. Grief and bitterness, suffering and hatred, had etched his flesh in this way. The white-hot rage generated by mental images of his pain and humiliation at the hands of the cruel horsesoldier Pinner renewed his will to survive—even under the most arduous of circumstances. No man could do more than kill him, and he was not afraid to die. He was just desperate to live—to complete the mission of vengeance at which he had failed so often: to kill the hated Cyrus Pinner of the White Eyes cavalry.

But always, Pinner and "Pinner's Indian" eluded the fatal bullet or knife thrust. They searched, came together, clashed and then were driven by circumstances onto different paths again and again, until . . . it finally happened . . . the death the Apache had waited for since he was a warrior of eighteen. With the first plunge of the mighty golden knife into Cyrus Pinner's evil flesh, Cuchillo Oro released his pent-up hatred for the horsesoldier, sending the fatally wounded cavalry officer over the cliffs and into the cold waters of the river.

It was over—the blood feud between himself and Pinner—he should be filled with a great satisfaction. He had prayed for it, longed to make the last atonement for his wife and child. . . . Yet, oddly, he felt empty, drained. The expected elation was not there. Cuchillo was suddenly angry. Somehow, he felt cheated. Was this all there was?

Avenging his avowed enemy is not enough for the embittered brave. As long as there are White Eyes left to ravage the land of his ancestors, the warrior must continue his battle. With his proud blood rising, Cuchillo Oro, the grandson of the wise chieftain Mangas Coloradas, renews his promise for revenge. This time there is no turning back—not for the Apache, and not for those who have persecuted his people!

More bestselling western adventure from Pinnacle, America's #1 series publisher. Over 5 million copies of EDGE in print!

Buy them at your local bookstore or use this handy coupon.

Clip and mail this page with your order